COLIN MACINNES (1914-76), son of novelist Angela Thirkell, cousin of Stanley Baldwin and Rudyard Kipling, grandson of Burne-Jones, was brought up in Australia but lived most of his life in London about which he wrote with a warts-and-all relish that earned him a reputation as the literary Hogarth of his day.

Bisexual, outsider, champion of youth, 'pale-pink' friend of Black Londoners and chronicler of English life, MacInnes described himself as 'a very nosy person' who 'found adultery in Hampstead indescribably dull' and was much more at home in the coffee bars and jazz clubs of Soho and Notting Hill.

A talented off-beat journalist and social observer, he is best known for his three London novels, *City of Spades*, *Absolute Beginners* and *Mr Love and Justice*. His other books include *To the Victor the Spoils*, a disenchanted view of the Allied occupation of Germany in the aftermath of the Second World War, *June in Her Spring* and *England, Half English*. Colin MacInnes's essays were published in *Out of the Way* in 1980 and a selection of the best of his fiction and journalism is available in *Absolute MacInnes*, edited by Tony Gould. MacInnes died of cancer in 1976.

By Colin MacInnes

City of Spades
Absolute Beginners
Mr Love and Justice

Absolute Beginners

COLIN MACINNES

Printed and bound by
CPI Group (UK) Ltd, Croydon, CR0 4YY

Allison & Busby Limited
12 Fitzroy Mews
London W1T 6DW
www.allisonandbusby.com

First published in Great Britain by Allison & Busby Ltd in 1980.
This edition published in 2011.

A CIP catalogue record for this book is available from
the British Library.

10 9 8 7 6

ISBN 978-0-7490-0998-4

Typeset in 11/15.5 pt Sabon by
Allison & Busby Ltd.

The paper used for this Allison & Busby publication
has been produced from trees that have been legally sourced
from well-managed and credibly certified forests.

For Alfred Maron

CONTENTS

IN JUNE   9

IN JULY   151

IN AUGUST   207

IN SEPTEMBER   231

IN JUNE

It was with the advent of the Laurie London era that I realised the whole teenage epic was tottering to doom.

'Fourteen years old, that absolute beginner,' I said to the Wizard as we paused casually in the gramophone section to hear Little Laurie in that golden disc performance of his.

'From now on,' said Wizard, 'he's certainly Got the Whole World in His Hands.'

We listened to the wonder boy's nostrils spinning on.

'They buy us younger every year,' I cried. 'Why, Little Mr L.'s voice hasn't even dropped yet, so who will those taxpayers try to kidnap next?'

'Sucklings,' said Wizard.

We climbed the white stair to the glass garden under the top roof of the department store, and came out on the glorious panorama, our favourite rendezvous.

I must explain the Wiz and I never come to this store to buy anything except, as today, a smoke-salmon sandwich and ice coffee. But in the first place, we have the opportunity to see the latest furnishings and fabrics, just like some married couple, and also to have the splendid outlook over London, the most miraculous I know in the whole city, and quite unknown to other nuisance-values of our age, in fact to everyone, it seems, except these elderly female Chelsea peasants who come up there for their elevenses.

Looking north you don't see much, it's true, and westward the view's entirely blocked up by the building you're inside. But twisting slowly on your bar stool from the east to south, like Cinerama, you can see clean new concrete cloud-kissers, rising up like felixes from the Olde Englishe squares, and then those gorgeous parks, with trees like classical French salads, and then again the port life down along the Thames, that glorious river, reminding you we're on an estuary, a salt inlet really, with crazy seagulls circling up from it and almost bashing their beaks against the circular plate glass, and then, before you know it, you're back again round a full circle in front of your iced coffee cup.

'Laurie L.,' I said, ''s a sign of decadence. This teenage thing is getting out of hand.'

The Wiz looked wise, like the middle feller of the three old monkeys.

'It's not the taxpayers,' he said, 'who are responsible. It's the kids themselves, for buying the EPs these elderly sordids bribe the teenage nightingales to wax.'

'No doubt,' I said, for I know better than ever to argue with the Wizard, or with anyone else who gets his kicks from an idea.

Mr Wiz continued, masticating his salmon sandwich for anyone to see, 'It's been a two-way twist, this teenage party. Exploitation of the kiddos by the conscripts, and exploitation of themselves by the crafty little absolute beginners. The net result? "Teenager" 's become a dirty word or, at any rate, a square one.'

I smiled at Mr W. 'Well, take it easy, son,' I said, 'because a sixteen year old sperm like you has got a lot of teenage living still to do. As for me, eighteen summers, rising nineteen, I'll very soon be out there among the oldies.'

The Wizard eyed me with his Somerset Maugham appearance. 'Me, boy,' he said, 'I tell you. As things are, I won't regret it when the teenage label's torn off the arse pockets of my drip-dry sky-blue jeans.'

What the Wiz said was at any rate partially true. This teenage ball had had a real splendour in the days when the kids discovered that, for the first time since centuries of kingdom-come, they'd money, which hitherto had always been denied to us at the best time in life to use it, namely, when you're young and strong, and also before the newspapers and telly got hold of this teenage fable and prostituted it as conscripts seem to do to everything they touch. Yes, I tell you, it had a real savage splendour in the days when we found that no one couldn't sit on our faces any more because we'd loot to spend at last, and our world was to be our world, the one we wanted

11

and not standing on the doorstep of somebody else's waiting for honey, perhaps.

I got off my stool and went and stood by the glass of that tottering old department store, pressed up so close it was like I was out there in the air, suspended over space above the city, and I swore by Elvis and all the saints that this last teenage year of mine was going to be a real rave. Yes, man, come whatever, this last year of the teenage dream I was out for kicks and fantasy.

But my peace was shattered by the noise I heard of Wizard in an argument with the conscript behind the counter bar.

I should explain the Wiz has for all oldies just the same kind of hatred psychos have for Jews or foreigners or coloureds, that is, he hates everyone who's not a teenager, except for short-pant sperms and chicklets, whom I suppose he regards as teenagers in bud. The Wiz just doesn't like the population outside the teenage bracket, and takes every chance he gets to make the oldies conscious of their hair-root dyes, and sing out aloud the anthem of the teenage triumph.

Wiz has the art of clawing the poor taxpayers on the raw. Even from where I stood I saw the barman's face was lurid as a point steak, and as I approached I heard that sharp, flat, dry little voice the Wizard has was needling him with, 'Oh, I suppose you're underpaid, boy, that's what's the matter with you. Don't like your work up here with these old hens.'

'You'd best settle up and 'op it,' said the conscript.

The Wizard turned to me. '"'Op it," he says – just

listen! This serf speaks authentic old-tyme *My Fair Lady* dialect.'

The Wizard's tactic always was to tempt the enemy to strike him, which, because he's small and seems so slender and so juvenile, arouses sympathy of other oldsters, the born aunts among them especially, who take his side and split the anti-teenage camp wide open. He often succeeds, because I can tell you he's completely fearless, a thoroughly vicious, dirty little pugilist, and only fails when sometimes they laugh at him, which makes him beside himself with rage.

The present argument, as I expected, was about the bill, which Wizard, when he's in the mood, will query even if it's for an item like a cup of tea. And often, even when he's loaded, he'll make out he's completely skint and say to them well, there you are, I've got no money, what you going to do about it? And this with the left breast pocket of his Continental casual jacket stuffed with notes and even visible, but his face so fierce and come-and-kill-me that it frightens them, and even me. It usually seems to work, because they say get to hell out, which he does in his own time, and at his own speed, as if it was an eight-course meal he'd had and paid for, not just bounced a bill.

I paid for him, and Wiz didn't mind my paying, only laughed that little ha-ha laugh of his as we walked down the white and silver metal stair. 'Boy,' he said, 'you're a born adult number. With your conventional outlook, you just can't wait to be a family man.'

I was vexed at him, but answered, 'Don't be like that,

Wizard. We all know you're loaded, so why do you play that kindergarten game?'

Which is a fact, I mean his being loaded, because the Wiz, in spite of his tender years, is, for his age, the number one hustler of the capital, his genius being in introducing A to B, or vice versa, that is to say, if someone has an article to sell, and someone else desires it, Wiz has a marvellous instinct for meeting them both and bringing them together. But, you might answer, that's what shops are for, which is exact. But not for exchanging the sort of article the Wizard's customers are interested in which, as you've guessed, are not so legal, and when I say 'article', I mean it may be the kind of services which might make you call the Wiz a pimp, or a procurer if you wanted to, not that it would worry him particularly.

I've wondered how the Wizard gets away with it, because, after all, he deals with male and female hustlers who must be wiser than he is, and certainly, at any rate, are stronger. But he handles them all right – in fact in a way that makes you proud to be a kid. And how he does it is, I think, that he's found out at a very early age what most kids never know, and what it took me years myself to discover – in fact it didn't dawn on me until this year, when the knowledge of it's come too late to use – namely, that youth has power, a kind of divine power straight from mother nature. All the old taxpayers know of this because, of course, for one thing, the poor old sordids recollect their own glorious teenage days, but yet they're so jealous of us, they hide this fact, and whisper it among themselves. As for the boys and girls,

14

the dear young absolute beginners, I sometimes feel that if they only *knew* this fact, this very simple fact, namely how powerful they really are, then they could rise up overnight and enslave the old taxpayers, the whole damn lot of them – toupets and falsies and rejuvenators and all – even though they number millions and sit in the seats of strength. And I guess it was the fact that only little Wizard realised this, and not all the other two million teenagers they say exist throughout our country, that makes him so sour, like a general with lazy troops he can't lead into battle.

'*He's got the whole wide world in his hands!*
He's got this crumby village drapers, in his hands!
He's got . . .'

This was the Wizard, singing his improvisation on the Laurie London number. And as the stairway cage was probably built of breeze blocks, there was a loudhailer echo up and down the flights which astonished the lady peasants who were using it to carry home their purchases.

'Easy now,' I said, laying my hand upon the Wizard's arm.

He wrenched it away, and glared at me as if I was what I certainly *was* just at that moment, his deadliest enemy.

'Don't *touch* me!' he said, if you can call it 'said', because 'screeched' would be more like it.

'All right, big boy,' I told him, mentally washing my hands of the whole damn matter.

We came out of the glass doors into an absolutely

15

fabulous June day, such as only that old whore London can throw up, though very occasionally. The Wizard stood looking up at me as if debating whether to insult me, or to call the cold war off.

'Dig this, Wiz,' I said to him. 'I'm not by nature given to interference, it's just that I think the way you're going on you'll kill yourself, which I'd regret.'

This seemed to please him, and he smiled. And when the little Wizard drops his guard it really is miraculous, because a really charming boy looks out at you from behind that razor-edge face of his, if only for an instant. But he didn't say anything to me.

'I got to go and see Suzette,' I told him. 'I hear she has a client for me.'

'You should like that,' said Wizard, 'after you've spent so much paying bills for *me*.'

'You're a horrid little creature, Wiz,' I told him. 'It's a wonder to me they don't use you for some experiment.'

'See you,' said Wizard. 'Please give my hate to little Suze.'

He'd hailed a cab, because Wizard only travels about in taxis, and will walk for miles rather than use the public transportation system, though I sometimes have known him take a late-night bus. He had a long argument with the driver before he got in – it seems Wizard was trying to persuade the citizen to leave one door open, so that the summer breezes could ruffle the Wizard's true-blond Marlon Brando hairdo on his journey.

But I couldn't wait to see if he succeeded, because with Suzette you have to be dead on time for this reason, that if she sees any Spade she likes the look of, she'll get up at once and follow him, come what may, though I will say for her that she'll sit like her bottom was glued to the seat till whatever time you've dated her for, even if Harry Belafonte should walk by. Her name, by the way, Suzette, has been given to her because that's what, according to Suze herself, a Spade lover of hers called her once when, gazing hungrily at her from top to toe, especially toe, this Spade, who was a Fang boy from French Gaboon, said to her, '*Chérie*, you are my *Crêpe Suzette*, I'm going to eat you.' Which I've no doubt he did.

The fact is, that little sweet seventeen Suzette is Spade-crazy. I've often explained to her that to show you're a friend of the coloured races, and free from race prejudice and all that crap, you don't have to take every Spade you meet home and drag him between sheets. But Suzette is quite shameless about it, enjoys the life, and naturally is very popular among the boys. She doesn't make any money out of her activities, because though I think she'd like to, and certainly would, and quite a bit of it if she happened to like whites, the Spades don't give her anything, not because they're not loaded or generous, both of which they very often are, but because every Spade believes, in spite of any evidence to the contrary (and there's a lot), that every woman in creation is thirsting for the honour of his company. So poor old Suzette, in spite of her being the belle of the Strutters' Ball, has to toil every day at a fashion house, which as a matter of fact is how she is so useful to me.

I now shall disclose my graft, which is peculiar. It's

not that I haven't tried what's known as steady labour, both manual and brain, but that every job I get, even the well-paid ones (they were the manual), denied me the two things I consider absolutely necessary for gracious living, namely – take out a pencil, please, and write them down – to work in your own time and not somebody else's, number one, and number two, even if you can't make big money every day, to have a graft that lets you make it *sometime*. It's terrible, in other words, to live entirely without hope.

So what I am, is a photographer: street, holiday park, studio, artistic poses and, from time to time, when I can find a client, pornographic. I know it's revolting, but then it only harms the psychos who are my customers, and as for the kids I use for models, they'd do it all down to giggles, let alone for the fee I pay them. To have a job like mine means that I don't belong to the great community of the mugs: the vast majority of squares who are exploited. It seems to me this being a mug or a non-mug is a thing that splits humanity up into two sections absolutely. It's nothing to do with age or sex or class or colour – either you're born a mug or born a non-mug, and me, I sincerely trust I'm born the latter.

So now you can see why, from time to time, I pay a call on Suze. For Suze, in the course of business at her fashion house, meets lots of kinky characters, usually among the daddies of the chicks who dress there, and acts as agent for me getting orders from them for my pornographic photos, drawing commission from me at the rate of twenty-five per cent. So you realise Suze is a sharp gal, and no doubt this is because she's not only English, but part Gibraltarian, partly Scotch and partly Jewish, which is perhaps why I get along with her, as I'm supposed to have a bit of Jewish blood from my mother's veins as well – at any rate, I know I'm circumcised.

I found Suze in her Belgravia coffee bar, just near her work, which was one of the weirdie varieties, called The Last Days of Pompeii, and done up to represent just that, with stone seats in dim nooks, and a ruined well as the centrepiece, and a mummified Roman let into a hole in one of the walls just for kicks, I dare say. Suze was allowing her cappuccino to grow cold, and nibbling at a cream cheese and gherkin sandwich, for Suze never eats middays, as she's inclined to plumpness, which I rather like, but makes up for it at evening time with huge plates of chicken and peas she cooks for her Spade visitors.

'Hi, darl,' she said.

'Hi, hon,' I answered.

That's how we heard two movie stars address each other at a film we went to ages ago that rather sent us, in the days when Suze and I were steady.

'How are the boys?' I asked her, sitting down opposite, and under that tiny table putting my knees to hers.

'The boys,' she said, 'are quite all right. Quite, quite okay.'

'Have you had your hundredth yet?' I asked her.

'Not yet a hundred,' Suze replied, 'not yet, no, I don't think so, not a hundred.'

I ordered my striped cassata. 'You ever think of marrying with one of them?' I asked her edgily, as usual

19

slipping into that groove of nastiness that affects me whenever I talk to Suze of her love life.

She looked dreamy, and actually flipped her eyelashes in the Italian starlet manner. 'If ever I marry,' she said, 'it will be exclusively for distinction. I mean to make a very *distinguished* marriage.'

'Not with a Spade, then.'

'No, I don't think so.' She blew a little brown nest in the white froth of her cappuccino. 'As a matter of fact,' she said, 'I've had an offer. Or what amounts to an offer.'

She stopped, and gazed at me. 'Go on,' I said.

'From Henley.'

'No!'

She nodded, and lowered her eyes.

'That horrible old poof!' I cried.

I should explain that Henley is the fashion designer Suzette works for, and old enough to be her aunt, quite apart from anything else.

Suze looked severe and sore at me. 'Henley,' she said, 'may be an invert, but he has distinction.'

'He's certainly got that!' I cried. 'Oh, he's certainly got that all right!'

She paused. 'Our marriage,' she continued, 'would of course be sexless.'

'You bet it would!' I yelled. I glared at her, seeking the killer phrase. 'And what will Miss Henley say,' I shouted, 'when the Spades come tramping in their thousands into his distinguished bridal chamber?'

She smiled with pity, and was silent. I could have smacked her down.

'I don't dig this, Suze,' I cried. 'You're a secretary in that place, you're not even a glamorous model. Why should he want *you*, of all people, as his front woman alibi?'

'I think he admires me.'

I glowered her 'You're marrying for loot,' I shouted out. 'With the Spades you were just a strumpet, now you're going to be a whore!'

She poked her determined, obstinate little face at mine. 'I'm marrying for distinction,' she replied, 'and that's a thing that you could never give me.'

'No, that I couldn't,' I said, very bitterly indeed.

I got up under pretext of spinning a record, pressed my three buttons wildly, and luckily got Ella, who would soothe even a volcano. I walked just a moment to the door, and really, the heat was beginning to saturate the air and hit you. 'This summer can't last,' said the yobbo behind the Gaggia, mopping his sweaty brow with his sweaty arm.

'Oh yes it can, daddy-o,' I answered. 'It can last till the calendar says stop.'

'No . . .' said the yobbo, gazing meanly up at the black-blue of that succulent June sky.

'It can shine on forever,' I hissed at him, leaning across and mingling with the steam out of his Gaggia. Then I turned away to go back and talk business with Suze. 'Tell me about this client,' I asked her, sitting down. 'Tell me the who, the when, and even, if you know it, the why.'

Suze was quite nice to me, now she'd planted her little

arrow in my lungs. 'He's a diplomat,' she answered, 'or so he says.'

'Does he represent any special country?'

'Not exactly, no, he's over here for some conference, so she told me.'

'She who?'

'His woman, who came in with him to see Henley and buy dresses.'

I gazed at Suzette. 'Please tell me a thing I've always wanted to know. How do you go about raising the matter?'

'What matter?'

'That you're an agent for my camera studies.'

Suze smiled.

'Oh, it's quite simple, really. Sometimes, of course, they know of me, I mean recommended by other clients. Or else, if not, I just size them up and show them some from my collection.'

'Just like that?'

'Yes.'

'And Henley, does he know?'

'I never do it if he's there,' said Suze, 'but I expect he knows.'

'I see,' I said, not pleased somehow by this. 'I see. And what of this diplomat? How do I fix the deal?'

'*Do you mind?*' was all Suzette answered, the reason being that by now I had one of her knees caught between my two. I let go, and said, 'Well, how?'

She opened her square-sac, and handed me a shop-soiled card, which said:

Mickey Pondoroso
12b, Wayne Mews West,
London (England), SW1

The address part was in printed copperplate, but the name was written in by hand.

'Oh,' I said, fingering this thing. 'Have you any idea what sort of snap he'll need?'

'I didn't go into any details.'

'Don't sound so scornful, Suze. You're taking my twenty-five per cent, aren't you?'

'Have you got it for me in advance?'

'No. Don't come the acid drop.'

'Well, then.'

I got up to leave. She came rather slowly after.

'I'll go out looking for this character,' I said. 'Shall I walk you back first to your emporium?'

'Better not,' she said. 'We're not supposed to bring our boyfriends near the building.'

'But I'm not,' I said, 'your boyfriend any longer.'

'No,' said Suzette. She kissed me quickly on my lips and ran. Then stopped running, and disappeared at walking pace.

I started off across Belgravia, in search of Mr Mickey P.

And I must say that, in its way, I rather dig Belgravia: not because of what the daddies who live there think of it, that is, the giddy summit of a mad sophistication, but because I see it as an Olde Englishe product like Changing the Guard, or Savile Row suits, or Stilton cheese in big brown china jars, or any of those things they advertise in *Esquire* to make the Americans want to visit picturesque Great Britain. I mean, in Belgravia, the flower boxes, and the awnings over doors, and the front walls painted different shades of cream. The gracious living in the red with huge green squares outside the window, and purring hired and diplomatic vehicles, and everything delivered at the door and on the slate, and little restaurants where camp creatures in cotton skintight slacks serve half an avocado pear at five bob, cover charge exclusive. All that seems missing from the scene is good King Ted himself. And I never cross this area without thinking it's a great white-and-green theatre with a cast of actors in a comedy I rather admire, however sad it may be to think of.

So there was I, in fact, crossing it in my new Roman suit, which was a pioneering exploit in Belgravia, where they still wore jackets hanging down over what the tailors call the seat. And around my neck hung my Rolleiflex, which I always keep at the ready, night and day, because you never know, a disaster might occur, like a plane crashing in Trafalgar Square, which I could sell to the fish-and-chip wrapper dailies, or else a scandal, like a personage seen with the wrong kind of man or woman, which little Mr Wiz would certainly know how to merchandise.

This brought me to Wayne Mews West, which, like often in these London backwaters, was quite rural, with cobbles and flowers and silence and a sort of a sniff of horse manure around, when I saw a Vespa cycle with a CD plate on it parked nearby a recently built white mews flat, and crouching beside a wooden tub outside a chrome front door, a figure in a mauve Thai silk summer suit who was, would you believe it, watering a fig tree growing in the tub.

I snapped him.

'Hullo there,' he said, looking up and smiling at me. 'You like me to pose for you beside my Vespa?'

'Can't they allot you anything with four wheels?' I said. 'You must come from one of those very corrupt, small countries.'

Mr Mickey P. was naturally not pleased. 'I smashed it up,' he said. 'It was a Pontiac convertible.'

'This rule of the left we have,' I said, 'is so confusing.'

'I understand the rules,' said Mr P., 'but got run into, just.'

'You always do,' I said.

'Do what?'

'Keep still, please, and smile if you like that kind of snap.' I clicked a few. He stood by his motor scooter as if it was an Arab pony. 'You always get run into,' I explained. 'It's always the other feller.'

Mr Pondoroso leant his scooter against the Wayne Mews wall.

'Well, I don't know,' he said, 'but there are a lot of very bad drivers in your country.'

I wound my spool. 'And what are they like in yours?' I asked him.

'In mine,' he said, 'it doesn't matter, because the roads are wide, and there are fewer autos.'

I looked up at him. I was curious to find where he came from, but didn't like asking direct questions, which seems to me a crude way of finding out things that, with a little patience, they'll tell you anyway. Besides, we were still at the sparring stage that always seems necessary with the seniors, whatever their race may be.

'You're a Latin American?' I asked him.

'I come from these parts, yes, but I live in the United States.'

'Oh, yes. You're representing both?'

He smiled his diplomatic smile. 'I'm in a UNO job,' he said, 'attached. Press officer to the delegation.'

I didn't ask which one it was. 'I wonder,' I said, 'if I could step inside out of this glare to change my spool?'

'To . . . ?'

'Recharge my camera. As a matter of fact,' I said, eyeing him under the portico, 'I believe I have to talk about photography to you. Suzette sent me, you met her at Henley's place.'

He looked cautious and blank a moment, then turned on the diplomatic grin again and battered me on the shoulder. 'Come right in,' he cried, 'I've been expecting you.'

Inside it looked cool and costly – you know, with glass-topped white metal furniture, oatmeal-stained woodwork, Yank mags and indoor plants and siphons, but as if none of it belonged to him, as in fact I don't suppose it did. 'You have a drink?' he said.

'Thank you, no, I won't,' I told him.

'You don't drink?'

'No, sir, never.'

He stared at me, holding a bottle and a glass, and genuinely interested in me for the first time, so it seemed. 'Then how do you get by?' he asked me.

I've had to explain this so often before to elder brethren, that it's now almost a routine. 'I don't use the liquor kick,' I said, 'because I get all the kicks I need from me.'

'You don't drink at all?'

'Either you drink a lot,' I told him, 'or else, like me, you don't drink anything at all. Liquor's not made for zips, but for orgies or total abstinence. Those are the only wise weddings between man and bottle.'

He shook his head, and poured himself some deadly brew. 'So you're the photographer,' he said.

I saw I'd have to be very patient with this character. 'That's me,' I said. 'What kind of print might you be needing?' I went on, not sure yet what kinkiness I had to cater for.

He drew himself up and flexed his torso. 'Oh, I would want you to photograph me.'

'You?'

'Yes. Is that unusual?'

'Well, it is, a-bit-a-little. My clients usually want photographs of models doing this and that . . .'

I was trying to make it easier for the cat. But he said, 'Me, I want no models – only me.'

'Yes, I see. And you doing exactly what?'

'In athletic poses,' he replied.

'Just you alone?'

'Of course.' He saw I was still puzzled. 'In my gymnastic uniform,' he explained.

He put down his glass and bottle, and stepped into the next room while I flicked Yank mags and had a tonic water. Then out he came wearing – and I swear I'm not inventing this – a white-laced pair of navy-blue basketball shoes, black ballet rehearsal tights, a nude chest thatched like a Christmas card, and, on his head, a small, round, racing-swimmer's cap.

'You can begin,' he said.

'How many poses do you want?'

'About a hundred.'

'Seriously? It'll cost you quite a lot . . . You want to be *doing* anything particular, or just poses?'

'I leave this to your inspiration.'

'Okay. Just walk about, then. Do whatever comes naturally to you.'

As I clicked away, I worked out what the most was I could ask him: and I wondered if he was perhaps insolvent, or a lunatic, or in trouble with the law, like so many in the capital these days. This crazy Latin-American number was lumbering all over the furniture of his apartment, striking narcissistic poses, as if he was already gloating over the prints I'd give him of such a glorious big hunk of man.

After a while of this in silence, he perspiring, I chasing him round clicking like a professor with a bug-net, he grabbed a drink, collapsed into a white shining leather chair, and said, 'Perhaps you can help me.'

'Mr Pondoroso, I thought I was.'

'You call me Mickey.'

'If you say so,' I said to him, playing it cool, and rapidly reloading my apparatus.

'It's like this,' said Mr Mickey P. 'I have a study to complete for my organisation on British folk ways in the middle of the century.'

'Fine,' I said, snapping him sitting down, his upper belly bulging over his ballet pants, so as to make my hundred quickly.

'Well, I've observed the British,' he said, 'but I've got very few interesting ideas about them.'

'How long have you been observing them?' I asked.

'Six weeks, I think, which I know is not very long, but even so, I just can't quite get perspectives.' Mickey P. peered at me between zips. 'Even the weather's wrong,' he said. 'It's reputed to be cold in the English summer, but just look at it.'

I saw what he meant. An old sun from the Sahara had crept up on us unawares, one we weren't at all ready for, and baked us into quite a different loaf from the usual soggy pre-sliced product.

'Try asking me,' I said.

'Well, let's take the two chief political parties,' he began, and I could see he was winding himself up for a big performance.

'No thank you,' I said quickly. 'I don't want to take any part of either.'

His face slipped a bit.

'They don't interest you, is that it?'

'How could they?'

'But your destinies,' he said, 'are being worked out by their initiatives . . .'

I clicked his unshaven face in a close-up horror picture. 'Whoever,' I said, 'is working out my destinies, you can be quite sure it's not those parliamentary numbers.'

'You mustn't despise politics,' he told me. 'Somebody's got to do the housekeeping.'

Here I let go my Rolleiflex, and chose my words with care.

'If they'd stick to their housekeeping, which is the only backyard they can move freely in to any purpose, and stopped playing Winston Churchill and the Great Armada when there's no tin soldiers left to play with any more, then no one would despise them, because no one would even notice them.'

Mr Pondoroso smiled. 'I guess,' he said, 'that fixes the politicians.'

'I do hope so,' I replied.

'Then take,' said Mr P., 'the bomb. What are you going to do about *that*?'

Clearly, I had a zombie on my hands.

'Listen,' I said to him. 'No one in the world under twenty is interested in that bomb of yours one little bit.'

'Ah,' said this diplomatic cat, his face coming all over crafty, '*you* may not be, here in Europe I mean, but what of young peoples in the Soviet Union and the USA?'

'Young peoples in the Soviet Union and the USA,' I told him, clearly and very slowly, 'don't give a single lump of cat's shit for the bomb.'

'Easy, son. How you know that?'

'Man, it's only you adult numbers who want to destroy one another. And I must say, sincerely, speaking as what's called a minor, I'd not be sorry if you did: except that you'd probably kill a few millions of us innocent kiddos in the process.'

Mr P. grew a bit vexed.

'But you haven't been to America, have you!' he exclaimed. 'Or to Russia, and talked to these young people!'

'Why do I have to go, mister? You don't have to travel to know what it's like to be young, any time, anywhere. Believe me, Mr Pondoroso, youth is international, just like old age is. We're both very fond of life.'

I don't know if what I said was crap, or if anyone in the universe thinks it besides me, but at all events, it's what I honestly believe – from my own observations and from natters I've had with my old Dad.

Mr P. was looking disappointed with me. Then he brightened up a bit, raised his brows eagerly, and said, 'That leaves us with only one topic for an Englishman, but a very important one . . . (here the pronk half rose in his ballet tights and saluted) . . . and that is, Her Britannic Majesty the Queen!'

I sighed.

'No, please, not that one,' I said to him politely but very firmly, 'Really, that's a subject that we're very, very tired of. One which I just can't work up the interest to have any ideas about at all.'

Mr Pondoroso looked like he'd had a wasted afternoon. He stood up in his gymnastic uniform, which with his movements round the room had slipped a bit to show a fold of hairy olive tum, and he said to me, 'So you've not much to tell me of Britain and her position.'

'Only,' I said, 'that her position is that she hasn't found her position.'

He didn't wig this, so giving me a kindly smile, he stepped away to make himself respectable again. I put a disc on to his hi-fi, my choice being Billie H., who sends me even more than Ella does, but only when, as now, I'm tired, and also, what with seeing Suze again, and working hard with my Rolleiflex and then this moronic conversation, graveyard gloomy. But Lady Day has suffered so much in her life she carries it all for you, and soon I was quite a cheerful cat again.

'I wish I had this one,' I said, when Mr P. appeared.

'Take it, please,' he told me, beaming.

'Wait till you get my bill for the snaps before you make me gifts as well,' I warned him.

His only answer, which was rather nice of him, was to put the record in its sleeve and stick it underneath my arm like as if he was posting a letter.

I thanked him, and we went out in the sun. 'When you're tired of your Vespa,' I said wittily, 'you can give me that as well.'

Boy, can you credit it, it functioned! 'As soon as my automobile's repaired,' he said, slapping his hand down on the saddle, 'this toy is yours.'

I took his hand. 'Mickey,' I said, 'if you mean that, you're my boy. And the photos, need I say, are complimentary.'

'No, no,' he cried. 'That is another, separate business. For the pictures, I shall pay you cash.'

He darted in. I tried sitting on the scooter saddle for the feel of it, and when he darted out, with this time his mauve Thai silk jacket on, he handed me a folded cheque.

'Thank you,' I said, unfolding it. 'But, you know, this isn't cash.'

'Oh. You prefer cash?'

'It's not that, Mickey – it's just that you *said* cash, didn't you, see? But let's look where the branch is. Victoria station, lovely. And I see it's not one of the ugly crossed variety, good boy. I'll go there before they put up the shutters, fare you well.'

With which I blew, reflecting this, that if by any fragment of a chance he meant it, that is, about the scooter, and if I wanted to act quick and get the snaps developed, so as to keep contact with him and work on his conscience, if he'd got one, to secure the vehicle, I'd have to go home immediately to my darkroom.

So off I set, but stopping on the way to raid the bank, which was getting ready to close as I arrived, in fact the clerk had half the door shut, and he looked me up and down, my Spartan hairdo and my teenage drag and all, and said just, 'Yes?'

'Yes what?' I answered.

'You have *business* here?' he said to me.

'I have,' I told him.

'*Business*?' the poverty-stricken pen-pusher repeated.

'Business,' I said.

He still had his hands upon the door. 'We're closing now,' he told me.

'If my eyes don't fail me,' I replied, 'the clock above your desk says 2.56 p.m., so perhaps you'll be kind enough to get back behind it there and serve me.'

He said no more, and made his way round inside the counter, then raised his brows at me across it, and I handed over Mr Pondoroso's cheque.

'Are you,' he said, after examining it as if it was the sort of thing a bank had never seen before, 'the payee?'

'The which?'

'Is,' he said, speaking slowly and clearly, as if to a deaf Chinese lunatic, 'this-your-name-written-on-the-cheque?'

Jawohl, mein Kapitan,' I said, 'it is.'

Now he looked diabolically crafty.

'And how,' he enquired, 'do I know this name is yours?'

I said, 'How do you know it isn't?'

He bit his lip, as the paperbacks say, and asked me, 'Have you any proof of your identity?'

'Yes,' I replied. 'Have you of yours?'

He shut his eyes, reopened them and said, 'What proof?'

'In the arse pocket of my jeans here,' I said to him, slapping my hindquarters briskly, 'I carry a perspex folder, with within it my driving licence, which is a clean one I'm surprised to say, my Blood Donor's Certificate, showing I've given two pints of gore so far this year, and tatty membership cards of more speakeasies and jazz clubs than I remember. You may look at them if you really want to, or you could get Mr Pondoroso on the blower and ask him to describe me, or, better still, you could stop playing games and give me the ten pounds your client has instructed you to pay me that is, unless your till is short of loot.'

To which he answered, 'You have not yet endorsed the document on the back, please.'

I scribbled out my name. He twiddled the cheque, began writing on it and said, without looking up, 'I take it you're a minor?'

'Yes,' I said, 'if it's anything to do with anything, I am.' He still said nothing, and he still didn't hand me over my loot. 'But now I'm a big boy,' I continued, 'I don't wet my bed any longer, and know how to hit back if I'm attacked.'

He gave me the notes as if they were two deformed specimens the bank happened to have it was ashamed of, then nipped round his counter and saw me out of the door, and locked it swiftly on my heels. I must admit this incident made me overheated, it was all so unnecessary and so old-fashioned, treating a teenager like a kid, and I headed away from Victoria towards my home in quite a rage.

I must explain the only darkroom I possess of my own, without which, of course, I'd have to get my printing done commercially, is at my old folks' residence in Belgravia South, as they call it, namely, Pimlico. As I expect you'll have guessed, I don't like going there, and haven't lived in the place (except when they're off on their summer seaside orgy) in years. But they still keep what they call 'my room' there, out in the annexe at the back, which used to be the conservatory, full of potted flowers.

The family, if you can call it that, consists of three besides myself, plus numerous additions. The three are my poor old Dad, who isn't really all that old, only forty-eight, but who was wrecked and ruined by the 1930s, so he never fails to tell me, and then my Mum, who's much older than she lets on or, I will say this for her, looks certainly three or four years older than my Dad, and finally my half-brother Vern, who Mum had by a mystery man seven years before she tied up with my poppa, and who's the number-one weirdie, layabout and monster of the Westminster city area. As for the numerous additions, these are Mum's lodgers, because she keeps a boarding house, and some of them, as you'd expect if you knew Ma, are lodged in very firmly, though there's nothing my Dad can do about it, apparently, as his spirits are squashed by a combination of my Mum and the 1930s, and that's one of the several reasons for which I left the dear old ancestral home.

Mum won't let me have a key and, as a matter of fact, is even tough about giving one to her paid-up boarders, as she likes to see them come and go, even late at night, so though as a matter of fact I've had a key made of my own, in case of accidents, I go through the form of ringing the front doorbell, just out of politeness, and also to show her I regard myself strictly as a visitor and don't *live* there. As usual, although she gets mad if you go down the area steps and knock on the basement door, where she almost always is, Mum came out from there into the area and looked up to see who it was, before she'd come up the stairs inside and open the front door for me which she might have done, if she'd been civilised, in the first place.

There she stood, her face lighting up at the sight of a pair of slacks, even her own son's, with that sloppy sexy expression that always drove me mad, because, after all, tucked away behind all those mounds of highly desirable flesh, my Mum has got real brains. But she's only used them to make herself more appealing, like pepper and salt and garlic on an overdone pork chop.

'Hello, Blitz Baby,' she said.

Which is what she calls me, because she had me in one, in a tube shelter with an air raid warden acting as midwife, as she never tires of telling me or, worse still, other people in my presence.

'Hullo, Ma,' I said to her.

She still stood there, pink hands with detergent suds on them on her Toulouse-Lautrec hips, giving me that come-hither look she gave her lodgers, I suppose.

'Are you going to open up?' I asked her, 'or should I climb in through your front parlour window?'

'I'll send you down your father,' she answered me. 'I expect he'll be able to let you in.'

This is the trick my Mum has, to speak to me of Dad as if he's only *my* relation, only mine, that she never had

37

anything whatever to do with (apart, of course, from having had sex with him and even marrying the poor old man). I suppose this is because, number one, Dad's what's known as a failure, though I don't regard him as one exactly, as anyone could have seen he'd never have succeeded at anything anyway, and number two, to show that her first husband, whoever he was, the one who goosed her into producing that Category A morbid, my elder half-brother Vernon, was the *real* man in her life, not my own poor old ancestor. Well, that's her little bit of feminine psychology: you certainly learn a lot about women from your Mum.

I was kept there waiting a considerable time, so that if it wasn't for the need of my darkroom they'd have never seen me, when Dad appeared with that dead-duck look not merely on his face, but hanging on his whole poor old scruffy body, which makes me demented, because really he's got a lot of character, and though he's no mind to speak of, he's read a lot like I do – I mean, tried to make the best of what he's got in a way my Mum hasn't tried to do at all, or even thought of trying. As usual, he opened the door without a word except 'Hullo,' and started off up the stairs again towards his room in the attic portion of the building, which is just an act because he knows, of course, I'll follow him up there for a little chatter, if only for politeness' sake, and to show him I'm his son.

But today I didn't, partly because I was suddenly tired of his performance, and partly because I'd so much work to do immediately inside my darkroom. So out I went and, would you believe it, found that horrible old weirdie Vernon had built himself a cuckoo's nest there, which was something new.

'Hullo, Jules,' I said to him. 'And how's my favourite yobbo?'

'Don't call me Jules,' he said. 'I've already told you.'

Which he has – perhaps 200,000 times or so, ever since I invented the name for him, on account of Vernon = Verne = Jules of *Round the World in Eighty Days*.

'And what are you doing in my darkroom, Julie?' I asked this oafo brother of mine.

He'd got up off the camp bed in the corner – all blankets and no sheets, just like my Vernon – and came over and did an act he's done with monotonous regularity ever since I can remember, namely, to stand up over me, close to me, breathing heavily and smelling of putrid perspiration.

'What, again?' I said to him. 'Not another corny King Kong performance!'

His fist whisked past my snout in playful panto.

'Do grow *up*, Vernon,' I said to him, very patiently. 'You're a big boy now, more than a quarter of a century old.'

What would happen next would be either that he'd push me around in which case, of course, it would be just a massacre, except that he knew I'd get in at least one blow that would really cripple him, and perhaps even harm him for life – or else he'd suddenly feel the whole thing was beneath his dignity, and want to talk to me, talk to anyone, in fact, whatever, since the poor old ape was such an H-Certificate product he was really very lonely.

So he plucked at my short-arse Italian jacket with his great big cucumber fingers and said, 'What you wear this thing for?'

'Excuse me, Vernon,' I said, edging past him to unload my camera on my table. 'I wear it,' I said, taking the jacket off and hanging it up, 'to keep warm in winter, and, in summer, to captivate the chicks by swinging my tail around.'

'Hunh!' he said, his mind racing fast, but nothing coming out except this noise like a polar bear with wind. He looked me up and down while his thoughts came into focus. 'Those clothes you wear,' he said at last, 'disgust me.'

And I hope they did! I had on precisely my full teenage drag that would enrage him – the grey pointed alligator casuals, the pink neon pair of ankle crêpe nylon-stretch, my Cambridge blue glove-fit jeans, a vertical-striped happy shirt revealing my lucky neck-charm on its chain, and the Roman-cut short-arse jacket just referred to . . . not to mention my wrist identity jewel, and my Spartan warrior hairdo, which everyone thinks costs me 17/6d in Gerrard Street, Soho, but which I, as a matter of fact, do myself with a pair of nail scissors and a three-sided mirror that Suzette's got, when I visit her flatlet up in Bayswater, W2.

'And you, I suppose,' I said, deciding that attack was the best method of defence though oh! so wearisome, 'you imagine you look alluring in that horrible men's wear suiting that you've bought in a marked-down summer sale at the local casbah.'

'It's manly,' he said, 'and it's respectable.'

I gazed at the floppy dung-coloured garments he had on. 'Ha!' was about all I said.

'What's more,' he went on, 'I've not wasted money on it. It's my demobilisation suit.'

My heaven, yes, it looked it – *yes*!

'When *you've* done your military service,' the poor old yokel said, his boot face breaking into a crafty grin, 'you'll be given one too, you'll find. *And* a decent haircut just for once.'

I gazed at the goon. 'Vernon,' I said, 'I'm sorry for you. Somehow you missed the teenage rave, and you never seem to have had a youth. To try to tell you the simplest facts of life is just a waste of valuable breath, however, do try to dig this, if your microbe minibrain is capable. There's no honour and glory in doing military service, once it's compulsory. If it was voluntary, yes, perhaps, but not if you're just sent.'

'The war,' said Vern, 'was Britain's finest hour.'

'What war? You mean Cyprus, boy? Or Suez? Or Korea?'

'No, stupid. I mean the *real* war, you don't remember.'

'Well, Vernon,' I said, 'please believe me, I'm glad I don't. All of you oldies certainly seem to try to keep it well in mind, because every time I open a newspaper, or pick up a paperback, or go to the Odeon, I hear nothing but war, war, war. You pensioners certainly seem to love that old, old struggle.'

'You're just ignorant,' said Vern.

'Well, if I am, Vern, that's quite okay by me. Because I tell you: not being a mug, exactly, I've no intention of playing soldiers for the simple reasons, first of all, that big armies obviously are no longer necessary, what with the atomic, and secondly, no one is going to tell me to do anything I don't want to, no, or try to blackmail me with that crazy old mixture of threats and congratulations that a pronk like you falls for because you're a born form-filler, taxpayer and cannon fodder . . . well, boy, just take a look in the mirror at yourself.'

That left him silent for a while. 'Come on, now,' I said. 'Be a good half-brother, and let me get on with my work. Why have you moved in this room, anyway?'

'You're wrong!' he cried. 'You'll have to do it!'

'That subject's exhausted. We've been into it thoroughly. Do forget it.'

'What we done, you gotta do.'

'Vernon,' I said, 'I hate to tell you this, but you really don't speak very good English.'

'You'll see!'

'All right,' I said, 'I'll see.'

I was trying, as you'll have realised, to drive him out of the room, but the boy is sensitive as the end of a truck, and just flopped back on his bed again, worn out by the mental effort of our conversation. So I put him out of my mind and worked on at my snaps in silence, till Dad knocked on the door with two cups of char; and standing there in the dark, with only the red light burning, we both ignored that moron, not bothering to wonder if he

42

was awake and eavesdropping, or dreaming of winning six Victoria Crosses.

Dad asked me for the news.

Now, this always embarrasses me, because whatever news I tell Dad, he always comes back again to his two theme songs of, number one, what a much better time I have than he had in the 1930s, and, number two, why don't I come back 'home' again – which is what Dad really seems to believe this high-grade brothel that he lives in means to me.

'You've found that he's moved in,' said Dad, pointing in the direction of the bed. 'I tried to stop it, but I couldn't. The room's still yours, though, I've always insisted on that all the way along.'

I imagined poor Dad insisting to my Mum.

'What's she put him here for, anyway?' I asked.

'He's been quarrelling with the lodgers,' Dad said. 'There's one of them in particular, doesn't get on with him at all.'

I didn't like to ask him which or why. So, 'And how's the book going?' I asked my poor old ancestor. Which is a reference to a *History of Pimlico* Dad's said to be composing, but nobody's ever seen it, though it gives him the excuse for getting out of the house, and chatting to people, and visiting public libraries, and reading books.

'I've reached Chapter Twenty-Three,' he said.

'When does that take us up to?' I asked him, already guessing the answer.

'The beginning of the 1930s,' he replied.

I gulped a bit of tea. 'I bet, Dad,' I said, 'you give those poor old 1930s of yours a bit of a bashing.'

I could feel Dad quivering with indignation. 'I certainly do, son!' he shouted in a whisper. 'You've simply no idea what that pre-war period was like. Poverty, unemployment, fascism and disaster and, worst of all, no chance, no opportunity, no sunlight at the end of the corridor, just a lot of hard, frightened, rich old men sitting on top of a pile of dustbin lids to keep the muck from spilling over!'

I didn't quite get all that, but concentrated.

'It was a terrible time for the young,' he went on, grabbing me. 'Nobody would listen to you if you were less than thirty, nobody gave you money whatever you'd do for it, nobody let you *live* like you kids can do today. Why, I couldn't even marry till the 1940s came and the war gave me some sort of a security . . . Just think of the terrible loss, though! If I'd married ten years earlier, when I was young, you and I would have only had twenty years between us instead of thirty, and me already an old man.'

I thought of pointing out to Dad that if he'd married so much earlier it might have been another woman than my Mum, in which case I wouldn't have existed, or not, at any rate, in my present particular form – but let it go. 'Hard cheese,' I said to him instead, hoping he'd got the subject out of his system for this visit. But no, he was off again.

'Just look around you, when you next go out!' he cried. 'Just look at any of the 1930s buildings! What they put up today may be ultramodern, but at any rate it's full of light and life and air. But those 1930s buildings are all shut in and negative, with landlord and broker's man written all over them.'

'Just a minute, Dad,' I said, 'while I hang up this little lot of negatives.'

'Believe me, son, in the 1930s they hated life, they really did. It's better now, even with the bomb.'

I washed my hands under the hot tap that always runs cold as usual. 'You're topping it up a bit there, Dad, aren't you?' I said.

Dad dropped his voice even lower. 'And then, there's another thing,' he said, '—the venereal.'

'Yeah?' I said, though I was really quite a bit embarrassed, because no one likes much discussing that sort of topic with a Dad like mine.

'Yes,' he went on, '—the venereal. It was a scourge – a blight hanging over all young men. It cast a great shadow over love, and made it hateful.'

'It did?' I said. 'Didn't you have doctors, then?'

'Doctors!' he cried. 'In those days, the worst types were practically incurable, or only after years and years of anxiety and doubt . . .'

I stopped my work. 'No kidding?' I said. 'It was like that, then? Well, that's a thought!'

'Yes. No modern drugs and quick relief, like now . . .'

I was quite struck by that, but thought I'd better change the subject all the same.

'Then why aren't you cheerier, Dad?' I said to him. 'If

you like the fifties better, as you say you do, why don't you enjoy yourself a bit?'

My poor old parent gulped. 'It's because I'm too old now, son,' he said. 'I should have had my youth in the 1950s, like you have, and not my middle-age.'

'Well, it's too late to alter that, Dad, isn't it. But hell, you're not yet fifty, you could get out into the world a bit . . . I mean, you're not really too old to get a job, are you, and travel around and see what sights there are? Others have done it, haven't they?'

My poor old Pop was silent.

'Why do you stay in this dump, for instance?' I said to him.

'You mean here with your mother?'

'Yes, Dad. Why?'

'He stays because he's afraid to go, and she keeps him because she wants the place to look respectable.'

This came from the bed and my charming half-brother Vernon, who we'd quite forgotten, and who evidently had been listening to us with both his red ears flapping.

'Ignore him, Dad,' I said. 'He's so easy to ignore.'

'He's nothing to do with *me*,' my father muttered, 'nothing whatever.' And he picked up the cups and made off out of the room, knocking things over.

'You,' I said to Vernon, 'are a real number one horror, a real unidentified thing from outer space.'

The trouble about Vernon, really, as I've said, is that he's one of the last of the generations that grew up before teenagers existed: in fact, he never seems to have been an absolute beginner at any time at all. Even

46

today, of course, there are some like him, i.e. kids of the right age, between fifteen or so and twenty, that I wouldn't myself describe as teenagers: I mean not kiddos who dig the teenage *thing*, or are it. But in poor Vernon's era, the sad slob, there just weren't *any*: can you believe it? Not any authentic teenagers at all. In those days, it seems, you were just an overgrown boy, or an under-grown man, life didn't seem to cater for anything whatever else between.

So I said all this to him.

'Oh, yeah?' he answered (which he must have got from old Clark Gable pictures, like the ones you can see revivals of at the Classics).

'Yeah,' I said to him. 'And that's what explains your squalid downtrodden look, and your groaning and moaning and grouching against society.'

'Is zat so,' he said.

'Zat is, half-brother,' I replied.

I could see him limbering up his brain for a reply: believe me, even I could feel the floor trembling with the effort.

'I dunno about the trouble with *me*,' my oafo brother finally declared, 'but *your* trouble is, you have no social conscience.'

'No what?'

'No social conscience.'

He'd come up close, and I looked into his narrow, meanie eyes. 'That sounds to me,' I said, 'like a parrot cry pre-packaged for you by your fellow squalids of the Ernie Bevin club.'

'Who put you where you are.'

'Which who? And put me where?'

And now this dear fifty per cent relative of mine came up and prodded my pectorals with a stubby, grubby digit.

'It was the Attlee administrations,' said my bro, in his whining, complaining, platform voice, 'who emancipated the working man, and gave the teenagers their economic privileges.'

'So you approve of me.'

'What?'

'If it was the Ernie Bevin boys who gave us our privileges like you say, you must approve of us.'

'No, I don't, oh no.'

'No?'

'That was an unforeseen eventuality,' he said. 'I mean you kids getting all these high-paid jobs and leisure.'

'Not part of the master plan?'

'No. And are you grateful to us? Not a bit of it.'

There I agreed with him at last. 'Why should we be?' I said. 'Your pinko pals did what they wanted to when they got power, and why should we nippers thank them for doing their bounden duty?'

This thought, such as it was, really halted him in his tracks. You could hear his brain racing and grinding behind his red, crunched face, till he cried excitedly, 'You're a traitor to the working-class!'

I took the goon's forefinger, which was still prodding me in the torso, and shook it away from me, and said:

'I am *not* a traitor to the working-class because I do

48

not belong to the working-class, and therefore cannot be a traitor to it.'

'N – h'n!' he really said. 'You belong to the upper-class, I suppose.'

I sighed up.

'And you reject the working-classes that you sprung from.'

I sighed some more.

'You poor old prehistoric monster,' I exclaimed. 'I do *not* reject the working-classes, and I do *not* belong to the upper-classes, for one and the same simple reason, namely, that neither of them interest me in the slightest, never have done, never will do. Do try to understand that, clobbo! I'm just not interested in the whole class crap that seems to needle you and all the taxpayers – needle you all, whichever side of the tracks you live on, or suppose you do.'

He glared at me. I could see that, if once he believed that what I said I really meant, and thousands of the kiddos did the same as well, the bottom would fall out of his horrid little world.

'You're dissolute!' he suddenly cried out, 'Immoral! That's what I say you teenagers all are!'

I eyed the oafo, then spoke up slow. 'I'll tell you one thing about teenagers,' I said, 'compared with how I remember you ten years ago . . . which is we wash between our toes, and change our vests and pants occasionally, and don't keep empty bottles underneath our beds for the good reason we don't touch the stuff.'

Saying which, I left the creature; because really, all

this was such a waste of time, a drag, all so obvious, and honestly, I don't like arguing. If they think that all cat's cock, well, let them think it, and good luck!

I must have been muttering this out aloud along the corridor, because a voice said, over the staircase balustrade, 'Counting your money, then, or talking to the devil?' and of course it was my dear old Mum. There she stood, holding the railings, like someone in a Tennessee Williams film show. So, 'Hullo, Madame Blanche,' I said to her.

For a moment she started to look flattered, like women do if you say something sexy to them, no matter how intimate it is, so long as they think it's flattering to their egos, until she saw I was ice-cold and sarcastic, and her closed-for-business look came over her fine face again.

But I got in my body blow before she could. 'And how is the harem-in-reverse?' I said to her.

'Eh?' said my Ma.

'The gigolo lodgers, the Pal Joeys,' I went on, to make my meaning clear.

As if to prove my point, two of them kindly passed by at that moment, making it hard for poor old Mum to flatten me, as I could see by her bitter glare that she'd intended, which was now transformed into a sickly simper, prim and alluring, that she turned on like a light for the two beefo Malts who walked between us, oozing virility and no deodorant.

As soon as they'd squeezed by her up the stair, with much exchanging of the time of day, she whipped round on me and said, 'You little rat.'

50

'Mother should know,' I told her.

'You're too big for your boots,' she said.

'Shoes,' I told her.

In and out she breathed. 'You've too much spending money, that's your trouble!'

'That's just what's *not* my trouble, Ma.'

'All you teenagers have.'

I said, 'I'm really getting tired of hearing this. All right, we kids have got too much loot to spend! Well, please tell me what you propose to do about it.'

'All that money,' she said, looking at me as if I had pound notes falling out of my ears, and she could snatch them, 'and you're only minors! With no responsibilities to need all that spending money for.'

'Listen to me,' I said. 'Who made us minors?'

'What?'

'You made us minors with your parliamentary what sits,' I told her patiently. 'You thought, "That'll keep the little bastards in their places, no legal rights, and so on," and you made us minors. Righty-o. That also freed us from responsibility, didn't it? Because how can you be responsible if you haven't any rights? And then came the gay-time boom and all the spending money, and suddenly you oldos found that though we minors had no rights, we'd got the money power. In other words – and *listen* to me, Ma – though it wasn't what you'd intended, admittedly, you gave us the money, and you took away our responsibility. Follow me so far? Well, okay! You majors find the laws you cooked up have given you all the duties, and none of the fun, and us the contrary, and you don't like it, do you. Well, as for us, the kids, we do like it, see? We like it fine, Ma. Let it stay that way!'

This left me quite exhausted. Why do I *explain* it to them, talking like a Method number, if they're not interested in me anyway?

Mum, who hadn't been taking this in (and I mean my ideas, though she naturally grasped the general gist), now changed her tactics, which made me wary, for she came down the stair in silence and beckoned me into her private parlour, as in the old way she used to for some trouble, and also as in the old way, I thought it best just not to follow her, and take my leave. But she must have guessed this, because she popped out of her parlour again, and caught me with the front door open, and grabbed my sleeve. 'I must speak to you, son,' she said.

'Speak to me outside, then,' I told her, trying to walk out of the door into the street, but she still clutched.

'No, in my room, it's vital,' she kept hissing.

Well, there we were, practically wrestling on the doorway, when she let go and said, '*Please* come in.'

I closed the door, but wouldn't move further than the corridor, and waited.

'Your father's dying,' Mum told me now.

Now, my first thought was, she's lying; and my second thought was, even if not, she's trying to get at me, because what does she care if he lives or dies? She's going to try to make me *responsible* in some way for something I'm not at all, i.e. the old blackmail of the parents and all oldies against the kiddos.

But I was wrong, it wasn't that, she wanted something from me. After a great deal of a lot of beating about the bush, she said to me, 'If anything should happen to your father, I'd want you to come back here.'

'You'd want me to,' I said. That's all.

'Yes. I'd want you to come back here.'

'And why?'

Because I really didn't know. But what gave me the clue was Mum dropping her eyes and looking modest and girlish and bashful, at first I thought for effect, but then I realised it was partly for true, and that for once she just couldn't help it.

'You want me back,' I said, 'because you'll want a man about the house.'

She mutely acquiesced, as the women's weeklies say.

'To keep the dear old place *respectable*, till you get married once again,' I continued on.

Still Ma was mute.

'Because old Vern, your previous product, is such a drip-dry drag that no one would ever take *him* for the male of the establishment.'

I got an eye-flash for that, but still no answer, while our thoughts sparred up there in silence in the air, unable to disconnect, because no matter how far you're cut off from a close relation, cut right off and eternally severed, there always remains a link of memory – I mean Mum *knew* a whole great deal about me, like nobody else did, and that held us.

'Dad's very much alive,' I said. 'He doesn't look like dying to me a bit. Not a bit, he doesn't.'

'Yes, but I tell you, the doctor's told me . . .'

'I'll take my instructions in that matter from Dad, and Dad alone,' I said. 'And if Dad ever dies, I'll take my instructions from myself.'

She could see that was that, and didn't give me, as you might have expected, a dirty look, but a puzzled one she couldn't control, such as she's given me about six times in my life, as though to say to me, what is this monster I've created?

With which I blew.

Down by the river, where I went to get a breather, I stood beside the big new high blocks of glass-built flats, like an X-ray of a stack of buildings with their skins peeled off, and watched the traffic floating down the Thames below them, very slow and sure (chug, chug) and oily, underneath the electric railway bridge (rattle, rattle), and past the power station like a super-cinema with funnels stuck on it. Peace, perfect peace, though very murky, I decided. Hoot, hoot to you, big barge, bon, bon voyage. There was a merry scream, and I turned about and watched the juveniles, teenagers in bud as you might call them, wearing their little jeans and jumpers, playing in their kiddipark of Disneyland items erected by the borough council to help them straighten out their thwarted egos. When crash! Someone thumped me very painfully on the shoulder blades.

I very slowly turned and saw the pasty, scabies-ridden countenance of Edward the Ted.

'Bang, bang,' I said, humouring the imbecile by pointing my thumb and finger at him like a pistol. 'Bad boy!'

Ed the Ted said nothing, just looked sinister, and stood breathing halitosis on me.

'And what,' I said, 'you doing pounding around down here?'

'I liv ear,' said Ed.

I gazed at the goon.

'My God, Ed,' I cried, 'you can actually talk!'

He came nearer, panting like a hippo, and suddenly twirled a key chain, that he'd been hiding in his fist and in his pocket, till it buzzed like a plane propeller between the two of us.

'What, Ed?' I said. 'No bike-chain? No flick knife? No iron bar?'

And, as a matter of fact, he wasn't wearing his full Teddy uniform either: no velvet-lined frock coat, no bootlace tie, no four-inch solid corridor-creepers – only that insanitary hairdo, creamy curls falling all over his one-inch forehead, and his drainpipes that last saw the inside of a cleaner's in the Attlee era. To stop the chain twirling, he tried to grab it suddenly with the same hand he was spinning it with, hit his own great red knuckles, winced and looked hurt and offended, then fierce and defiant as he put the hand and the chain in his smelly old drainpipes once again.

'Arve moved,' he said. 'Darn ear.'

'And all the click?' I asked him. 'All the notorious Dockhead boys?'

'Not v' click,' said Ed-Ted. 'Jus me.'

I should explain (and I hope you'll believe it, even though it's true) that Edward and I were born and bred, if you can call it that, within a bottle's throw of each other off the Harrow Road in Kilburn, and used to run around together in our short-pant days. Then, when the Ted-thing became all the rage, Edward signed up for the duration, and joined the Teddy boy wolf cubs, or whatever they're called, and later graduated through the Ted high school up the Harrow Road to the full-fledged Teddy boy condition – slit eyes, and cosh, and words of one syllable, and dirty fingernails and all – and left his broken-hearted Mum and Dad, who gave three rousing cheers, and emigrated down to Bermondsey, to join a gang. According to the tales Ed told me, when he left his jungle occasionally and crossed the frontier into the civilised sections of the city and had a coffee with me, he lived a high old life, brave, bold and splendid, smashing crockery in all-night caffs and crowning distinguished colleagues with tyre levers in cul-de-sacs and parking lots, and even appearing in a telly programme on the Ted question where he stared photogenically, and only grunted.

'And why, Ed,' I said, 'have you moved darn ear?'

''Cos me Mar as,' he said. 'She's bin re-owsed.'

He blinked at the effort of two syllables.

'So you still live with Momma?' I enquired.

He beetled at me. 'Course,' he said.

'Big boy like you hasn't got his own little hidey-hole?' I asked.

Ed bunched his torso. 'Lissen,' he said. 'I re-spek my Mar.'

'Cool, man,' I said. 'Now, tell me. What about the

mob, the click? Have they been re-owsed as well?'

'Ner,' he said.

'Ner? What, then?'

At this point, our valiant Edward looked scared, and glancing round about him at the flat blocks, which towered all round like monsters, he said, 'The click's split up.'

I eyed the primitive.

'You mean,' I said, 'that bunch of tearaways have thrown you out?'

'Eh-y?' he cried.

'You heard, Ed. You've been expelled from the Ted college?'

'Naher! Me? Espel me? Wot? Lissen! Me, Ar lef *them*, see? You fink I'm sof, or sumfink?'

I shook my head at the poor goof and his abracadabra. 'Do me a favour, Ed,' I said. 'You're scared of the boys, why not admit it? Old style Teds like you are wasted, anyway: they've all moved out of London to the provinces.'

Edward the Ted did a little war dance on the cracked concrete paving. 'Naher!' he kept crying, like a ten-year-old.

'The trouble is, Ed,' I said, 'you've tried to be a man without having been a teenager. You've tried to miss out one of the flights of stairs.'

At the mention of 'teenager', Ed came to a standstill and stood there, his body hunched like a great ingrowing toenail, staring at me as if his whole squashed personality was spitting.

'Teenagers!' he cried out. 'Kid's stuff. Teenagers!'

I just raised my brows at the poor slob, gave a little one-hand one-arm wave, and said bye-bye. As I was crossing the yard between the house blocks, like an ant upon a chessboard, a hunk of rock, clumsily aimed, of course, thank heaven, flew by and hit the imitation traction engine in the kiddipark. 'Yank!' Ed yelled after me, 'Go ome, Yank!'

Sad.

Up out in Pimlico, the old, old city raised her bashed grey head again, like she was ashamed of her modern daughter down by the river, and I went up streets of dark purple and vomit green, all set at angles like ham sandwiches, until I reached the Buckingham Palace road, so called, and the place where the air terminal stands opposite the coach station.

And there, on the one side, were the glamour people setting off for foreign countries, mohair and linen suits, white air-liner vanity bags, dark sun-spectacles and pages of tickets packed to paradise, every nationality represented, and everyone equal in the sky-dominion of fast air-travel – and there, on the other side, were the peasant masses of the bus terminal shuffling along in their front-parlour-curtain dresses and cut-price tweeds and plastic mackintoshes, all flat feet and fair shares and you-in-your-small-corner-and-I-in-mine; and then, passing down the middle of them, a troop of toy soldiers, all of them with hangovers after nights of rapture down on the Dilly, and wearing ladies' fur muffs on their heads and sweaty red jackets that showed their vertebraes from neck to coccyx, and playing that prissy little pipe music like a bird making wind – and I thought, my God, my Lord, how horrible this country is, how dreary, how lifeless, how blind and busy over trifles!

After which, feeling maybe it perhaps was *me*, I walked into the little square behind the terminal, where there was the usual assortment of mums and prams and bubble-blowing occupants, and old men with boots and dandruff, and rolled fags with the tobacco dripping out at the ends, and I sat down on a wood bench beneath enormous planes, they must have been, with decorative beds and even a fountain, which is practically unknown in England, where they always remember to turn the taps off and economise with water, and noticed that hosing away there was a West Indian gardener, surrounded by a swarm of kids, all pulling at his hose, and he doing the benevolent adult performance I must say very well, and also the coloured man at ease among the hostile natives.

Now myself, I've nothing against kids, I realise that they have to be so that the race can continue, but I can't say that I like them, or approve of them. In fact, I mistrust them, and consider they're a menace, because they're so damned wilful and *energetic*, and, if you ask me, in spite of their charming little childish habits, they know perfectly well what they're up to, and see they get it, and one day, mark my words, we'll wake up and find the little horrors have risen in the night and captured the Bank of England and Buckingham Palace and the BBC. But this West Indian, he must have had paternal instincts, or something, or been trained as a lion tamer, because he handled these little atom bombs without effort, either kidding them so that they all screamed with laughter (and him as well), or else cracking down on them in a fury, and getting immediate results. And all between this, and the hosing, he'd say a word or two to the mums and the old geezers, flaunting his BWI charms, for which I don't blame him, but was also attentive to the old chatterboxes of both sexes, till everyone I do declare actually beamed.

In fact, this coloured character struck me as so bloody *civilised*.

With which thought, I heaved myself up, there in that scented garden in the height of summer, feeling oh! so somehow saddened, and caught myself a bus. It took me across London to my manor in the area of W10 and 11.

I'd like to explain this district where I live, because it's quite a curiosity, being one of the few that's got left behind by the Welfare era *and* the Property-owning whatsit, both of them, and is, in fact, nothing more than a stagnating slum. It's dying, this bit of London, and that's the most important thing to remember about what goes on there. To the north of it, there run, in parallel, the Harrow Road I've mentioned, which you'd hurry through even if you were in a car, and a canal, called the Grand Union, that nothing floats on except cats and contraceptives, and the main railway track that takes you from London to the swede counties of the West of England. These three escape routes, which are all at different heights and levels, cut across one another at different points, making crazy little islands of slum habitation shut off from the world by concrete precipices, and linked by metal bridges. I need hardly mention that on this north side there's a hospital, a gasworks with enough juice for the whole population of the kingdom to commit suicide, and a very ancient cemetery with the pretty country name of Kensal Green.

On the east side, still in the W10 bit, there's another railway, and a park with a name only Satan in all his splendour could have thought up, namely Wormwood Scrubs, which has a prison near it, and another hospital, and a sports arena, and the new telly barracks of the BBC, and with a long, lean road called Latimer Road which I particularly want you to remember, because out of this road, like horrible tits dangling from a lean old sow, there hang a whole festoon of what I think must really be the sinisterest highways in our city, well, just listen to their names: Blechynden, Silchester, Walmer, Testerton and Bramley – can't you just smell them, as you hurry to get through the cats-cradle of these blocks? In this part, the houses are old Victorian lower-middle tumble-down, built I dare say for grocers and bank clerks and horse-omnibus inspectors who've died and gone and their descendants evacuated to the outer suburbs, but these houses live on like shells, and there's only one thing to do with them, absolutely one, which is to pull them down till not a one's left standing up.

On the south side of this area, down by the W11, things are a little different, but in a way that somehow makes them worse, and that is, owing to a freak of fortune, and some smart work by the estate agents too, I shouldn't be surprised, there are one or two sections that are positively posh: not *fashionable*, mind you, but quite graded, with their big back gardens and that absolute silence, which in London is the top sign of a respectable location. You walk about in these bits, adjusting your tie and looking down to see if your shoes are shining, when – wham! suddenly you're back in the slum area again – honest, it's really startling, like where the river joins on to the shore, two quite different creations of dame nature, cheek by thing.

Over towards the west, the frontiers aren't quite as definite, and the whole area merges into a drab and shady and semi-respectable part called Bayswater, which I would rather lie in my coffin, please believe me, than spend a night in, were it not for Suze, who's shacked up there. No! Give me our London Napoli I've been describing, with its railway scenery, and crescents that were meant to twist elegantly but now look as if they're lurching high, and huge houses too tall for their width cut up into twenty flatlets, and front façades that it never pays anyone to paint, and broken milk bottles *everywhere* scattering the cracked asphalt roads like snow, and cars parked in the streets looking as if they're stolen or abandoned, and a strange number of male urinals tucked away such as you find nowhere else in London, and red curtains, somehow, in all the windows, and diarrhoea-coloured street lighting – man, I tell you, you've only got to be there for a minute to know there's something radically *wrong*.

Across this whole mess there cuts, diagonally, yet another railway, that rides high above this slum property like a scenic railway at a fair. Boy, if you want to admire our wonderful old capital city, you should take a ride on this track some time! And just where this railway is slung over the big central road that cuts across the area north to south, there's a hole, a dip, a pocket, a really unhappy valley which, according to my learned Dad, was formerly at one time a great non-agricultural marsh. A place of evil, mister. I bet witches lived around it, and a lot still do.

And what about the human population? The answer is, this is the residential doss-house of our city. In plain words, you'd not live in our Napoli if you could live anywhere else. And that is why there are, to the square yard, more boys fresh from the nick, and national refugee minorities, and out-of-business whores, than anywhere else, I should expect, in London town. The kids live in the streets – I mean they have *charge* of them, you have to ask permission to get along them even in a car – the teenage lot are mostly of the Ted variety, the chicks mature so quick there's scarcely such a thing there as a *little* girl, the men don't talk, glance at you hard, keep moving, and don't stand with their backs to anyone, their women are mostly out of sight, with dishcloths I expect for yashmaks, and there are piles and piles of these dreadful, wasted, negative, shop-soiled kind of *old people* that make you feel it really is a tragedy to grow grey.

You're probably saying well, if you're so cute, kiddo,

why do you live in such an area? So now, as a certain evening paper writes it, 'I will tell you.'

One reason is that it's so cheap. I mean, I have a rooted objection to paying rent at all, it should be free like air, and parks, and water. I don't think I'm mean, in fact I know I'm not, but I just can't bear paying more than a bob or two to landlords. But the real reason, as I expect you'll have already guessed, is that, however horrible the area is, you're *free* there! No one, I repeat it, no one, has ever asked me there what I am, or what I do, or where I came from, or what my social group is, or whether I'm educated or not, and if there's one thing I cannot tolerate in this world, it's nosey questions. And what is more, once the local bandits see you're making out, can earn your living and so forth, they don't swing it on you in the slightest you're a teenage creation – if you have loot, and can look after yourself, they treat you as a man, which is what you are. For instance, *nobody* in the area would ever have treated me like that bank clerk tried to in Belgravia. If you go in anywhere, they take it for granted that you know the scene. If you don't, it's true they throw you out in pieces, but if you do, they treat you just as one of them.

The room I inhabit in sunny Napoli, which overlooks *both* railways (*and* the foulest row of backyards to be found outside the municipal compost heaps), belongs to an Asian character called Omar, Pakistani, I believe, who's regular as clockwork – in fact, even more so, because clocks are known to stop – and turns up on Saturday mornings, accompanied by two countrymen who act as bodyguards, to collect the rents, and you'd better have yours ready. Because if you haven't, he simply grins his teeth and tells his *fellahin* to pile everything you possess neatly on the outside pavement, be it rain, or snow, or mulligatawny fog. And if you've locked the door, it means absolutely nothing to him to smash it down, and even if you're in bed, all injured innocence and indignation, he still comes in with his sickly don't-mean-a-thing kind of smile. So if you're going to be away, it's best to leave the money with a friend, or better still, pay him, as I do, monthly in advance. And when you do, he takes out a plastic bag on a long chain from a very inner pocket, and tucks the notes away, and says you must have a drink with him some time, but even when I've once or twice met him in a pub, he's never offered it, of course. Also, if you make any complaint *whatever* – I mean, even that the roofs falling in, and the water cut off – he smiles that same smile and does positively sweet bugger-all about it. On the other hand, you could invite every whore and cut-throat in the city in for a pail of gin, or give a corpse accommodation for the night on the spare bed, or even set the bloody place on fire, and he wouldn't turn a hair – or turn one if anybody complained to him about you. Not if you paid your rent, that is. In fact, the perfect landlord.

The tenants come and go, as you might expect, but among the regular squatters I have a few particular buddies, of whom I'd specially name the following three.

The first of them, on the floor below me (I'm on the

top), is a boy called The Fabulous Hoplite. I'm hoping you'll not scoff at his name, because Hoplite would certainly not care for it if you did, as he's a most sensitive and dignified character, who was formerly a male whore's male maid, if the truth be told, but has now retired from that particular scene. According to report, the Hoplite has been in business with some of the city's top poof raves, and was even more in demand by the gentry than the costly glamorosos he'd shacked up with. How I know him, is on account of his being a friend of Wiz's who he admires (but nothing doing), and it was through them that I actually got my room. What the Hoplite does for a living now, apart from a bit of freelancing on the side when conditions get too rough, is act as contact man for various gossip columnists, because though you might not think this credible, considering his background, Hoplite gets around on the Knightsbridge-Chelsea circuit in quite an important way, no doubt owing to his being very handsome in an elfin, adolescent sort of style, and certainly very witty, or should I say sharp-tongued, but most of all, because he's really very *friendly*: I mean, he really *does like* people, which a lot of people think they do, but which it seems, as a matter of fact, is really very rare.

Next, on the first floor, is in fact the best room, but I somehow don't think he'll last there, on account of really critical moments with Mr Omar, is a young coloured kid called Mr Cool (which I need hardly say is not his baptismal name, I don't suppose). Cool is a local product, I mean born and bred on this island of both races, and he wears a beardlet, and listens to the MJQ, and speaks very low, and blinks his big eyes and occasionally lets a sad, fleeting smile cross his kissable lips. He's certainly younger than I am, but he makes me feel about nine or so, he's so very poised and paternal, though what the hell he does to keep himself in MJQ LPs I haven't an idea – I really haven't. I don't think it's anything illegal, which is what you might expect, because the kid is always so skint, he's only one suit (a striped Italian black), and no furniture to speak of except for his radiogram, so that either business, whatever it may be, is bad, or else, for reasons best known, he's covering up.

I miss out various rooms and floors, and come now to my particular pal, who lives in the basement and really is a horror, called Big Jill. Now Jill is a Les. and, what is more, you may not believe this, but a Les. ponce, that is to say, she keeps a string of idiotic chicklets on the game, and just sits back in her over-heated, over-decorated, over cooking-smelling basement and collects. She's in all day, and goes out as sun sets to an overnight club where she's behind the counter, and holds her court among her little Les.-ette fans. And then, in the wee small hours, she has a way, when she comes home, of stopping in the area before she goes in and yelling at the upper windows at the Hoplite or myself, to ask if we want to come down and have anything to eat. Which, as a matter of fact, we quite often do, not really for the food, but because old Jill is very wise, in spite of being not far in her twenties, and is my chief and only confidant about Suzette who I ask her advice about but, as I need hardly tell you, haven't produced for her inspection, for all my contacts with Suze are at her place over there in W2.

So by now, of course, I had arrived there, and shot up the flights of no-lino stairs, which nobody keeps swept and ever lit (and the front door's always open) into my loft, which is one big room right across the whole top of the establishment, plus bathroom on the landing minus a bath (I use the municipal), but with basin and a convenient. And I've decorated it all in what I call anti-contemptuous style, i.e. ancient aunt Fanny wallpapers I got from some left-overs in a paint shop in the Portobello Road. I've got a bed, too, a triple one, and the usual chair and table; but no other chairs, and instead a lot of cushions spread out on the floor and on top of what is my only luxury, a fitted carpet. My clothes I hang on ropes with polythene covers for the BR soot, the rest I keep in my metal cabin trunk. I don't have curtains because I like to look out, specially at night, and I'm too high for anyone to look in. The only other objects are my record-player, my pocket transistor radio, and stacks of discs and books that I've collected, hundreds of them, which every New Year's Day I have a pogrom of, and sling out everything except a very chosen few.

I was having a wash down, at the bathroom sink, when up came the Hoplite, nervously patting his hair which was done in a new style of hairdo like as if a large animal had licked the Hoplite's locks down flat, then licked the tip of them over his forehead vertical up, like a cockatoo with its crest on back-to-front. He was wearing a pair of skintight, rubber-glove thin, almost transparent cotton slacks, white nylon-stretch and black wafer-sole casuals, and a sort of maternity jacket, I can only call it, coloured blue. He looked over my shoulder into the mirror, patting his head and saying nothing, till when I said nothing too, he asked me, 'Well?'

'Smashing, Hoplite,' I said. 'It gives you a rugged, shaggy, Burt Lancaster appearance.'

'I'm not so sure,' the Hoplite said, 'it's me.'

'It's you, all right, boy. Of course, anything is, Fabulous. You're one who can wear *anything*, even a swimsuit or a tuxedo, and look nice in it.'

'I know you're one of my fans,' the Hoplite said, smiling sadly at me in the mirror, 'but don't mock.'

'No mockery, man. You've got dress sense.'

The Hoplite sat down on the lavatory seat, and sighed. 'It's not dress sense I need,' he said, 'but horse sense.'

I raised my brows and waited.

'Believe it or not, my dear,' the Hoplite continued sadly, 'but your old friend Fabulous, for the first time in his life – the *very* first in nineteen years (well, that's a lie, I'm twenty, really) – is deep, deep, deep in love.'

'Ah,' I replied.

There was a pause.

'You're not going to ask me with who?' he said, appealingly.

'I'm so sure you're going to tell me, Hop.'

'Sadist! And not *Hop*, please!'

'Not me. No, not a bit, I'm not. Well – who is it?'

'An Americano.'

'Ah.'

69

'What does this "Ah" mean?' the Hoplite said suspiciously.

'Several things. Tell me more. I can see it coming, though. He doesn't care.'

'Misery! That's it.'

'Doesn't care for the angle, Hoplite, or doesn't care for you personally, or just doesn't care for either?'

'The angle. Not bent at all, though I had hopes that perhaps he dabbled . . . And he's so, so understanding, which makes it so, so, so much worse.'

'You poor old bastard,' I said to the Hoplite, as he sat there on my John, and almost crying.

He plucked at a piece of sanitary tissue, and blew his nose. 'I only hope,' he said, 'it doesn't turn me anti-American.'

'Not that, Hoplite,' I said. 'Not you. It's a sure sign of total defeat to be anti-Yank.'

'But I thought,' said lovelorn Fabulous, rising from his seat and strolling across to gaze out on the railway tracks, 'you didn't approve of the American influence. I mean, I know you don't care for Elvis, and you do like Tommy.'

'Now listen, glamour puss,' I said, flicking his bottom with my towel. 'Because I want English kids to be English kids, not West Ken Yanks and bogus imitation Americans, that doesn't mean I'm anti the whole US thing. On the contrary, I'm starting up an anti-anti-American movement, because I just despise the hatred and jealousy of Yanks there is around, and think it's a sure sign of defeat and weakness.'

'Well, that's a relief,' said Fabulous, a bit sarcastically. So, really to hurt him, I made as if to use my towel again, and didn't.

'The thing is,' I said, 'to support the local product. America launched the teenage movement, there's no denying, and Frankie S., after all, was, in his way, the very first teenager. But we've got to produce our own variety, and not imitate the Americans – or the Ruskis, or anybody, for that matter.'

'Ah, the Russians,' said the Hoplite, with a dreamy look coming over his pretty countenance. 'You think they have teenagers over there as well?'

'You bet they have,' I said. 'Haven't you talked to any of the boys who've been over for the Congresses? They've got them just like us. But where the Russians fail, is sending us propaganda, and not sending us anyone in the flesh to look at, or to talk to.'

The Hoplite was getting a bit bored, as he does when it goes off the gossip kick into ideas. 'You're such a clever boy,' he said, patting me on the shoulder, 'and such a hard judge of the rest of us poor mortals . . . And deep down, I do believe, you're quite a patriot.'

'You bet I'm a patriot!' I exclaimed. 'It's because I'm a patriot, that I can't bear our country.'

The Hoplite was at the door. 'If you're interested at all,' he said, 'there's a party tonight, mine hostess being Miss Lament.'

'I'm not sure I care for that gimmicky girl,' I said. 'What sort of party – is it special?'

Dido Lament, I should explain, is a female columnist,

and that actually is her name, or rather, her maiden name. Lament is known among us kids because she did a big investigation round the coffee bars in the days when the Rock thing first broke, and got taken up by all her clients in High Society – or rather, by the bus-queue masses who read about them in her column.

'Oh, the usual SW3 trash,' said Hoplite, waving his hands about disdainfully, though I know full well he just couldn't wait to go. 'Advertising people, and television people, and dressmaking people and show business fringe people – all the parasites,' he said. 'Henley, I know, is going, and have reason to believe, is taking Suze.'

'He is?' I said, showing no sign of grief to this bit of pure camposity called Hoplite.

'And Wizard should be there,' he went on, 'up to no good, I doubt not, the dear lad . . .'

'YOU STUDS UP THERE!' came a great yell from the stairs. 'Come down and see your doll!'

This was Big Jill from her basement sector.

'Oh!' Hoplite cried. 'I do wish that female talent-spotter wouldn't shout so! Go to her if you want to, child, but me, I've got much better things to do.' And blowing me a kiss, he tripped off down the stairs, very sadly singing.

'Five minutes, Jill girl!' I yelled over the top of them.

Because, first of all, I wanted to glance at a snap of Suze that was taken of us both one day up on top of the Monument there in the City by a kid I handed my Rolleiflex to, to snap us, and which shows us, she standing in front, and me standing round behind her, holding her arms, and looking over her head just after kissing her on the neck. And as I wandered round, putting on a garment here, and a garment there, I carried this photo, and propped it up somewhere when I had to use both hands, and gazed at the bloody thing and thought 'Oh Christ, it was only just one single summer ago, what's the use of being young if you're not loved? Well, all right – what *is* the use? What is it? Or is that obvious, I mean my question?'

So that was that, and down I went to see Big Jill.

But on the first floor landing, opposite Mr Cool's room, I noticed the door was left open, which was a sign I know that Cool had something he'd like to say to me, but was too damn proud to ask me to step in. If it had been anyone else, I would have just let the hint he dropped there where it lay, but with the coloured boys you've got to be so careful, or otherwise they put it down to prejudice. So I put my head around the door, and jeepers-creepers, nearly had a fit because would you believe it, there were *two* Mr Cools, one coloured, and one white, or so it seemed.

'Oh, hi,' said Mr Cool, 'this is my brother, Wilf.'

'Hi, Wilf,' I said. 'That's crazy!'

'What is?' said this Wilf.

'You being the brother of my favourite Mr Cool. It nearly shook me rigid when I saw the pair of you.'

'Why did it?' said this white-skinned number, who struck me, I must say, as not being at all a swinging character like his brother – in fact, quite *un*-cool.

'Wilf's on his way,' said Mr Cool.

'Yem,' said this Wilf, and 'see you.' And he shook hands with his brother, and went out past me with not so much as a genuflection or a curtsy.

As soon as he'd gone, I said, 'Cool, please excuse me, but I don't quite dig the scene. I was quite polite to your brother, wasn't I? but he just didn't want to know.'

Mr Cool was standing very still, and very lean, and very all-by-himself, and said, 'My brother's come to warn me.'

'Of what? News me up, please.'

'Wilf's Mum's by another man, as you'll have guessed.'

'Well . . . Yes . . . So . . . ?

'He doesn't like me much, and my friends he likes even less, specially my white ones.'

'Charming! Why, please?'

'Let's not go into that. But anyway, he gets round the area and knows the scene, and he says there's trouble coming for the coloureds.'

I laughed out loud, but a bit nervously. 'Oh Cool, you know, they've been saying that for years, and nothing's happened. Well, haven't they? I know in this country we treat the coloureds all like you-know-what, but we English are too lazy, son, to be violent. Anyway, you're one of us, big boy, I mean home-grown, as much a native London kid as any of the millions, and much more so than hundreds of pure pink numbers from Ireland and abroad who've latched on to the Welfare thing, but don't belong here like you do.'

My speech made no impression on Mr Cool. 'I'm just telling you what Wilf says,' he answered. 'And all I know is, he likes coming here so little it must be *something* that makes him feel he ought to.'

'Perhaps your mother told him to,' I suggested, because I always like to think that *someone's* female parent has maternal instincts.

He shook his head. 'No, it was Wilf's idea,' he said, 'to come.'

I looked hard at Mr Cool.

'And if anything should happen,' I asked, 'whose side would your brother himself be on?'

Mr Cool blew out some smoke and said, 'Not mine. But he felt he had to come and tell me.'

As I stood there looking at the Cool, it struck me so hard how absolutely lonely the poor fucker was – standing there all on his Pat Malone, and yet so resolute, so touch-me-if-you-dare . . . And the nasty question grew up also in my mind as to what I might be doing if there should be trouble here in Napoli – I, the sharp kid, the pal of the whole wide world. Were those really my principles, or was it all on top? And although I knew it was the wrong thing to say, and knew it positively at the very moment, I found myself saying to Cool, 'Tell me, Cool, you're not short of anything, are you? I mean, I couldn't help you out with any loot?'

He just shook his head, which was quite awful, and I was really relieved that Big Jill hooted up the stairs – much louder, this time, was only two floors away – 'STUD! Are you coming down to me?'

'Coming, doll,' I shouted and, with a wave to Cool, went down to Jill in her nether regions.

It needs a bit of an effort of imagination to see what the little Les. butterflies see in Jill because she is, to say the very least of it, so massive, and though I know she's blatant and masterful and all the rest of it, and wears slacks, of course, and even would do to a wedding at St. Paul's, I'm sure, she isn't beautiful in any way that I can see, or even *glamorous*. In fact, if it wasn't she's a city girl, you'd somehow imagine her handling horses – and perhaps, come to think of it, that is the appeal to the young chicks.

'You're late,' she said, 'you horrid little studlet.'

'What do you mean, "late", Big Jill? Did you and me have any sort of an appointment?'

She grabbed me abruptly like an ourang-outang, lifted me two feet off the floor, and banged me down again. 'If you were a chick,' she said, 'I'd eat you.'

'EASY, lady-killer,' I cried. 'You'll get me entangled in your cactuses.' Because it's true Jill is a great collector of indoor plants, in fact they sprout and dangle all over her basement rooms, and in the area as well.

She pushed a cup of coffee in my hands and said, 'Well, how's your sex life, junior, since the last time we met?'

'We met two days ago, Big Jill. It hasn't changed since then.'

'No? Nothing to report?'

Big Jill was standing looking at me, legs apart, with that sort of kindly, 'understanding' look that irritates you when the person just doesn't dig anything whatever about your inner character and pursuits.

'You don't understand as much as you think, Big Jill,' I said, voicing my thoughts to her.

'Oh!' she said huffily. 'Please pardon me for existing.'

'All that I mean, dear,' I said, to soften up the absurd old cow, 'is that your attitude to all those kicks is much too expert. You know so damn much, you know so damn little.'

Big Jill now dropped the wise old elder sister thing, and said, 'Clue me then, teenager. My big ears are flapping.'

'All I mean, Big Jill, is that you can't say, "How's your sex life?" just like you say, "How's the weather?"'

She sat down wrong way round on the chair, with her arms resting on the back of it, and her big tits resting on her arms. 'Obviously,' she said.

'The whole thing about sex,' I said to her, 'is that it's all very easy, and all very difficult indeed.'

'Ah . . .' said Big Jill, looking tolerant and amused, as if I was putting on a show for her.

'I mean, anyone can have a bash, that's obvious, there's nothing to it, but is there any pleasure?'

'Well, isn't there, big boy?' she asked me, giving a great, fat smile.

'Oh, of course there is, in that way, yes, but there isn't really, because you can't have it just like that without messing something else that matters up, and this brings you badly down.'

'Even if you like the party of the second part, it brings

you down?' said Jill, getting interested, as I could see.

'If you *like* the other number, I mean like the looks of them, really dig them sexually – and I mean really – then it isn't quite so bad, because at least you're only acting like a pair of animals, which isn't a bad thing to do . . . But even then, you're still wrought badly down.'

'Wrought down because you might lose them?'

'No, no, not that. Because you've not really got them, because they aren't the person.'

'What person?'

'The person you really dig, with all of yourself, your other half you'd give your life to.'

'You're not referring to marriage, are you?'

'No, no, no, no, no, Big Jill.'

'*To love*?'

'Yep. That's it. To it.'

Big J.'s eyes were pale, so that she seemed to be staring into herself, and not out into the room at me.

'You ever had that combo?' she enquired.

'No.'

'Not even with Suzette?'

'No. Me, yes, I was ready for that everything stage of it, but for Suze it was only a head, bodies and legs thing, when it happened.'

Big Jill looked wise, and said, 'So it was really you who broke it up, then.'

'I suppose you could say so, yes. I wanted more from Suze than she wanted to give me, and I just couldn't bear anything that was less.'

'Then why you still trail round after her? You hope she'll change?'

'Yes.'

Big Jill heaved herself up, and said, 'Well, boy, I can tell you something, which is she won't, Suzette. Not for ten or fifteen years she won't, anyway, I can promise you that. Later on, when you're both a big boy and girl, you might be able to wrap a big thing up . . .'

I'd moved away, and was looking out into her area Kew gardens. 'If I can work up the strength of will,' I said, 'I'm going to cut out seeing Suze at all.'

'Don't turn your back when you're talking, son. You mean live on your visions like a monk?'

I turned round and said, 'I mean shut my gate to all that nonsense.'

Big Jill came over too. 'You're too young for that,' she said. 'If you do, you'll only do yourself an injury. You shouldn't give up kicks till they don't mean a thing to you any more.' But she was quite a bit edgy, I could see. 'You're a romantic!' she said. 'A second feature Romeo!' and she took back my coffee cup as if I'd tried to rob her of it.

Well, there it is. That's what always happens if you try to tell the *truth*, they always want to know it, and nag you and persuade you against your better sense to tell it, and then they're always angry with you when they hear it, and dislike you for it. And, as a matter of fact, it wasn't even the truth I'd told Big Jill, in one respect: and that is, Suze and I hadn't made it, actually, though we'd sailed right up close so often. But even when the scene was set, and we both meant business, it hadn't happened, and I'm not sure if the real reason for this was her, or me.

I thought of all this, as I climbed out of Napoli into London, up towards N. Hill Gate. And straining up the Portobello Road, I passed a crocodile of infants, and among them a number of little Spadelets, and I noticed, not for the first time, how, in the underground movement of the juveniles, they hadn't been educated up yet to the colour thing. Fists and wits, they were what mattered, and the only enemy was teacher. And as I walked on along the Bayswater Road, just inside that two miles of gardens, so pretty and kind by day (but not by night), I went on thinking, as my Italian casuals carried me on.

Perhaps Big Jill's right, I think too much, but the sight of these school-kids reminded me of the man who really taught me to think at all, and that was my elementary schoolmaster, called Mr Barter. I know it's un-sharp to admit a schoolteacher ever taught you anything, but this Mr Barter, who was cross-eyed, did. I got in his clutches when I was eleven, and the glorious 1950s had just begun. On account of schools being blitzed when I was an infant (which I can hardly remember, only a bit of the buzz-bombs at the end), I had to walk a mile up into Kilburn Park, to the place where this Mr Barter gave his performance. Now, dig this – because this was it. Old Mr Barter was the only man (or woman, too) in all the schools that I attended, before I packed that nonsense in three years ago, who actually made me realise two things, of which number one is, that what you learnt had some actual value to you personally, and wasn't just dropped on you like a punishment, and number two, that everything you learnt, you hadn't learnt until you'd really dug it: i.e. made it part of your own experience. He'd tell us things – for example, like that Valparaiso was a big city in Chile, or that x+y equals something or other, or who all the Henrys were, or Georges, and he'd make us feel this crazy stuff really *concerned* us kids, was something to do with us, and had a value. Also, he made me kinky about books: he managed to teach me – to this day, I don't know how – that books were not just a thing like that – I mean, just *books* – but somebody else's mind opened up for me to look into, and he taught me the habit, later on, of actually *buying* them! Yes – I mean real books, like the serious paperbacks, which must have been unknown among the kids up in the Harrow Road those days, who thought a book's an SF or a Western, if they thought it's anything.

Since we're on the subject, and I can't cause any more red faces than I already have, I'd also like to mention that the second great influence of my life was something even more embarrassing, and this is that, believe it or not, I actually was, for two whole years a *wolf cub*! Yes – me! Well . . . this is the fable. I got swung into that thing when, like all kids do, I was called up for the Sabbath school, and I soon told that Sunday lot it could please take a walk, but somehow got latched on to this wolf cub kick, because it started to fascinate me, for the following reasons. The first week I attended, dragged there by Dad, the old cub master, who I now realise was a terrible old poof, said that he wanted my attendance to be voluntary, not forced, and if after a full month I found they made it so attractive I'd want to come of my own free will, then would that show? I said, sure, yes it would, thinking, naturally, the month would soon pass by, and they began to teach me a lot of crap I found, even at that age, absolutely useless and ridiculous, like lighting fires with two matches when matches are about the cheapest thing there are to buy, and putting tourniquets on kids' legs for snake-bites when there aren't any snakes in London, and anyway, what if they bit kids on the head or other sensitive parts? Yet gradually, all the same, to everyone's astonishment, I did actually begin to be a raver for those weekly meetings in the Baptist corrugated iron temple, because I really felt – don't laugh – that for the first time, here was a family: at any rate, a lot, a mob, a click I could belong to. And though that dreadful old cub master with his awful shorts, and his floppy khaki hat, was queer as a coot and even queerer, he didn't interfere with any of us kids in any way, and actually succeeded in teaching us *morals* – can you believe it? Well – he did! He really did. I can honestly say the only ideas on morals I know anything of, were those that bent old cub master made me believe in, chiefly, I think, because he made us feel that he liked us, all us grubby-kneed little monsters, and cared what happened to us, and didn't *want* anything from us, except that we look after ourselves decently in the great big world hereafter. He was the first adult I'd ever met – even including Dad – who didn't come the adult at us – didn't use his strength, and won us over by persuasion.

That brings me to today, and to the third item in my education, my university, you might say, and that's the jazz clubs. Now, you can think what you like about the art of jazz – quite frankly, I don't really care *what* you think, because jazz is a thing so wonderful that if anybody doesn't rave about it, all you can feel for them is pity: not that I'm making out I really understand it *all* – I mean, certain LPs leave me speechless. But the great thing about the jazz world, and all the kids that enter into it, is that no one, not a soul, cares what your class is, or what your race is, or what your income, or if you're boy, or girl, or bent, or versatile, or what you are – so long as you dig the scene and can behave yourself, and have left all that crap behind you, too, when you come in the jazz club door. The result of all this is that, in the jazz world, you meet all kinds of cats, on absolutely equal terms, who can clue you up in all kinds of directions – in social directions, in culture directions, in sexual directions, and in racial directions . . . in fact, almost anywhere, really, you want to go to learn. So that's why, when the teenage thing began to seem to me to fall into the hands of exhibitionists and moneylenders, I cut out gradually from the kiddo waterholes, and made it for the bars, and clubs, and concerts where the older numbers of the jazz world gathered.

But this particular evening, I had to call at a teenage hut inside Soho, in order to contact two of my models, by names Dean Swift and the Misery Kid. Now, about Soho, there's this, that although so much crap's written about the area, of all London quarters, I think it's still one of the most authentic. I mean, Mayfair is just top spivs stepping into the slippers of the former gentry, and Belgravia, like I've said, is all flats in houses built as palaces, and Chelsea – well! Just take a look yourself, next time you're there. But in Soho, all the things they say happen, do: I mean, the vice of every kink, and speakeasies and spielers and friends who carve each other up, and, on the other hand, dear old Italians and sweet old Viennese who've run their honest, unbent little businesses there since the days of George six, and five, and backward far beyond. And what's more, although the pavement's thick with tearaways, provided you don't meddle it's really a much safer area than the respectable suburban fringe. It's not in Soho a sex maniac leaps out of a hedge onto your back and violates you. It's in the dormitory sections.

The coffee spot where I hoped I'd find my two duets was of the kind that's now the chicest thing to date among the juniors – namely, the pigsty variety, and adolescent bum's delight. I don't exaggerate, as you'll see. What you do is, rent premises that are just as dear as any other, rip up the linos and tear out the nice fittings if there happen to be any, put in thick wood floors and tables, and take special care not to wipe the cups properly, or sweep the butts and crusts and spittle off the floor. Candles are a help or, at a pinch, non-pearl 40-watt blue bulbs. And a jukebox just for decoration, as it's considered rather naïve to *use* one in these places.

This example was called Chez Nobody, and sure enough, sitting far apart from each other at distant tables, were the Dean and the Misery Kid. Though both are friends of mine, and, in a way, even friends of each other, these two don't mix in public, on account of the Dean being a sharp modern jazz creation, and the Kid just a skiffle survival, with horrible leanings to the trad. thing. That is to say, the Kid admires the groups that play what is supposed to be the authentic music of old New Orleans, i.e. combos of booking office clerks and quantity-surveyors' assistants who've handed in their cards, and dedicated themselves to blowing what they believe to be the same note as the wonderful Creoles who invented the whole thing, when it all long ago began.

If you know the contemporary scene, you could tell them apart at once, just like you could a soldier or sailor, with their separate uniforms. Take first the Misery Kid and his trad. drag. Long, brush-less hair, white stiff-starched collar (rather grubby), striped shirt, tie of all one colour (red today, but it could have been royal-blue or navy), short jacket but an old one (somebody's riding tweed, most likely), very, very, tight, tight, trousers with wide stripe, no sox, short *boots*. Now observe the Dean in the modernist number's version. College-boy smooth crop hair with burnt-in parting, neat white Italian rounded-collared shirt, short Roman jacket *very* tailored (two little vents, three buttons), no-turn-up narrow trousers with 17-inch bottoms absolute maximum, pointed-toe shoes, and a white mac lying folded by his side, compared with Misery's sausage-rolled umbrella.

Compare them, and take your pick! I would add that their chicks, if present, would match them up with: trad.

boy's girl – long hair, untidy with long fringes, maybe jeans and a big floppy sweater, maybe bright-coloured never-floralled, never-pretty dress . . . smudged-looking's the objective. Modern jazz boy's girl – short hemlines, seamless stockings, pointed-toed high-heeled stiletto shoes, crêpe nylon rattling petticoat, short blazer jacket, hair done up into the elfin style. Face pale – corpse colour with a dash of mauve, plenty of mascara.

I sat down just beside the Misery Kid, who was eating a gateau and had everything horrible about him, spotty, unpressed, unlaundered, but with the loveliest pair of eyes you ever saw, brown and funny and appealing, I can only say, not that the Kid ever asks you for anything, as he only speaks in sentences of four words at his most voluble.

'Evening, Kid,' I said. 'There's been a small disaster.'

He just gazed like a fish: brows up, but not really curious.

'You recollect the snaps I took of you as the poet Chatterton with your bird as your Inspiration in some nylon net?'

'So?' said the Kid.

'It's all right, my client's not bounced the order, but I've developed the stuff, and your chick came out too indistinct by far.'

'She not meant so?'

'She's meant to be vague, Misery Kid, but she's meant to be visible behind that nylon net. Well? I expect she must have moved.'

'You pay us for a second take?'

'Certainly, Mr Bolden. But I can't pay for anything till I give the prints to Mr X-Y-Z.'

'Who he?'

'The client.'

The Misery Kid picked his nose and said, 'This client no deposit?'

'No. We've just got to do it all again, Mr Kid, to get our money. Can you raise your partner?'

'I dunno I know,' he said. 'Bell me tonight, I tell you.'

He got up, not showing his feelings, which was really rather heroic, because here was this trad. child, alone among the teenagers, in the days of prosperity, still living like a bum and a bohemian, skint and possibly even hungry, but still not arguing about the loot. If he'd argued, he'd have got some out of me, but to argue when the dirt dropped down on your head was contrary to his whole trad. ideology. As the Misery Kid passed by the Dean on his way out, Dean Swift looked up and hissed at him, 'Fascist!' which the Kid ignored. These modern jazz boys certainly do feel strongly about the trad. reaction.

The Dean came over and sat down with me. I should explain I haven't seen the Dean for several weeks, although he's my favourite and most successful model. The Dean's speciality's an unusual one, which is posing always fully dressed, and yet, somehow, managing to look pornographic. Don't ask me how! In the studio, exactly when he shouted out, 'Now!' I throw the switch, though he looks quite ordinary to me, and then, behold!

when he's developed, there he is – indecent. Snaps of the Dean sell like hot ice-cream among vintage women with too many bosoms and time on their hands, and even my Ma, when she saw some photos of him was impressed – he looks so damn available, the Dean does. She actually asked to meet him, but Dean Swift is not interested in this, the chief reason being that he's a junkie.

If you have a friend who's a junkie, like I have the Dean, you soon discover there's no point whatever discussing his addiction. It's as senseless as discussing love, or religion, or things you only feel if you feel them, because the Dean, and I suppose all his fellow junkies, is convinced that this is 'a mystic way of life' (the Dean's own words), and you and I, who don't jab hot needles in our arms, are just going through life missing absolutely everything worthwhile in it. The Dean always says, life's just kicks. Well, I agree with him, so it is, but personally, it seems to me the big kick you should try to get by how you live it sober. But tell that to the Dean!

Why I'd not recently seen him, is that he'd until then been away inside. This has fairly often happened to the Dean, owing to his breaking into chemists' shops, and as he suffers a lot when he's cut off from the world and all it gives in there, he doesn't like you to refer to it when he emerges. At the same time, he *does* like you to say you're glad to see him once again, so it's all a trifle dicey.

'Hail, squire,' I said. 'Long time no see. How is you are we? Won't you say tell?'

The Dean smiled in his world-weary way. 'Doesn't this place stink?' he said to me.

'Well certainly, Dean Swift, it does, but do you mean its air, or just its atmosphere?'

'The both. The only civilised thing about it,' the Dean continued, 'is that they let you *sit* here, when you're skint.'

The Dean gazed round at the teenage products like a concentration camp exterminator. I should explain the Dean, though only just himself an ex-teenager, has sad valleys down his cheeks, and wears a pair of steel-rimmed glasses (which he takes off for our posing sessions), so that his Dean-look is habitually sour and solemn. (The Swift part of the thing comes from his rapid disappearance at the approach of any cowboys. You're talking to him and then, tick-tock! he's vanished.) I could see that now the Dean, as usual when skinned and vicious, was going to engage in his favourite theme, i.e. the horror of teenagers. 'Look at the beardless microbes!' he exclaimed, loud enough for everyone to hear. 'Look at the pram products at their plotting and their planning!'

And, as a matter of fact, you could see what he meant, because to see the kids hunched over the tables it *did* look as if some conspiracy was afoot to slay the elder brethren and majorities. And when I'd paid, and we went out in the roads, even here in this Soho, the headquarters of the adult mafia, you could everywhere see the signs of the un-silent teenage revolution. The disc shops with those lovely sleeves set in their windows, the most original thing to come out in our lifetime, and the kids inside them purchasing guitars, or spending fortunes on the songs of the Top Twenty. The shirt-stores and bra-stores with ciné-star photos in the window, selling all the exclusive teenage drag I've been describing. The hairstyle saloons where they inflict the blow-wave torture on the kids for hours on end. The cosmetic shops – to make girls of seventeen, fifteen, even thirteen, look like pale rinsed-out sophisticates. Scooters and bubble-cars driven madly down the roads by kids who, a few years ago, were pushing toy ones on the pavement. And everywhere you go the narrow coffee bars and darkened cellars with the kids packed tight, just whispering, like bees inside the hive waiting for a glorious queen bee to appear.

'See what I mean,' the Dean said.

And the chicks, round the alleys, on that summer afternoon! Heavens, each year the teenage dream-girl has grown younger, and now, there they were, like children that've dressed up in their fashionable aunties' sharpest clothes – and suddenly you realise that it's not a game, and that these chicks mean business, and that it's not so much you, one of the boys, they aim their persons at, as their sheer, sweet, energetic legs walk down the pavement three by three, but no, at quite adult numbers, quite mature things, at whose eyes they shoot confident, proud looks there's no mistaking.

'Little madams,' said the Dean.

'There you go!' I answered.

Here Dean Swift stopped us in his tracks.

'I tell you,' he said, pulling his US-striped and rear-buckled cap down over his eyes, 'I tell you something. These teenagers are ceasing to be rational, thinking, human beings, and turning into mindless butterflies. And they're turning into butterflies all of the same size and colour, that have to flutter round exactly the same flowers, on exactly the same gardens. Yes!' he exclaimed at a group of kiddos coming clicking, cracking, prattling by. 'You're nothing but a bunch of butterflies!'

But the kidettes took no notice of the Dean whatever, because just at that moment . . . there! in his hand-styled car with his initials in its number, there sped by the newest of the teenage singing raves, with beside him his brother, and his composer, and his chicklet, and his Personal Manager, so that all that was missing was his Mum. And the kids waved, and the young Pied Piper waved his free hand back, and everyone for a few seconds was latched on to the glory.

'Singer!' cried the Dean out after him. 'Har, Har!'

He was standing out there in the road, gesticulating at the departing vehicle. Abruptly, though, he sheered off at an angle, and I had to catch him up across the way. He looked back over his neck, gripped my arm, and hurried on. 'Cowboys,' he explained.

I looked back too. 'They didn't seem to me like cowboys,' I told the Dean.

But to tell him this, was like telling some expert in Hatton Garden that you don't think that stone there is a diamond.

'I tell you this,' the Dean said fiercely. 'I can smell a copper in the dark, a hundred feet away, blindfolded. And anyway,' he continued pityingly, 'didn't you see those two were dressed in casual clothes, but with their *shoes mended?'*

That clinched the matter for the Dean.

'You don't like coppers, do you,' I said to him.

The Dean paused on his tracks. 'The only good thing about the bastards,' he said gently, 'is that they've all got themselves together into the same cowboy force. Just imagine what the world would be if monsters like them were out among the rest of us, without a label!'

The poor old Dean! He really hates the law although, unlike most that do, he doesn't fear it, really doesn't, though he's been given the matchbox treatment on more than one night occasion. Of course, all the jobs he's ever done have brought him into conflict with the cowboys – e.g. faith-healer, dance-hall instructor, club escort, property consultant and old-lady sitter.

We'd now reached a street down near 'the Front', as the girls on the game call the thoroughfare, and here the Dean whispered, 'I must have a fix very shortly, and I need a new whosit for my whatsit.' So we went into a chemist's shop nearby.

Behind the counter was a female case who didn't like the appearance of the Dean, and went into that routine that shopkeepers have perfected in the kingdom, that is, to get on the busy thing and bustle about with very necessary tasks, and when you cough or something, look up as if you'd broken into their private bedroom. And when they speak, they use a new kind of 'politeness' that's very common in our city, i.e. to say kind and courteous words, with a bitchy edge of nastiness, so they disarm you as they beat you down. To open the thing, of course, she asked us, 'Can I help you?'

Ah! but in the Dean she'd met her equal, because he has perfected, and almost patented, a style of being terribly polite in a way that doesn't mean a thing, and is in fact a mockery of the person he's polite to, though not easy for them to pin down, because the Dean acts so serious and earnest they couldn't quite make up their minds if it was sarcasm.

'Yes, Mad-ahm!' he answered, 'you certainly *can* help me, if you please, and if I'm not taking up too much of your time.'

And then they began their duel of politeness, their eyes blazing hatred at each other, and there you are, I thought, that's what happens when people grow to think that politeness, which is so lovely, is a form of weakness. And when the Dean had succeeded in luring the old slut to get out all sorts of products he didn't really need at all, he suddenly said, 'Thank you, Mad-ahm, so much,' and dipped his cap at her and went out in the sun saying, 'One of the fellow sufferers at the Dubious will lend me what I need.'

The Dubious, I should explain, is of all the drinking clubs that fester in Soho, the one that's in fashion just at present with the sharper characters, and there, sure enough, when I came in with the Dean, I saw, among others, Mr Call-me-Cobber, and his friend the ex-Deb-of-Last-Year: he being a telly personality from the outer colonies, and she one who slipped effortlessly off the pages of the weekly social glossies on to those of the monthly fashion ones. As a matter of fact, the ex-Deb's rather nice in a hunt ball way, but the same cannot be said of Call-me-Cobber, who really flogs that dinkum Aussie thing too hard, though on the telly screen it looks terrific, so sincere.

While the Dean went rambling off into dark corners, I snapped this drunken loving couple, propping my Rolleiflex upon the bar.

'Oh, hullo, reptile,' said the ex-Deb, 'perhaps you can help my paramour with his new series.'

'It's called,' the Cobber said, '*Lorn Lovers*, and we're looking for persons deeply in love who fate has sundered.'

'You're too young for tears, I suppose,' the ex-Deb said to me, 'but maybe among your somewhat older companions . . . ?'

I nominated the Hoplite as Lorn Lover of the year.

'And who's he in love with?' Call-me-Cobber asked. 'We want to confront the frantic pair in front of the cameras, without either knowing beforehand what's going to hit them.'

'He's in love with an American,' I said.

'A good angle, though we'll have to pay the fee in dollars . . . Yes, confront the pair of them, and get them in a clinch.'

'It'll be sensational,' I said.

'*His* trouble,' said the ex-Deb, pointing a princess-size cigarette-holder at her lover, 'is his success. Ever since that fabulous series on the Angries, when the thing first broke, they expect the highest from him.'

'And they'll get it!' Call-me-Cobber cried. 'It's my aim, my mission, and my achievement to bring quality culture material to the pop culture masses.'

'He's the culture courtier of all time,' his lady said, as they both gulped the firewater down, then tried to kiss each other.

Call-me-Cobber looked around the basement room, where parties crouched on plastic covered seats with dim rose lights shining reflected up at them from the parquet floor. 'Today,' he announced, 'each woman, man and child in the United Kingdom can be made into a personality, a star. Whoever you are – and I repeat, whoever – we can put you in front of cameras and make you live for millions.'

But no one seemed interested in this idea down there in the Dubious, so Call-me-Cobber slipped off his stool and went searching for the toilet. And the ex-Deb turned all her attention to myself, and started suddenly to get 'maternal'. Because a woman, if she's high and a bit frustrated, and you're young, is very apt, I've found, to want to show she 'understands' – though what, you never quite discover, and it's most embarrassing.

'Tell me about your camera,' the ex-Deb said, leaning across and fondling the thing and breathing spirits on me though, I must say, looking smashing.

'What you want to know about it?' I enquired.

'How did you learn to use it?' she said mysteriously.

'By trial and error.'

'Ah!'

I didn't get that 'Ah!'

'When you were young?' she said. 'A boy?'

That's it.'

She gazed at me as if I was straight out of Dr Barnardo's. 'You've had a hard life, I can see,' she said 'sympathetically'.

'No, I wouldn't say so' – and I wouldn't, really.

'Ah, but I can see you have!' she nattered on.

I gave up. 'Well – you win,' I told her.

'Your mother must have been a bitch,' she said.

Now, though I quite agreed with this, it made me furious! Who the hell did she think she was, this fashion model – Mrs Freud?

'I'll tell you something,' I said, 'about my mother. She may have her defects – who hasn't? – but she's got a lot of courage, and she's kept her looks, which are terrific.'

'You're loyal, kid,' said the ex-Deb, her swish-skirt nearly sliding her off the stool in her emotion.

'You bet,' I said, heaving her on to it again.

She held my arm, and said, 'Tell me a secret about you teenagers. Do you have a very active sex existence?'

They can't keep off it. 'No,' I replied, 'we don't.'

And, as a matter of fact, what I said was true, because although you often seen teenagers boxed up together in a free-and-easy, intimate sort of way, it doesn't very often reach the point of no return. But in this kingdom we reside in, the firm belief of the venerables seems to be that, if you see kids out and about enjoying themselves, then fleshy vices must be at the bottom of it all, somewhere, not just as it often is – frisking and frolicking, and having a carefree ball.

So as this wasn't the ex-Deb's business, anyway, I changed the subject round and said to her, 'Where will you take your holiday this year, Miss Sheba?'

'Who, me? Oh, I dunno . . . I always get taken some place or other where there's sand, and quarrels, and a quick flight home . . . And you, child? I hear all you brats are hitch-hiking across the Continent these days.'

'No longer,' I said, firmly.

'Why no longer?' she asked me, coming into focus.

'The hitch thing's out. We're tired of being molested, and arriving at destinations we didn't mean to. We pay our own fares now, like everybody else, in fact a lot of the new travel panders depend on teenage travellers.'

'So you've been in all those Continental places?'

Now, it's a funny thing . . . why should I be ashamed that I've never left our island yet? Why should I? because the reason is, although I've had opportunities enough (well, only last summer, the Marxists tried to ship me to a Youth thing in Bulgaria – think of that!), I've just not wanted to . . . Or rather . . . Well, as a matter of fact, I haven't even ever yet left London, except for once, of which I have the vaguest recollection, when I was trundled down to Brighton for the day, beside the sea, in connection with one of my Ma's manoeuvres, and all I remember of it is being parked here and there, upon the beach and up on bar stools with ginger beer, while she disappeared to mess about with the easy-money-boy who was her escort. As for the country, that great green thing that hangs around outside the capital, with animals, I've never seen it, because even when the bombs fell thickest in war-time, my old Ma refused to leave her manor, and refused to have Vern and me evacuated, come what may. And all I remember of that journey up and down to Brighton, is getting into trains and getting out – the rest was lying rocking on the hot and smelly seat, or vomiting.

Yet I must get away some day, and see the world. Not just that Continent they speak of – Paris and Rome, and all that crap – but the great wide one, like Brazil, say, or Japan, and that is why I *must* be sensible and save some loot, boy, hustle up some big stuff and depart in peace aboard some jet. So,

'No,' I replied, 'not all of them. I'm happiest in my manor, taking sunbathes in the Hyde, or doing swallows from the top board at the Hampstead ponds.'

She peered at me, her eyes swimming with the lush that she'd consumed. 'You're a poet, infant, in your way,' she said.

'Oh, I dunno about that,' I answered her.

While this ridiculous conversation of the ex-Deb and myself was still proceeding, some musicians there in the Dubious had begun to have a blow, because apparently a character called Two-Thumbs Tumbril, who plays bass, was holding some auditions for an out-of-city gig he thought might happen, if he could recruit a combo. There in the Dubious which, as I think I've said, is in a cellar, the instruments resounded with a thunderous effect, and as I listened to the sweet and soothing sound I once again reflected, thank the Lord I was born into the jazz age, what on earth could it have been when all they had to listen to was ballad tunes and waltzes? Because jazz music is a thing that, as few things do, makes you feel really at home in the world here, as if it's an okay notion to be born a human animal, or so.

A cat at the counter said, 'Nice, but they'll not make Bewley-Ooley.' Another answered, 'Well, who cares? That, garden party's for the ooblies and the Hooray Henries, anyway.' A third just said, 'Great,' with a soft dream in his eyes – but that may have been because he'd just been dragging on a splif inside the toilet.

From that same toilet, not quite yet fully adjusted before leaving, now reappeared the dinkum Call-me-Cobber number, who eyed the performers as if he was Mr Granz in person, like all these telly personalities do, acting the universal impresario to mankind. And after the bliss of hearing the boys blow in the proper company, the sight of the dinkum wrought me down a bit, because in the jazz thing, the audience is half the battle, even more than half.

'Nice,' he decided, 'but it falls between two stools. They're neither pop nor prestige-worthy.'

'That's two good stools,' I said, 'to fall between,' and slid off my own to leave them.

The ex-Deb-of-Last-Year grabbed me by the port pocket of my strides. 'Are you going to Miss Lament's?' she asked me.

'Yes, maybe I catch you there,' I told her, as I unhooked her vermilion claws.

'You leaving us?'

'Just for a moment, Knightsbridge girl,' I said.

Because I'd seen the Wiz come in the place, and wanted a swift word with my blood brother.

The Wiz was wearing a gladiator Lonsdale belt with studs on it, and this he unbuckled as he came into the Dubious, like a soldier that's been relieved from guard. But still he looked wary, as he always did, and no doubt in his sleep as well, as if the world was in the other corner of the ring where he did battle, and himself a lonesome hunter on the London jungle trail. 'Come over behind the music,' I said to him, and we got on the other side of the performers, so that their sound made a barrier that hedged us from the lush-swilling visitors around the counter.

'What's new?' I asked the Wiz.

A nice thing about Wizard is that he forgets a quarrel absolutely. A battle, with the Wiz, is always for a purpose, like a meal, and once it's over, he just doesn't seem to think of it any more at all. He eyed me with approval, and I could see that once again I was his old reliable, perhaps the only one he had outside eternity.

'I've news for you,' he said.

I must admit at feeling anxious, because the Wiz's bits of news are apt to sweep you out to sea until you can get adjusted to them.

'I'm thinking,' he said, 'of going into business with a chick.'

'Oh, are you. Clever boy. I'll visit you at Brixton,' I said, disgusted.

'You don't approve?'

'How can I? You're not that kind of hustler.'

'Try anything once . . .'

'Oh, sure. Oh sure, oh sure. Next thing is breaking and entering.'

I got up to fetch some drinks, and also to have time to think of this. Because I'd always imagined one day Wiz might go that way, but always decided he had brains enough to do better than that, and not get himself into some bower-bird's clutches. Because say what you like, in that set-up it's the female party who controls the situation, even if she gives the male one all her earnings, and he crunches her on Sunday evenings after the weekly visit to the Odeon. The simple reason being that her own activity, whatever you may think of it, is legal, and the boy's is not, and all she has to do if there's an argument is dial Detective Sergeant Someone round the corner.

'Health, wealth and happiness,' he said sarcastically.

'Happiness! You should talk!'

There was a silence. Then,

'Go on,' said Wiz. 'Let's have it.'

'What use, if you've decided?'

'Let's have it all the same.'

I groaned, I really did.

'It's just, Wiz, that it's not your kind of thing. Tell me one ponce you know who's got real brains.'

'I know of several.'

'I don't mean craft or cunning, I mean *brains*. Constructive brains.'

The Wiz said, 'I could introduce you to several bookies, club owners, car-hire proprietors, who've built up their business by loot they made when on the game before retirement.'

I said, 'I could introduce you to several Saturday-midnight-at-the-chemist's, and several in-and-out boys, and several corpses, who've had just the same idea.'

'Ah. Well, we disagree.'

I said to the lunatic, 'It may be all right for creatures who are young in *mind*, as well as age, but, let's face it, Wiz, you're too mature already. You *know* too much what you'd be doing.'

The Wizard smiled, if you can call it that. 'And this,' he said gently, 'comes from a kiddo known around the town for flogging pornographic photos.'

Oh well, hell!

'In the first place,' I said . . .

'And don't forget the second – and the third . . .'

'In the first place,' I continued, 'you know very well only *some* of my snaps are pornographic, and I'm on that kick for giggles as much as loot. In the second, as you say, you know I'm pulling out of that activity as soon as ever – as I've often told you. And in the third, yes, as you also say, are you really comparing poncing with what I do?'

'Not really,' the Wizard said, 'because it's more straightforward, and it's better paid.'

'Oh, if you say so, Sporting Life.'

There was another pause for refreshments between rounds.

'And who's the lucky chick?' I asked him.

'Oh, girl I know. Of course,' he said, 'you'll

understand it's not wise to say *who*, specially to anyone who disapproves.'

'How right you are, young Wizard. Anyway, whoever it is, I pity her. You'll have a dozen on the game before you're nicked.'

'I'd not be surprised,' the Wizard said.

I drained my non-alcoholic beverage.

'Well, let me tell you, genius,' I said, 'two things, and do just listen. The first is, cute little number though you may be, you're really not the fixer type, the hustler type, because you're too damn delighted by the sport of it to take it seriously enough. The other, which you know full well, and should be ashamed of yourself for, is that you really have got brains, and if you'd had even a fragment of education, you'd have done big things, boy, and it's not too late. It's really not too late: why don't you study?'

'The school of life,' Wiz answered.

'Brixton class.'

'So what? Each occupation has its risks.'

'Fool.'

'Yeah? Oh, well . . .'

The Wizard looked up at the ceiling, because the combo had stopped its operations for a moment. And me, I really felt I must say *something* to stop this thing: not because I disapproved of it (although I did), but because I knew that, if the Wizard did it, then I'd lose him.

But he got in first, now. 'I'll tell you something,' the Wizard said to me. 'I've thought it over carefully – and I'm safe as houses. Look!' And I looked at him. 'Imagine me in the dock! What mug – even a magistrate, let alone a jury – is going to believe a baby-face like me could be a ponce?'

I waited, then said, 'If you could see yourself in a mirror now, this very moment, you'd realise you don't look young at all. Not at all, Wiz, you don't – you look damn old.'

'Oh, I do?' said Wiz. 'Well, then, let me tell you something else. This is an old, old thing, this whore, and ponce, and client business. Since A. and Eve, there's always been the woman, and the visitor, and the local male.'

'Be the visitor, then.'

'Nobody likes the easy-money boy, there I agree. But the reasons he's disliked for, kiddo, are all very hypocritical. The client shifts his shame on to the ponce, see, and the ponce is willing to carry it for him – give him a clear, social, respectable alibi. Then, no man likes paying for what the ponce is paid for. And most of all, boy, the world is jealous of the ponce! Well, kid, and rightly!' And he smiled a great big aren't-I-clever smile.

'Fine, fine,' I cried. 'We'll have to get you testifying before those Wolfenden creations.'

'Oh, *them*' said the Wizard. 'The last person they'd ever want to ask about the game is anyone who *knows* about it . . . a whore, a ponce, even a client. You know what the Wolfenden is for?' he went on, leaning across and grinning at me. 'It's so as to play down the queer thing in our country, and hide it behind the kosher game. It's so as to confuse the two, and get all the mugs muddled, so that if they call down fire and brimstone, they don't know on what.'

'Not so loud, Wiz,' I cried, because the combo had broken up, and someone hadn't yet put on the pick-up once again.

So there it was. Already, I was speaking *secretly* to the Wiz, like I had never done before, becoming a part of his squalid little plot, and, believe me, I was revolted.

'Christ!' I exclaimed. 'What's happening to me? My girl, I've lost her to the Spades and queers, and now my friend, I'm losing him to the girls.'

'Don't compare me with Spades,' said Wiz.

'Now, be intelligent, I wasn't. I was comparing Suze with you.'

'Nice! Perhaps it's you who's worrying most about all this, little latchkey kid.'

'Oh, perhaps!'

'Well,' said the Wizard, making as if to rise, 'when the cowboys start to fill me in, I'll have you buzzed immediately for bail.'

'Don't talk to me like that, Wiz, *please*!'

'Oh, I know you'll come running . . . you adore me!'

This was evidently it, and I reached up and slapped the Wiz real hard. Real hard, I did. He didn't look all that surprised, and he didn't retaliate at all. He just rubbed his cheek and walked off over to the bar, so that I realised this was how he wanted it to be. Oh, fuck, I thought.

So I went out of the Dubious to catch the summer evening breeze. The night was glorious, out there. The air was sweet as a cool bath, the stars were peeping nosily beyond the neons, and the citizens of the Queendom,

105

in their jeans and separates, were floating down the Shaftesbury Avenue canals, like gondolas. Everyone had loot to spend, everyone a bath with verbena salts behind them, and nobody had broken hearts, because they all were all ripe for the easy summer evening. The rubber plants in the espressos had been dusted, and the smooth white lights of the new-style Chinese restaurants – not the old Mah Jongg categories, but the latest thing with broad glass fronts, and dacron curtaining, and a beige carpet over the interiors – were shining a dazzle, like some monster telly screens. Even those horrible old Anglo-Saxon public-houses – all potato crisps and flat, stale ale, and puddles on the counter bar, and spittle – looked quite alluring, provided you didn't push those two-ton doors that pinch your arse, and wander in. In fact, the capital was a night-horse dream. And I thought, 'My lord, one thing is certain, and that's that they'll make musicals one day about the glamour-studded 1950s.' And I thought, my heaven, one thing is certain too, I'm miserable.

And then, who should I see, wandering along the Soho thoroughfare, but the Kid-from-Outer-Space, who doesn't know that is his name, because I haven't told him so. This kid, who is extremely nice and that, and who I know from school days and even from the Baden-Powell contraption, belongs entirely to the Other World, i.e. as I've explained, the outer world that doesn't dig the scene, although, in many ways, they keep the whole scene going. This Outer-Space kid works for the municipal, doing whatever he does, and somehow I meet him every year or so, just once, by accident, like this, when sometimes he strays out of his four-square manor into mine, or I do, vice versa. And then we meet like travellers, and I tell him of the wonders of my section of the capital, real and fabled, and he tells me of his sports activities, and of his saving for a motor scooter, and of which side of the books a debit item goes in at the municipal, or a credit does. He's sweet, but rather dull, though not a drag, exactly.

'What knot would you use,' I said, coming up beside him, and speaking from the corner of the mouth into his ear, 'to tie two ropes of unequal thickness, supposing you had two such ropes, and wanted to join the pair of them together?'

'Oh-ho, it's you, boy Mowgli,' said this Outer-Space creation, stopping and slapping my shoulder till I sank four inches into the Soho pavement.

'Me, me! How are the national problems shaping up? Give me the loaded gossip from the accountancy cats in the town hall.'

'The budget's balanced,' said the O.-S. kid, 'but the money it's balanced up with is worth only a third of itself, these days.'

'Dig! And how's the scooter whatsit? How many legs you broken besides your own?'

The O.-S. kid looked sad. 'I not got the scooter,' he replied, 'because my Ma preferred a telly.'

'Boy – you a traitor? You let old Ma tell you how to spend your personal earnings?'

'Well, son, she's getting on, she is.'

'Likes to sit there in her wicker rocker, with her eyes crossed on the commercials?'

'Don't be sarky, now. You sore about something or other?'

'Very so, I am. Oh, yes!'

'Don't spread it round about, then. Not on me.'

'Okay, colonel. I shall keep it private.'

'Say what you like, see, there's lots to be learnt from television. I know it's for profits, but in its way it's a big universal education.'

'The population's seeing through the door at last, you think?'

'Well, isn't it? Tell me.'

'It's seeing only digests, slants and angles.'

'They kidding us then, those people? All those professors and authorities?'

'Why, sure they are! You think they tell us any secrets that's worth knowing? You think a professor who's studied twenty years can pop up in a studio and tell you something *real*?'

'It looks real, there up on the screen . . .'

'Oh, oh well . . . I tell you, Wolverine,' I explained to this simple, trusting soul, as we started walking down the boulevard, dodging prowlers, dodging gropers, dodging layabouts and tarts, 'I tell you. All these things – like telly witch-doctors, and advertising pimps, and show business pop song pirates – they despise us – dig? – they sell us cut-price sequins when we think we're getting diamonds.'

The boy stopped. 'Listen,' he said, 'you got to believe *something* in this world.'

'All right – you say so. Well, look right there!' I said, and pointed at a coffee bar that's even listed now in serious guidebooks, because the legend is, the top pop teenage rages were all 'discovered' there. 'See this establishment?' I said. 'See all the kids jam-packed in there beside the jukes, looking like they feel in at the prize-giving, the authentic big event?'

'I know the place. I been there.'

'I bet you have! It's made for mugs like you. Well, let me tell you – no teenage nightingale ever was "discovered" in that place until the telly cameras and the journalists moved in there for the massacre. The singing kids had all found out themselves, across the river, south, or anywhere, before those vultures gathered round to peck the kitty. I tell you, Tarzan, that fishbowl over there is just as real as nothing.'

I could see what was happening: on account of my argument with the Wizard, and my earlier cul-de-sac with Suze, I was coming the acid drop with this young feller. So I did what I've found best on these occasions, namely, cut the umbilical, and I dashed into a club entrance with a wave and crying, 'Moment!', and picked up the telephone and dialled the operator, and said hullo to her and asked her how I made a call to the prime minister, as I was a tourist from New Zealand and had the same name as Mr M., and wanted to ask the poor old geezer if we were possibly related. And after she'd sorted me out – quite nicely, I must say – I hung up and dashed out again, and found the Outer-Space kid still standing there, with his mouth open, and asked him about his sporting activities, because he was a boxer, though the singlet kind.

He said there were good fights billed south of the river soon, with some boys from his club, so why not go together? I said, oh, yes. Then he said meanwhile, what about we take in a film this evening? But that was no good to me, because you don't go into Soho to see films, because Soho *is* a film, and anyway, most times I go to cinemas I walk out half way through because all I see is a sheet hanging up there, and a lot of idiots staring at it, and hidden up behind all this there's just a boy operating the machinery with a fag hanging in his mouth even when he puts the record on for the 'God Save', and the cattle down there rise up on their corns, but not he, no! *Life* is the best film for sure, if you can see it as a film. So when I explained this, he said what about a bite? – a steak was what he actually suggested. And I said sorry, I was a vegetarian, which I am, not because of the poor animals or anything, but just because you belch much less, and red meat gives me the horrors.

So clearly, it wasn't going to be a big night out with the O.-S. kid, and now, as always happened, after being so pleased to see each other once again, we were just as glad to say farewell . . . isn't that like so many human relations? 'Remember me to your old Ma,' I said, 'and don't let her get ideas about a second telly.'

And all of a sudden I thought, I must get out of this fairground area, and have a bit of calm and meditation, so I hailed a cab and told the driver would he take me down by the Embankment, end to end, first one way, and then the other. He didn't enjoy this much, because taxi-drivers, like everyone that has ponce activities, like to pretend they're necessary and useful as well as for hire, but he naturally agreed, because the adults love to take your money and make you feel they're doing you a favour, both combined.

Whoever thought up the Thames Embankment was a genius. It lies curled firm and gentle round the river like a boy does with a girl, after it's over, and it stretches in a great curve from the parliament thing, down there in Westminster, all the way north and east into the City. Going in that way, downstream, eastwards, it's not so splendid, but when you come back up along it – oh! If the tide's in, the river's like the ocean, and you look across the great wide bend and see the fairy advertising palaces on the south side beaming in the water, and that great white bridge that floats across it gracefully, like a string of leaves. If you're fortunate, the cab gets all the greens, and keeps up the same steady speed, and looking out from the upholstery it's like your own private Cinerama, except that in this one the show's never, never twice the same. And weather makes no difference, or season, it's always wonderful – the magic always works. And just above the diesel whining of the taxi, you hear those *river* noises that no one can describe, but you can always recognise. Each time I come here for the ride, in any mood, I get a lift, a rise, a hoist up into joy. And as I gazed out on the water like a mouth, a bed, a sister, I thought how, my God, I love this city, horrible though it may be, and never ever want to leave it, come what it may send me. Because though it seems so untidy, and so casual, and so keep your-distance-from-me, if you can get to know this city well enough to twist it round your finger, and if you're its son, it's always on your side, supporting you – or that's what I imagined.

So when we returned again to Westminster, with the driver's neck all disapproval, I asked this coachman to turn south, across the stream, down to the Castle: because the thought had come to me it would be nice, after so many mixed emotions, to look in on Mannie Katz and his spouse Miriam.

Mannie I first met at a jellied eel stall near the Cambridge Circus, when we both reached for the vinegar and said pardon. As you'll have guessed, the boy is Jewish, likewise Miriam (and their one offspring), but I don't think it's only because I am a bit myself, as I've explained, on my Mum's side, that I admire this couple so. Here I must explain my attitude to the whole Jewish thing which in a word is, thank God (theirs and ours) they're here. I know all the arguments about them, back to front, and quite see what the Gentiles mean who are disturbed by them – but really! Add up all the defects that you can think of, please, and put them beside the great fact that the Jewish families *love life*, are on its side, are rinsed right out with it . . . and what do those debit things amount to? Just go inside a Jewish household, anywhere, I tell you, and however *dreadful* you may find them, what sticks out six miles and strikes you in your consciousness is that they're *living*. It's all a great noisy, boasting, arguing, complaining mess all right, but they're *alive!* And how they handle whatever stuff life's made of, like it was a material they were sampling, makes you realise immediately that they're an old, old, senior people who've been in the business of existence for a very long while indeed. I love London all right, as I've explained. But when the Jewish population have all made enough loot to take off for America, or Israel, then I'm leaving too. It would be turning out the light.

Mannie, as a matter of fact, has been to Israel, on a writers' congress there, and just missed that two-day battle with the Pharaohs we're all trying to forget. But being a Cockney kid, he's not as aggressive as the genuine Israelis who, when you meet them round the coffee bars, describe the orange-grove they live in as if it was a continent, and know the answers to absolutely everything before you've even asked the questions. Mannie's an authentic Cockney, by the way, not one of the suburban variety-bandbox imitations, and he's hard, and sad, and humorous, and sentimental, just like they are. Miriam's his second lady, and he must have married the first one from the cradle (she was one of ours – they came unstuck), because he's only just now hitting twenty, like we all are. There's also a young warrior of two years old called Saul who, in spite of all I've said in favour of Jewish family existence, is a bloody nuisance, and needs some of that Israeli discipline instead of being spoilt by the entire Katz clan, of every generation, and there are plenty.

This getting inside a Jewish home, if you yourself are not one, is a delicate operation, because although the place is yours once you're inside it, they take their time before they ask you round, and don't like sudden

113

unexpected visits, as at present. But this I can do to the Katzes, because some time ago I did Emmanuel a big, big favour without meaning to, i.e. I introduced him to a kinky character I'd photographed, called Adam Stark, who turned out to be a crazy let's-make-a-big-loss publisher, and printed a bunch of Mannie's poems, which hit the literary headlines for a while. So that, for Auntie This and Grandma That down in the Borough Road, I'm Fix-it Charlie, the clever boy who gave their young soothsayer a needful hoist. In this world, if you do the little kindly deed just at the right moment, the dividend's enormous: otherwise, it's soon forgotten. All the same, I took the precaution of stopping the cab down by St. George's circus, and giving young Shakespeare four-pence worth of warning I was on my way.

The Katz lot – at least three dozen of them – live in a fine old reconditioned derelict, and Mannie himself came down there to admit me, wearing his uniform of blue-black corduroys, and brought me up into the best front room which I wish he wouldn't, because that meant, as soon as they heard a visitor was coming, the rest of the Katzes made it over to the favourite son to entertain his honoured guest, and disappeared themselves into the purlieus. And there, looking just like someone straight out of the O.T. – those illustrated copies with Rebecca, or maybe Rachel, hearing something marvellous, three thousand years ago, beside a well – was Miriam K., and there, doing his berserk performance on the parquet, was their youthful warrior product, Saul. Neither of them asked me why I'd come, or why I'd not been for an eternity, which in my book are two signs of civilised human beings – because, believe me, most hosts are bullies holding pistols at your head, but not this couple.

'And how are the Angries?' I enquired.

Actually, Mannie wasn't in on the Angries kick, though he appeared in print about the same time that bunch of cottage journalists first caught the public nostril. Mannie's verse, of which I can dig the general gist, I think, is angry only about the grave, which he disapproves of, but for the life of the kiddos living round the Borough and in Bermondsey, he pens nothing but approval. His poems are songs of praise of youthful London: but his conversation doesn't approve of anything at all. In conversation, Mannie disapproves of *everything*, particularly of what you last said, whatever it may be.

'I see they gave you that Memorial Prize thing,' I said. 'I meant to send you a Greetings through the post, but I forgot.'

'They didn't *give* it to me, son. I won it,' Mannie said.

'Next, they'll be making you an O.B.E., or naming a street after you.'

'An O.B.E.! You think I'd accept that?'

'Yes,' said Miriam, who was making some false curls out of her infant's real curls.

'Well, what's high enough for you?' I asked. 'A life peer, would that do?'

'It's not a laughing matter,' Mannie told me. 'In

England, they don't bribe you by money, but by trashy *honours*. People prefer them to mere money.'

'Not me, I'd settle for a bribe.'

'Flattery and respectability are sweeter than L.S.D.'

'You'd better change your mind then, and accept.'

'He will,' said Miriam, who was changing junior.

'Never. Not even the Laureateship.'

'Duke – you'd like that. Duke Katz of Newington Butts would suit you fine. I can see you in your robes and ping-pong titfer.'

'Unlike all my countrymen, I don't care for fancy dress,' said Mannie haughtily.

'Why you wear that velveteen creation, then?'

'Don't expect Mannie to be logical,' said his better half.

'So I'm not logical.'

'No.'

'You sure of that?'

'Yes.'

'And when I married you, I wasn't logical?'

'No. You were desperate.'

'Why was I desperate?'

'Because you'd messed up your first marriage, and wanted someone to put you together again.'

'So I messed it up.'

'You certainly helped.'

'Make a mess once, you can make another.'

'You mean us? I don't think so. Besides, I won't let you mess us up.'

'No? You won't let me?'

'No.'

As this little bit progressed, the loving pair got nearer and nearer to each other, till they were kneeling nose to nose, bawling each other out, and both clutching portions of the pride-and-joy.

'Miriam,' I said, 'your product's p——g on the parquet.'

'That's not unusual,' said his loving Mum, and they busied themselves with rescue operations.

As I gazed down at this domestic scene, all bliss, I thought the corny old thought, why shouldn't all marriages be like this – a quarrel that goes on forever and ties the couple up in closer, tighter knots? And why can't all mums be like Miriam, young and beautiful and affectionate – and all girls, for that matter? Old Mannie certainly was a picker.

'You like a herring?' he said to me, looking up from behind his son's behind.

'Naturally, boy.'

'I get some. Don't pin Saul to the floor,' he told his wife, who gave him one of those 'Oh, well' glances, and started a little mum-and-son thing with the juvenile – we understand each other, don't we, man-child-born-of-woman?

I heard Mannie beckoning me from outside the door, with a whisper you could hear down as far as Southwark bridge, and out in the corridor he said – as if continuing a conversation we'd already started – 'So it's a touch? You need a bit dinero? Five pounds do? Or three?'

'No, man. Not me.'

'Trouble? The bailiffs in? Got syphilis? The law? Need bail?'

'*No*, man. This is a sociable visit.'

'Girl trouble? Boy trouble? Horse trouble? Anything like that?'

'Oh, well . . . no, not exactly – but you know Suze.'

'Certainly, I do. Nice girl – a bit promiscuous, if you don't mind a frank opinion.'

'She's marrying Henley, so she says.'

'Yes? There'll be a quick divorce, I prophesy.'

'Why?'

'Because Suze will discover, in the course of time, that *she's* bringing more into the kitty than the rag merchant.'

'Of course! I wish you'd tell her so.'

'Not me! Never advise a woman – never advise anyone, for that matter.'

'And till she finds out – I suffer?'

Mannie laid his hands upon my shoulders, like a rabbi blessing a young foot-soldier before a hopeless battle.

'*She's* got to suffer, son,' he said, 'before you can get her, and stop suffering.'

'Nice lot of wasted suffering all round.'

Mannie looked at me with his great big oriental seen-it-all-ages-ago eyes. 'Sure,' he said. 'I'll get that herring for you.'

Out in the kitchen there, I could hear him singing – there's one, at least, I thought, who'll never be a teenage vocal star. And back in the big room, Miriam got out some photographs to show me of Emmanuel, in a white shirt, collecting his award.

'Splendid,' I said. 'He looks like that Shelley number, crossed with Groucho Marx.'

'He's sweet,' said Miriam, running a finger down her husband's photographic image.

'Bad snaps,' I told her. 'Why didn't you get me?'

She didn't answer that one, and said – turning suddenly upon me that way women do, to catch you unawares, and as if *all* the conversations that they've had with you hitherto were meaningless – 'You think he's got talent, really? You think Mannie's got real talent?'

The answer came out before the thought, which is the only kind of true one. 'Yes,' I said, and she said nothing more.

In came the herrings, and the poet.

'The trouble about this country,' he explained to us, picking up a train of thought he'd dropped somewhere earlier on and left to ripen up a bit wherever it was he'd dropped it, 'is the total flight from reality in every sector.'

Miriam and I munched, waiting.

'For centuries,' this Southwark Shakespeare said, 'the English have been rich, and the price of riches is that you export reality to where it is you get your money from. And now that the marketplaces overseas are closing one by one, reality comes home again to roost, but no one notices it, although it's settled in to stay beside them.'

Short pause. Seemed that a question was demanded. And so,

'And so?' I said.

'A rude awakening is due,' Emmanuel said, smacking

his lips around his herring, and gobbling it down like a performing seal.

I took up the old, old cudgels.

'A minute, Cockney boy,' I said. 'You talk of "the English" – aren't you one of us?'

'Me? Certainly. If you're born in this town, you're marked by it for life: specially by this area, you are.'

'And so what happens to *the English*, happens to you too?'

'Oh, positively. I'm booked on the same flight, whatever the direction.'

'So long as I know,' I said. 'I want you to be around when the big bills come in for payment.'

The chat had taken on suddenly an ever-so-slightly awkward edge, as chats will do, particularly when the tribal drums start beating in the distance – and I wanted Mannie to understand I *did* think him every bit a local, just as much as me and more, and needed him, and only feared he might get tired of us, and skip. But now he had grabbed prince Saul, and clutched him like that Epstein thing up by Oxford Circus, and said to me,

'I write in the English language, boy. You take that away from me, and the whole world it and I come out of, and you cut off my strong right arm and other vital parts as well – let alone my livelihood and hopes of fame. Three of my own grandparents didn't speak a word of it. But me, I do, your speech is mine.'

'Grandmother Katz spoke English very well,' said Miriam.

'Never to me, she didn't.'

120

Here young Saul belched.

'Listen,' said Mannie solemnly. 'I tell you a secret: England is dreadful, and the English – they're barbarians. But three things of theirs I cherish most sincerely – the lovely tongue they thought up God knows how and I try hard to write in, and the nosey instinct of their engineers, and seamen, and explorers and scientists, to enquire, to find out why, and their own radicals that bounce up every century to flay and slay them, never mind the risk. So long as they have those things I'm glad to be with them, and will defend them . . . and everything else I can forget.'

Mannie said this so seriously, like he was taking an oath that might land him in a gas chamber, but he'd keep it. Admitted, he was a bit conscious of saying it all, and of us his audience (particularly Saul) – but me, I believed him, and was impressed. 'I could do with a cup of tea,' I said, and this time Miriam went out to get it.

M. Katz arose and stretched himself and said, 'Heigh-ho – it's the human element. It's a wicked world.'

I by this time was wandering around this ghastly front abode – ghastly, I mean, in its furnishings and whatnot, which hadn't caught up with the contemporary kick, but nice and cosy-comfy and well used, as front room furnishings not always are. Over in one corner, almost hidden like a chamber pot behind a curtain, was a small selection of select volumes, including several of Mannie's two productions, one copy of each of these being bound in the hide of some rare animal, and enclosed in an outer covering of velours.

'They're not a bookish lot, your elders and betters,' I suggested.

'Not on my side,' said Mannie K., stepping over to finger his thin, beloved books. 'But come round to Miriam's father's place, and you'll see a whole public library, even stacked in the kitchen and the mod. cons., and most of them in German and in Russian.'

'Your folk are traders, Mannie?'

'Yes, but we have *four* rabbis in the family, if you include cousins,' he said with a ferocious grin, half pride, half horror.

'They didn't like it when little Emmanuel got on the writing kick?' I asked.

'There was a struggle. In Jewish families, Gentile boy, there always must be, over all major decisions, particularly about sons, a struggle. But as I went on working down the market, and in fact still do most of the week, they soon ungraciously surrendered. Especially when they first saw me on the telly.'

'And Miriam's lot?'

'They liked it even less. You see, I was supposed to be a bad match for the girl, and they thought, well, even if he's a peasant, at least he'll make the girl some money.'

'And so now?'

'Oh, they approve. Miriam's poppa's translated me into German and into Yiddish – but he's only got me published in the latter.'

'And they nice?'

Mannie gazed at the ceiling, stroking his tomes.

'I tell you one nice thing about them. The only three

questions they asked Miriam when she dropped her bombshell were, "Is he healthy, is he a worker, do you love him?" – in that order. They didn't mention money till they saw *me*.'

Young Saul, feeling ignored, had joined us.

'They're pleased about this one, anyway,' I said.

'What? With twelve grandchildren already? Perhaps they'll take a bit of notice when *we* have our twelfth.'

'Not on your Nelly, we won't,' said Miriam, coming in bearing us the char.

So there it was: my visit to Mannie and Miriam had set me up, and given me the fortitude to have another bash at Crêpe Suzette. After all, even if it's undignified for a man to chase a girl, what had I got to lose in my position? So I asked the Katz pair if I could use their blower, and called up Suze's W2 apartment where, quite surprisingly – or perhaps not, because boldness often *is* rewarded – she answered quite politely, and said to me, why didn't I come round and catch her before she left for the Lament performance down in SW3?

This time I took the metro, because I wanted to ruminate on what the best tactics would be to approach Suze – whether to try and force a showdown over Henley, or whether just to bank the fires, but keep them kindled till my turn came round one day. But this was a mistake, I mean the tube thing, because by the time I arrived outside her W2 address, I saw Henley's vintage Rolls was parked there, and the lights blazing happily on Suze's floor upstairs.

Suze lives in a trio of Victorian bourgeois palaces

that have been made over into flatlets for the new spiv intellectual lot, and on the old pillars underneath the porticos, instead of numbers 1, 2 and 3, or whatever it should be, they've written *Serpentine House*, this 'House' thing being the new way of describing any dump the landlords want to make a fast fiver out of. You press a bell, and a constipated voice answers down a loud-hailer thing (or sometimes doesn't), and you state your business into a grille as if you were broadcasting to the nation, and then there are quite a lot of clicks, and buzzes, and in you go to a hall where your bollocks freeze, even in summer, and climb in an upended coffin called the 'elevator', and jerk up past blank walls like a pit shaft till you stop with a late lurch at the requested number. At the lift gates – which it needs a strong man to open, but which close themselves before you're out – there, on the landing, rather to my surprise, stood Henley.

You'll dig Henley straight away if I describe him as a *cold* queer: i.e. he's not the swing-my-hips camp chatterbox variety, or a side-eyed crafty groping number, or the battle-scarred parachutist nail-biting type, but the smooth, collected, let's-talk-this-thing-over one.

'Good evening,' he said politely, trying to help me out of the elevator contraption.

'Well, and good evening to you,' I said. 'You've pinched my girl.'

Henley smiled just so slightly, and shook his head ever so slightly too, and said to me seriously, 'Naturally, when we're together, you can still come and see her.'

'*Can* I!' I said. 'You think I'd go near her in those circumstances?'

'Yes,' he said gently.

'Well, mister, then you don't know me!' I cried.

Hearing this frank exchange of greetings in the passage, Suzette herself emerged and stood there looking radiant: I mean, it is the only word to use that I can think of, she really shone, and wore a brittle Cinderella-in-the-ballroom-scene creation, one of those fragile things that girls, who really are so tough, as we all know, adore to climb into, to make us think they're sweet seventeen in person (which, in her case, in fact she was). She saw we'd got off to a dodgy start in our conversation, so she came out and grabbed us both, one hand apiece, and pulled us into her apartment, and did all those things with drinks, and fags, and radiograms that are supposed to melt a polar situation.

But I was not wearing that.

'You don't mind, Henley,' I said, crunching some pretzels and refusing the glass of Coke I hadn't asked for, 'if I speak my mind.'

The cat sat on an armchair, legs crossed, all laundry and hairdresser and dry-cleaner's, looking like a superior footman on his day off, but still horribly polite. 'Not a bit,' he said. 'That is, if Suzette doesn't mind.'

'We may as well have it,' Suzette said, flopping onto some cushions, and opening up a 2,000-page Yank mag.

'In the first place,' I said, beginning with the least obvious weapon, 'Suzette is working-class, like me,'

'And me,' said Henley.

'Eh?'

'My father, who's still living, was a butler,' the cat said.

'A *butler*,' I told him, 'is *not* working-class. No disrespect to your old Dad, but he's a flunkey.'

Suzette slammed down the mag, but Henley reached out what I think that he'd call a 'restraining arm', and said to me 'Very well, I'm not working-class. And so?'

'Those cross-class marriages don't work,' I told him.

'Nonsense. What next?'

'Suzette,' I continued, warming up, 'is young enough to be your great-great niece.'

'Please don't exaggerate. I know I'm much older, but I'm not yet forty-five.'

'Forty-five! You're ripe for Chelsea hospital!' I cried.

'Really,' said Henley, 'you *do* exaggerate. Take all the top film stars – Gable, and Grant, and Cooper. How old do you think they are?'

'They're not trying to marry Suze.'

'Very well,' he said. 'You think I'm senile. Anything else?'

'Point number three,' I said, 'I leave to your imagination.'

Henley uncrossed his legs, put neat, clean, effective fingers on either knee (I hope the creases of his pants didn't slice him), and said to me, 'Young man . . .'

'None of that "young man".'

'Oh, you're a *pest*,' cried Suzette.

'You bet I am!'

Slightly raising his voice, Henley continued, 'As I was about to say . . . do you know that a great many marriages between completely normal people are never consummated?'

'Then why wed?' I shouted.

'It's what the French call . . .'

'I don't care a fuck what the French call it,' I yelled. 'I call it just plain disgusting.'

Suzette was up, flashing fire. 'I do think you'd better go,' she said to me.

'Not yet. I haven't finished.'

'Let him go on,' said Henley.

'Let me my arse,' I said. 'What I want to ask you is, do you really suppose a set-up of that kind will make Suzette happy? I mean *happy* – do you understand that word?'

Henley had also risen. 'I only know,' he said very slowly to me, 'she'll make *me* happy.' And he went over and collected himself another drink.

I grabbed hold of Crêpe Suzette. 'Suzie,' I said. 'Do think!'

'Let go.'

I shook the girl. 'Do *think*,' I hissed at her.

She stood quite still, and rigid as a hop pole. Henley, from across the little room, said, 'Honestly, I do think Suzette's mind is made up, and I do think it best if you accepted the situation, at any rate for the time being.'

'You've bought her,' I said, letting go Suzette.

She aimed a swipe at me, but down I ducked. I moved over towards Henley.

'I suppose,' he said, 'you want to fight me.'

'I suppose I ought,' I said.

'Well, if you really want to, I'm quite agreeable, though I should warn you I'm a dirty fighter.'

'You're dirty all right,' I said.

'Well, go on,' he said to me, putting down his glass. 'Do for heaven's sake either begin, or, if you don't want to, sit down and not spoil everybody's evening.'

I noticed he had one hand inside his pocket. 'Key ring,' I thought, 'or maybe a lighter in the fist.' But I was only making excuses, because I knew I really didn't want to hit the man – it was Suzette I wanted to hit, or hit myself, bash my head against a concrete wall.

'We're not going to fight,' I said.

'Bravo,' he answered.

Suzette said very slowly to me, 'This is absolutely the last scene of this kind I want to see. One more, and I just won't see you ever at all, and please believe I mean it.'

'Thank you,' I said, 'for making yourself so clear. Goodbye for now, if I recover my temper I may see you down at the Lament's.'

'Just as you think,' Suze said.

Henley held out his hand, but this was too much, so with a sort of wave I stumbled out of the door and had to wait several minutes in the passage there, hearing them nattering behind me, because that bloody elevator kept going up and down with Serpentine House residents packed in it, and wouldn't even stop when I managed to get the steel grille open while it was between floors, and stared down after it dropping into the abyss.

When finally I got out of that front door, aching like in a nightmare, as I dived down the streets, I heard a kind of death-rattle breathing just behind my ear, and whipped round to look, but there was nobody – was me. 'None of that!' I cried, and broke all my regulations and went into a boozer and had a quick double something, and shot out again. I thought I'd go over the park, across the wide, open, lonely spaces, which also would be a short cut to Miss Lament.

On this north front of the Hyde, the terraces are great white monsters, like the shots you see in films of hotels at the Côte de France. There's the terraces for miles, like cliffs, then the Bayswater speedway with its glare lights and black pools, and the great dark green-purple park stretching on like a huge sea. The thing about the parks is, in day time they're all innocence and merriment, with dogs and perambulators and old geezers and couples wrapped up like judo performers on the green. But soon as the night falls, the whole scene reverses – into its exact opposite, in fact. In come the prowlers and the gropers and the cops and narks and whores and kinky exhibition numbers, and the thick air is filled with hundreds of suspicious, peering pairs of eyes. Everyone is seeking someone, but everyone is scared to meet that him or her they're looking for. If you're out of it, you want to go inside to see, and once you're in, you're very anxious to get out again. So in I went.

I tried not to think of Suze in there – and did. 'Suze, Suze, Suzette,' I said, and stopped, and I swear the thought of her was more me then than I was. I sat down

129

on a bench, and my voice said, 'Boy, do be reasonable.'

One thing was right, I had to admit, in Suze's smelly plans. Until you know about loot – I mean really know, know how to handle the big stuff, know what the difference is between, let's say, five thousand pounds and ten (which are exactly the same to me), or what it's like to look at anything and say, 'I'll buy it,' or how the mugs will dance for you if you fling them down a shower of sixpences – then certainly you're still a mug yourself. The hard little biting brain inside Suzette was decided to understand this money kick, and my lord, she was going to do so, come what may.

I can't say I really minded about Henley in particular, and that twin-bed marriage thing that he was offering. What I minded was that it should be *anyone* but me – anyone at all. When she played me up with her Spade Casanovas, it was just as bad . . . except for this very big except, that I knew those adventures had no permanence attached to them. I still had my way in.

Mannie had said, 'Wait,' but how could I possibly be that wise? Would he have waited long for Miriam?

Perhaps Suze isn't me, I thought out suddenly. Perhaps I'm mistaken about this – she isn't really Juliet for my Romeo. But what does it matter, even if she isn't, if I feel she is?

'Fuck!' I cried out in a great bellow.

Three or so special investigators, who'd been approaching my bench cautiously from out of the dark green, stopped in their tracks at this, and some melted. I got up. 'Can I have a light?' the boldest said, as I passed by.

'Don't take a liberty,' I said, and hurried on.

I got on a stretch of curving roadway that was so damn black I kept walking off it, and getting tangled in the whatsits that they put there to say please-keep-off-the-thing. A light shaft suddenly appeared from nowhere, and by me there flashed a pair of mad enthusiasts in track-suits, puffing and groaning and looking bloody uncomfortable and virtuous. Good luck to them! 'God bless!' I shouted after.

Then unexpectedly, I came out on a delightful panorama of the Serpentine, lit up by green gas, and by headlamps from the cars whining across the bridge. I picked my way down by the water, and trod on a lot of ducks, they must have been, who scattered squawking sleepily. 'Keep in your own manor, where you belong,' I told them, chasing the little bastards down into the lake.

I was now beside the waves, and I could just make the sign out, 'Boats for Hire', and saw them moored fifteen feet away from me out there. So thinking, why not? anything to relieve the agony, I sat on the grass, and took off my nylon stretch and Itie clogs, and rolled up my Cambridge blues, and stepped into the drink like King Canute. By the time I reached the first boat, I was up to my navel like the hero in an Italian picture, and hoisted myself into the thing and, after a lot of bother untying a skein of greasy cables, I managed to put out to sea. As soon as I was in the middle, I let her just float along.

I lay there, ruddy uncomfortable, gazing at the stars, and thinking again of Suze, and of how absolutely nice it would be if she was there, she and me. 'Suzie, Suzette,' I said, 'I love you, girl.' And I washed my face off in the muddy, invisible slop.

Then I sat up inside that boat, and thought, how can I make a lot of money quickly, if that's what she wants to get? Naturally, I thought of Wiz, of his plans for his prosperity, but knew I could never make it that way – honest, not because of morals, or anything like that, but because that life, though it may be glamorous in its way, is so really *undignified*, if that's the word. I want to be rich all right, but I don't want to be *hooked*.

Wham! we slapped into the bottom of the bridge, the boat and I. I looked up and saw a geezer looking over, and I waved up to the silly sod, and shouted out, '*Bon soir, Monsieur!*' and he said nothing in reply, but started throwing pennies down on me, or maybe they were dollar bits, I couldn't see, and didn't care to, because this character's idea of having a ball struck me as most dangerous. So I rowed on to the other bank, and disembarked just at the Lido, and had to climb a fence to get out of the enclosure, and ripped myself in several painful places.

The law, as anyone who knows it will agree, has a genius for showing up not when you're *doing* something, as it should, presumably, but when you're quite innocent and *have* just done something. This cowboy flashed his lighthouse on me as I was putting on my shoes and socks, and stood there saying nothing, but not dowsing that annoying glim.

But I was determined he'd have to say the opening

word, which he did by asking, after several long minutes, 'Well?'

'Having a paddle, officer,' I said.

'A paddle.'

'That's what I told you.'

'That's what you tell me.'

'In the old Serpentine.'

'Yeah.'

'Down there.'

'Down there, you say.'

This conversation seemed to me quite mental, so I got up, and said, 'Goodnight, officer,' and started off, but he said to me, moving up, 'Come here.'

So naturally, I ran.

One thing you learn about the law is that they don't like running because their helmets usually fall off. What's more, they don't like any kind of physical effort – in fact, the one thing coppers all have in common, apart from being tramps, is that they have a horror of physical labour of any kind, particularly manual. Just look at the expression on their faces when you see a photo of them in the papers, digging among the rushes for the killer weapon! So if you're fast on your feet, and there's only one of them, you can fairly easily elude them, which I did now by dodging behind that Peter Pan erection, and diving in some smutty bushes.

'Further on, mate – get further on,' a voice said, as I'd inconsiderately got entangled with a bird and client, which of course wasn't my intention, so I bowed myself out, and got up on the road again and over it among

133

the great dark trees, far darker than the dark sky up behind them, and I started walking normally, like some serious kiddo who's gone out nocturnal birdwatching, or learning poetry by heart for a dramatic evening at the borough hall. After trampling by mistake over some flower beds, for which I apologise, I came out on the south side of the Hyde, and escaped through the ornamental gate into the embassy section that starts up round about there.

If attending a teenage party, or in fact one of any other kind, I'd naturally wear my sharpest, coolest ensemble – possibly even my ivy-league outfit a GI got for me last year from his PX. But the Lament would be disappointed if, billing me to her public as a teenage product, I didn't show up in my full age-group regalia. So I wasn't embarrassed by my non-Knightsbridge clobber, but only a bit at being drenched downwards from the hips: however, I was hoping they'd accept that as just a bit of teenage fun.

So I rang the Dido bell. And, as often happens when you attend a party, another cat arrived on the doorstep at the same moment. Usually, they don't address you until properly introduced within, but this one was something of an exception, because, without even telling me his name, or anything, he smiled and said, 'You for the tigress's den as well?'

I didn't answer that, but smiled back just as politely (and with just as little meaning) as the cat – who was one of those young men with an old face, or old ones with a young one, hard to tell which: anyway, he had a very sharp top-person suit on, which must have cost his tailor quite a bit.

'You've known our remarkable hostess long?' he said.

'That's how it goes,' I answered, and we passed inside the block together.

No need for a lift this time, because Dido has a ground floor thing around a patio out the back, which is even selecter than a penthouse, in my opinion, because it's somehow more unexpected: I mean the patio, which was very large for London, and still full of gaps in spite of a fair number of hobos already milling around there. Lament's one of those persons who, when she throws a party, and you've just arrived, you don't have to hunt around for her under the cushions or in the toilet, to say hullo, because she's felt you directly you come in, and is on the scene immediately with a merry word of greeting. Up she glid, wearing a white hold-me-tight creation, like an enormous washable contraceptive, and with her ginger hair wind-tossed and tousled (I'll bet it took her all of half an hour), and with her radar-eyes gleaming on the target, and with her geiger-ears pinking big discoveries, and with her Casualty-Ward-10 hands slicing through the hospitable summer air, and with her feet, claws withdrawn inside the pads just for the present, very successfully and snakily carrying the lot.

'Oh, hul-*lo*, infant prodigy,' she said to me. 'You've already met my ex-lover Vendice? Are you hungering for something? Have you wet your pants?'

'Yes, yes, and no,' I told her. 'I've come straight up to your tenement from a bathe.'

'But of *course*,' she cried out, but in a low, rasping voice, as if someone had cut six of her vocal chords. Then she leant her head until her carroty locks swept by my neck, and said, 'Any items for the column?'

'Lots. How's the price these days?'

She put her lips on my neck skin without kissing, actually. 'You'll tell me for love,' she said.

'Yes. All the dirt. A bit later,' I assured her. But she didn't hear me, because she'd swept on along her mossy hostess's track.

I think Dido's the most unscrupulous person I've yet met, though I don't mean especially about money. What I mean is, she believes everything in existence is a *deal*. For example, when she came pounding around the teenage ghetto, collecting material for her articles I've referred to, she gave all the kiddos the impression that she wanted to *buy* the teenage thing, like somebody booking a row of ringsides at the circus. And when she looks at you – and she's always very pleased to see you – her eyes say she knows just how much your price will be. She's somewhere between thirty-eight and fifty-eight, I'd say, and this flat of hers in the Knightsbridge red-light district must be worth a bit more than ever her column pays her, so there are no doubt other items in reserve. The sex angle, so the chatter goes, isn't bent in any direction, and no one in particular's in evidence around her garret, though there are said to be favourites, and sometimes the industrial daddies from the North move in a while to look around.

I gazed at the saleroom, to see what sorts of customers

she'd mustered. I don't know if I can convey this idea exactly, but the general impression they all gave was of being well stoked with nourishment, well decked out in finery, but all on someone else's money. This is a curious thing – that you can usually tell who has their own loot, who not: rather as you can the really sexual numbers, boys and girls, from all the others, I mean the serious operators, by a sort of quietness, of purpose, of relaxation they possess.

Up came the Hoplite. He had on some Belafonte-style, straight-from-the-canefield (via the make-up room) kind of garments, with too many open necks, and tapering wrists, and shoes like tin-openers, all in light colours except for some splashes of mascara that gave his eyes melancholy and meaning. He plucked at my arm, and told me, with an agonising sigh, 'Look, yon's the Nebraska boy.'

I saw, chatting away beneath the pergola, a perfectly ordinary young US product – fresh, washed and double-rinsed as they manufacture them in thousands over there.

'Cute,' I told Hoplite.

'*Cute!* Oh, lordy me!'

'Well – dynamic, then.'

'That's a bit better.'

'You hitting it off, you two?'

'Ah, woe . . . !'

The Hoplite gripped my arm, gazing to and fro languorously from the Nebraskan one to me, and said, 'It's ghastly, you know. He's ever so friendly to me, and cheerful, and sometimes even grins and reaches out and *ruffles my hair.*'

137

'Painful. I feel for you.'

'Have pity! Ah me, ah me!'

'Ah you, all right. Where's the lush hidden?'

'It's not. You help yourself from the sideboard, just like that.'

I worked my way over with young Fabulous, who eased aside the multitude with his shapely tail.

'Ah-ha, you remind me,' I told Hop. 'The Call-me-Cobber number wants to sign you up for a television thing' – and I told him about the Lorn Lover programme project. The Hoplite looked very dubious indeed. 'Of course, you know I'd love to have my face and figure up there in between the commercials,' he told me, 'and naturally, I'd love to appear before the nation to tell it all about Nebraska. But do you think, really, public opinion's ripe yet for anything so bold?'

'You could say it's a deep and splendid friendship that unites you.'

'Well, in a sense it is.'

'I'll speak to C.-me-C., then.'

'And I will to Adonis.'

Standing there alone, clutching my lime-and-tonic, I was accosted by one of those numbers you always meet up with at a party, and she opened up to me with,

'Hullo, stranger.'

'Hi.'

'How are you called?'

'And you?'

'You tell me.'

'David Copperfield.'

138

She shrieked. 'I'm Little Nell.'

'There you go!'

'What do you do?'

'Only on Saturdays.'

'Naughty. No, I mean your job.'

'Photographic work.'

'For Dido?'

'I'm freelance.'

'Plenty of windmills to tilt at?'

'That's how it goes.'

'Which end of town you live?'

'The end I sleep in.'

'No, seriously.'

Here they always give you the, 'But I'm *interested* in you,' look.

'Round W10.'

'Oh, that's unusual.'

'Not to those who live in W10.'

Here, having a little *thought* to wrestle with, her brain started pinking.

'Know everyone here?'

'Everyone except you.'

'But you *do* know me. I'm Little Nell.'

You see what I mean? Honestly, that's what parties always turn out to be. All the pleasure of a party is going there, up as far as the front door only.

Bits of the company had started dancing, but I didn't want to join in this activity, because either they were doing that one-two, one-two ballroom thing, which makes everybody look like waiters and usherettes out on their annual rave, or else, if they were jiving, they were all of them frantic and alarming, like a physical culture demonstration by a bunch of cats with colic, knocking themselves out quite unnecessarily, because the real way to jive is to swing your body, not your legs and arms. I must admit some of the birds tried to get a hold of me, on account of the prestige of the teenage performance, but I pleaded not guilty, and made it over to the pergola. There I unhitched my Rolleiflex, and took a few pictures just to keep my hand in, and for a rainy day.

'I'd like some of those, if they're successful,' said a gent standing there beside me.

This gent, who wore a north-of-Birmingham suiting, was the one exception to the thing I said earlier on about their all, myself included, being a lot of parasites and ponces: I mean, he looked as if it was on himself that he depended – you know, substantial, and not throwing it all up at once. And this turned out to be the case, because he told me he was a businessman, a manufacturer in the motor industry, and believe me, I got quite a kick out of knowing him, as I had never actually met a businessman before – in fact, hardly believed that they existed, though realising, of course, they must do, somewhere.

'Good for you, chairman!' I said to him, pumping his business-manly paw. 'If you ask me, you commercial cats are the only ones that really keep the nation sliding off its arse.'

'You think so?' the number asked me, giving the 'amused smile' the seniors turn on whenever anything intelligent is said by an absolute beginner.

'Naturally, I think it,' I told him, 'if I've just said it.'

'Not many would agree with you,' he said, beginning to latch on to my conception.

'You don't have to tell me! Turn on your telly, or your radio, and do you ever catch anything about businessmen? Does anyone write books about them in the paperbacks? And yet, don't we all live off what you do? Without you tycoons, there just wouldn't be the money for the rent.'

'You're very flattering,' this industrial number said.

'Oh, shit!' I cried. 'Will *no* one ever take my ideas seriously?' The balance sheet product started to laugh soothingly, so I grabbed him by the lapel of his family-tailor hopsack, and said, 'Look! England was an empire – right? Now it isn't any longer – yes? So all it's got to live on will be brains and labour, i.e. scientists and engineers and businessmen and the multitudes of authentic toilers.'

The cat looked surprised and pleased.

'Mind you,' I added, just to bring him down a bit, 'I'm not saying business is *difficult*. I don't think it's difficult to coin loot, provided you're really interested in it – provided it's your number-one obsession.'

'I'll not disagree with you altogether there,' the boardroom product said.

'Most of us *think* we're interested in making money, but we're not: we're only interested in getting our hands on someone else's.'

He looked at me approvingly, as if he'd sign me up immediately as chief teacup boy in his twelve-storey office block.

'And how is the car trade?' I continued.

'Don't tell a soul,' he said, looking around him, 'but it's prospering.'

'Crazy!' I said. 'But of course,' I went on, 'you know you automobile producers are a bunch of murderers?'

'Oh, yes? Would you say so?' he said, smiling 'tolerantly' again.

'Well, in a sense you are. You read the figures of the slaughter on the highways?'

'I try to forget them. What are we to do?' This automotive one was still looking a bit 'amused', but I could see I'd touched him on a nerve. 'After all,' he said, 'if you took the cars off the roads tomorrow, the whole economy would collapse. Have you considered that?'

'No,' I said.

'In addition, the export industry on which, as you've said, this country lives, requires a healthy home consumption to sustain it.'

'There you go!'

'So death on the roads is the price we pay for moving the goods around, and earning currency abroad.'

I looked at the cat. 'You've said all this before,' I told him, 'to the assembled shareholders.'

'Good heavens, no!' the number said. 'As a matter of fact, son, I say it chiefly to myself.'

'Well,' I told this industrial chieftain, 'you know as well as I do, if you're a driver, which I expect you are, that there's stacks of goons sitting behind steering-columns who *like* the idea they may mow some victim down.' I waited, but he didn't answer. 'An accelerator and a ton of metal,' I went on, 'bring out the Adolf Hitler in us all. They know there's no danger to themselves, sitting up there inside that tank, and if they make a kill, they know nobody's going to hang them.'

The profit-and-loss one now began to look a bit uneasy – I mean, not at my ideas, but *me* – which always happens if you let loose an idea.

'Car driving,' I told him, twisting my knife round in the wound, 'is the licensed murder of the contemporary scene. It used to be duelling and cut-throats, now it's killing by car.'

I saw I mustn't keep on rucking him, because, after all, this was a party, so I patted him on his hopsack, just like he'd done me, and struggled across to cut in on Call-me-Cobber, and have a spin round with the ex-Deb-of-Last-Year. But: 'Fair goes, now, fair goes,' the Cobber said, and he pulled the ex-Deb out of reach, and all I got for my attempt was her making apologetic faces at me over the Aussie's beefo shoulders.

'Aboriginal!' said Zesty-Boy Sift.

This Zesty, who had come up now beside me, was the only other teenage product present at the barbecue, and I hadn't spoken to him yet for two reasons: first, because I meant to borrow five pounds from him, and wanted to choose my moment, and second, because this Z.-B. Sift had come up very abruptly in the world since I first knew him, and I didn't want to show I was impressed.

But in actual fact, I was. In the far dawn of creation when the teenage thing was in its Eden epoch, young

Zesty used to sing around the bars and caffs, and was notorious for being quite undoubtedly the crumbiest singer since – well, choose your own. *But* – here's the point – the songs he sung, their words as well as harmonies, were his invention, thought up by him in a garage in Peckham, where he used to toil by day and slumber in an old Bugatti. And though Zesty caught all the necessary US overtones to send the juveniles that he performed for, the words he thought up were actually *about* the London teenage kids – I mean not just 'Ah luv yew, Oh yess Ah du' that could be about anyone, but numbers like *Ugly Usherette*, and *Chickory with my Chick*, and *Jean, your Jeans!*, and *Nasty Newington Narcissus* which all referred to places and to persons which the kids could actually identify round the purlieus of the city.

So far, so bad, because nobody was interested in Zesty-Boy's creative efforts – particularly the way *he* marketed them – until one of the teenage yodellers who'd hit the big time remembered Zesty, and sold the whole idea of him (and of his songs) to his Personal Manager, and his A. & R. man, and his Publicity Consultant, and his Agency Booker, and I don't know who else, and behold! Zesty-Boy threw away his own guitar and saved his voice for gargling and normal speech, and started writing for the top pop canaries, and made piles – I mean literally piles – of coin from his sheet, and disc, and radio, and telly, and even filmic royalties. It was a real rags-to-riches fable: one moment Z.-B. Sift was picking up pennies among the dog-ends and spittle with a grateful grimace, the next he was installed in this same Knightsbridge area with a female secretary and a City accountant added to his list of adult staff.

'Those Aussies!' he said, 'have moved in for the slaughter. Did you know there's 60,000 of them in the country? And ever seen any of them on a building site?'

I didn't reply (except for a wise nod), because the matter of the five pounds was now uppermost in my mind, and about borrowing and lending, of which of both I have a wide experience, I could tell you several golden rules. The first is, come straight up smartly to the point: to lead up tactfully to the kill is fatal, because the candidate sniffs your sinister intention and has time to put up barricades. So I said, 'I want a fiver, Zesty.'

Zesty-Boy, I was glad to see, observed, on his side, the first golden rule of lending, which is to say yes or no *immediately* – if you don't, they'll hate you if you refuse, and never be grateful if you agree. He took out the note, said, 'Any time,' and changed the subject. As a matter of fact, in this case we both knew it was actually a gift, because in his Cinderella days I've often enough handed Zesty-Boy the odd cigarette-machine money, and as a shilling then was worth what a pound is to him now, this really was only a repayment. And I could add – since we're on this topic – that if you're in a position, ever, to be a *lender*, the two kinds of people you should most watch out for are not, as you might expect, the dear old boyhood pals of Paradise Alley days, but any newcomer (because borrowers are attracted to fresh faces), or anyone you've just done a favour to (because borrowers think there where the corn grows, there's sugarcane as well).

'Eh?' I said to Zesty-B. because, with these meditations, I hadn't been following attentively the trend his conversation had been taking.

'I said Dido's out for blood this evening. She's got the needle into Vendice, because he's not buying any more space in her fish-and-chip organ, and she's losing her cut on all the full-page spreads.'

'Bad,' I said, glancing over at the number he referred to, who was the one I'd met earlier outside the door, and who was under the arcade that ringed the patio, strip-lit with lamps all hidden, so that you always got only a reflection, and couldn't read a book there, supposing that you'd wanted to.

'What does he do, this Vendice?' I asked Zesty-Boy. 'And is that his baptismal name?'

Zesty said yes, it was, and that Vendice Partners' job was well up somewhere in the scaffolding of one of those advertising agencies that have taken over Mayfair, making it into a rather expensive slum.

'And why has Partners' pimpery taken their custom away from Dido's toilet-paper daily?' I asked Zesty-Boy.

'It may be that Dido's slipping, or the paper's slipping, or just that everything these days is falling in the fat laps of the jingle kings.'

'I wonder why Dido doesn't do a quick change and crash-land in the telly casbah?'

'Well – could she? I mean, can a journalist really do anything *else*?'

'I see what you mean.'

The time had now come for me to flatter the young Mozart in him a little. 'I heard one of your arias on the steam, last evening,' I told him. 'Separate Separates', if I remember. Very nice.'

'Which of the boy slaves was it sung it? Strides Vandal? Limply Leslie? Rape Hunger?'

'No, no . . . Soft-Sox Granite, I think it was . . .'

'Oh, that one. A Dagenham kiddy. He's very new.'

'He sounded so. But I loved the lyric, and enjoyed the lilt.'

Zesty-Boy shot a pair of Peckham-trained eyes at me. 'Yeah?' he said.

'I tell you, man. I don't flatter.'

'Compliment accepted.' I could see the cat was pleased. 'You heard they gave me my first Golden?' he said cautiously.

'Boy, I was delighted. For 'When I'm Dead, I'm Gone', wasn't it? A million platters, man – just fancy that!' How could the Sift kid fail to be delighted? 'How long will it all last, do you suppose?' I said to him.

'Companion, who knows? I gave it only a year, two years ago. And still they come – performers and, what's more, cash customers.'

'Still only boys for singers? No signs of any breasted thrushes?'

'We've tried one or two of them, but the kids just don't want to know. No, for the minors, it's still males.'

'And all those boys from Dagenham and Hoxton and wherever. You have to teach them how to sing American?'

'Oh no, they seem to pick it up – get the notes well up there in their noses when they sing . . . Though when they *speak*, even in personal appearances, it's back to Dagenham again.'

'Weird spiel, isn't it.'

'Weird! Child, I'm telling you – it's eerie!'

You know the way that, when things start to go amiss at a function, everyone notices it long before they actually stop doing whatever it was they're doing – drinking, dancing, talking and etcetera – and this was what now occurred, because a battle was developing between our hostess and the Partners number. But soon, just as no one can resist listening to a bit of hot chat over the blower, we all turned ourselves into spectators at the gladiatorial show.

They started off with the mutes on, playing that English one-up game they teach you at Oxford, or is it Cambridge, anyway, one of those camp holiday camps, with Dido saying, at the point I managed to tune in, 'I didn't say barsted, I said bastard.'

'It's not your pronunciation. Dido, that I'm questioning,' the copywriting cat was saying, 'but your definition.'

'Very well, I withdraw it,' Dido said, 'and say you're just a harlot.'

'Really, my dear, I don't think I'm a woman. Surely, I've given you proof positive of that . . .'

'Only just, Vendice, only just,' she said.

And so and so forth, guest and hostess, both very cool and, what was really rather horrible, without any emotion in it I could see – and the friends looking on and listening with that kind of grin the mob wear at a prize fight in the municipal baths. I must be a prude at heart, because this thing really shocks me – not bawling-outs and even fights, of course, but this methodical, public blood-letting. And I must be a snob, because I really do think that when an educated English voice is turning bitchy, it's a quite specially unpleasant sound, besides being fucking silly, and an utter drag. So I was much relieved, and I think one or two others were, when into the middle of all this stepped wedding-bells Henley with my Suze.

As it happened, I was adjacent to the stereo, so I slipped on some Basie, turned on the juice well up, and, with a low bow to Henley, grabbed the girl. Now if there's one thing among many Suze has learnt from her Spade connections, it's how to dance like an angel, and enjoy it, and I myself, though perhaps a bit unpolished, have studied on hard floors around the clubs and palais and in all-night private sessions, and besides which, we know all each others' routines backwards – and sideways and front as well – so before long, there we were, weaving together like a pair of springs connected by invisible elastic wires, until we reached that most glorious moment of all in dancing, that doesn't come often, and usually, admittedly, only when you're whipping it up a bit to show the multitude – that is, the dance starts to do it for you, you don't bloody well know what you're up to any longer, except that you can't put a limb wrong anywhere, and your whole damn brain and sex and personality have actually become that dance, *are* it – it's heavenly!

When just a second we were in an electric clinch, I said, 'Where you dine? He take you somewhere nice?' And she said, 'Oh, *him!*' Boy! Can you believe it? She said it just like that! So when we were close again a second, and the Count playing wonderfully in our ears, and the whole Lament lot standing round us thirty miles or so away, I cried out to her, 'Is he you? Is he really you?' And Suzette said, 'No, you are! But I'm going to marry him!' And at that moment the music stopped, because I'd jabbed the sapphire down too near the middle in the earlier excitement of the moment.

So I bid everyone good-night, and do sleep well, and thanks for having me, and went out of the flat into the London dawn. It *was* dawn, as a matter of fact, already: or rather, to be exact, it was that moment when the day and night are fighting it out together, but you've no doubt whatever who will triumph. A cab was passing by, and slowed down politely for the wayfarer, but I didn't want to break into Zesty-Boy's fiver at the moment, and also wanted to remember what Suze said about 10,000 times, so I set off to foot it back across the city to my home up the north in Napoli.

IN JULY

Picture me, up to the calves in mud at low tide beside the river, trying to pose the Hoplite and the ex-Deb up on a stranded barge. 'Don't *fuss* us,' the Hoplite said; and, 'Do hurry,' said the ex-Deb-of-Last-Year.

This was the spiel. Events of the last month had convinced me that the only way I could ever hope to make some swift dinero was by cracking into the top-flight photographic racket – i.e. produce some prints that would be so sensational that I'd make the big time in the papers and magazines, and even (this was my secret dream) succeed in holding a fabulous exhibition somewhere to which all my various contacts would bring their loaded friends. When you come to ponder on it, like I did for days, you'll see it's not so wild a notion as it might appear. After all, kids do make big money these days, as I've explained, and as for photography, well, it seems very fashionable just now to treat photographers like film stars, the reason being, I expect, that the culture-vultures get all the art kick they want out of snapshots, although actually they're damn easy to understand – and, need I say, so far as that goes, to manufacture.

But, as in everything here below, I had to find my gimmick, my approach, my slant, my angle. And after days of brooding on the problem, I hit on a plan that, so far as I can see, can't miss. It simply is, to weave a story round the two contemporary characters that everyone is interested in – i.e. the teenagers and the debs. You dig? The teenager, of humble origin – Prince Charming in reverse – encounters the Poor-Little-Rich-Girl debutante. Daddy and Pop both disapprove (as well as Mum and Mummy), so Teenage Tom and Diana Debutante have to meet clandestinely in selected spots about the capital (which I would choose for their crazy picturesqueness), and the whole collection, when completed, would comprise a stark, revealing portrait of the contemporary scene.

My chief difficulty was casting the two star parts, because although I know stacks of teenagers and a deb or two, I wanted persons I could rely on to keep the secret, and who would give me a lot of valuable time without immediate remuneration, and who, most of all, would look sensational when recorded for posterity by my Rolleiflex. The ex-Deb was the obvious selection for the female rôle, since her looks, though, to my taste, completely meaningless, are simply gorgeous – I mean, she's so damn glorious she isn't *real* – but the big question was, of course, would she accept? Well, thanks to Dean Swift, she did. Because the ex-Deb, though you couldn't precisely describe her as a junkie, climbs on the needle when being beautiful is just too much for her, and the Dean, when I introduced them, was able to help her in the matter of supplies. If you're going to tell me hooking her this way is unethical, I'm perfectly willing to agree to that, but please understand my situation in regard to Suze is urgent and rather desperate, as the performance at the registry totalizator can't be long delayed, although I haven't succeeded yet in discovering exactly when it is to be.

Now as for the boy, the obvious choice was Wiz – or, in fact, anyone at all within the age bracket other than The Fabulous Hoplite. But Wiz isn't my best friend, unfortunately, at the moment, so it was the Hop I picked. The reason is that, though Hoplite doesn't consider himself, correctly, to be an authentic teenager at all, or, for that matter, exactly a Prince Charming, he really is extremely handsome and delicious and photogenic, and the boy always has a load of spare time lying heavy on his hands. The deal here was rather dodgy, because I had to reject on Hoplite's part what the courts call a certain suggestion, and fixed it with him on the promise of a deluxe album of himself in classic poses, which he could offer as a birthday gift to his Americano.

If you've ever tried to assemble two colourful characters like the Fabulous and the ex-Deb in the same place, on several occasions, for a certain length of time, you'll realise what I've been up against these last weeks.

Particularly as, to get the London fairy-story atmosphere I'm aiming for, I've had to take them in a tanker down in Surrey docks, and in the reptile house at the zoological, and in both an ambulance and a hearse (that wasn't as difficult as it might seem), and also, actually inside the stables where our national toy soldiers groom their animals – which was a Day-to-Remember I believe I shall never forget.

'No, no, no, no,' I shouted from the foreshore, because the ex-Deb and the Hoplite had actually turned their backs on me.

'No – what?' cried my heroine, tossing her locks about, and turning in a practised pose that pointed all her salient features.

'You do *fuss* so,' the Hoplite said again, standing up to adjust his slacks, and looking like an are-you-weedy? be-like-me, advertisement.

I waded forward, and appealed to their better natures. 'Listen, *amateurs!*' I cried. 'It's your *fronts* that I'm paying for – the parts where you show some expression.'

'Paying us, infant!' said the female lead.

'If it's *expression* you want . . .' the Hoplite added. 'Besides, you've cut short a delightful conversation.'

I knew what that was. The Hop never tired of hearing of transactions in the debutante market, and chatted his leading lady endlessly on this subject, especially when I asked him for a heroic or a grief-ridden expression.

'Just one more try,' I pleaded, 'and do please recollect the script. The current situation is that Lord Myre is going to horsewhip his daughter's young heart-throb, and she's breaking the news to him that daddy's on the way down with his posse.'

'Delicious,' the Hoplite said.

'It's daddy who gets horsewhipped these days,' said the ex-Deb-of-Last-Year.

Picture, to recap, the scene. There, on the wharf, stood the ex-Deb's bubble-car and M. Pondoroso's Vespa (because yes, Mickey P. really had delivered the promised goods), and a band of onlookers with complimentary tickets, and up on the bridge above us, the City citizens scurrying to and fro, the men looking like dutiful school kids with their briefcases and brollies, the women as if they were hurrying to work in order to hurry home again, and out in the stream, the craft like Piccadilly circus-on-the-water, and there in the quagmire me, and this temperamental Old Vic duo. The fact is, it *was* rather difficult to concentrate, because the whole panorama was so splendid, with the sun hitting glass triangles off the water, and the summer with the season really in its grip, making the thought of those short, dark, cold days long ago seem just a nightmare.

So we decided to break off for *déjeuner*.

This we partook in a Thames-side caff up in a lane that, though I know the river frontage intricacies like the veins on my own two hands, I'd never discovered – but then, after all, who *does* know London? We found the caff by following some river toilers in there, and when we entered there was a mild sensation (whistles, stares, and dirty remarks made sideways), because, of course, the Hop and Deb are both exotic spectacles in

155

any setting, and the more so, obviously, here. But both were more than equal to the situation, neither being the least put out by blinkless stares, and neither being, in spite of all their camp and blah, the least bit snobbish – socially, I mean, at any rate – which is one reason why I like them.

So the ex-Deb, between whiles of her salt beef, swedes and dumplings, chatted anyone who chatted her, and even did a tango with a hefty belted character when someone put some silver in the juke. And Fabulous, surrounded by gigantic, sweaty manual workers, did a great act of borrowing salt and pepper and miscellaneous sauces from lots of tables, giving as good as he got to the resident wittery, till some sour, quite exceptional, customer asked him, how was trade?

There was a slight hush at this, and Fabulous asked the customer just why he wanted to know.

'I thought you might fancy me,' this troublemaker said, looking round for the applause which, actually, he didn't get.

'*You*?' said the Hoplite, gazing at the monster.

'That's what I said,' the cat rejoined.

'*Well*, now,' said Hop, in tones loud for all to hear. 'I don't really think so, no, I don't really think that you're exactly me. But if you bring your wife along, or your grandmother, or your sister, I dare say you'll find they'll prefer even me to anything they've had from you.'

'Prefer a poof?' the number said.

The Hoplite smiled round the room, rallying his supporters.

'Am I really the very first you've met?' he asked the character. 'You'd better go straight home and tell your mother you've seen one, before she changes you.'

This got a laugh, and the cat couldn't keep it up, and everybody changed the subject because, say what you like, although I know English workingmen are as crude as it's possible to be, they can be very civilised, when they feel like it, in the matter of behaviour.

A nautical cat, wearing a baseball cap and a bare chest marked, 'Pray for Me, Mother' told the ex-Deb that his boat did weekly trips up to Scandinavia, and why didn't she come along on one – everyone on board would be delighted, he assured her. The ex-Deb said she'd certainly consider this (and I believe she meant it), and the Hop asked if he could sign on as deckhand for the trip, and the nautical numbers all said greaser would suit him better – and all this chat about the sea, and seafaring, and ships sailing out of London, made me begin to feel that, hell, it really was ridiculous that here was I, nearly nineteen, and never yet left the city of my creation, so I determined there and then the very next thing I'd do, would be get myself a brand new passport.

When the place had cleared a bit, we got together to decide on the next location, which I wanted to be on the tea-terrace of an open-air swimming pool, with Hop explaining artificial respiration methods to the debutante. I could see that the Hoplite, in spite of his little victory, was a bit upset by the earlier occurrence, so I said, 'Never mind, Hop, small minds live in small worlds.'

'Don't they, though!' said Fabulous.

'Speaking personally,' said the ex-Deb, 'and I may be wrong, because I've no moral sense whatever – or so all the men I leave or don't like in the first place tell me – I think this game of putting everyone you meet in precise sexual categories, is just a bit absurd.'

'A drag, at any rate,' I suggested.

'No, just *absurd*. I mean,' said the ex-Deb, running her graceful fingers through her luscious locks, 'if everyone's entire life, every twenty-four hours, was filmed and tape-recorded, who exactly *would* seem normal any more?'

'Not me, for one,' said Hoplite, emphatically.

'Not you, darling, but not *anyone*,' the ex-Deb said. 'I mean, where does normality begin, and where does it definitely end? I could tell you a tale or two about *normal* men, if I felt inclined,' she added.

The Hoplite accepted courteously a Woodbine from an adjacent table. 'The world where they make laws and judgements,' he told us all, 'is way up above my poor bleeding baby head. But all I would ask is this, please: is there any other law in England that's broken every night by thousands of lucky individuals throughout the British Isles, without anything being *done* about it? I mean, if the law knew that thousands of crimes of any other kind whatever were to be committed by persons of whom they know the names and addresses and etcetera, wouldn't they take *violent* action? But in our case, although they know perfectly well what's happening – who doesn't, after all? It's all so notorious, and such a bore – except for the sordid happenings in parks, and the classical choir-boy manoeuvre that every self-respecting bitch most cordially disapproves of, they ignore the law they're paid to enforce every bit as much as we do.'

'Occasionally,' I reminded Hop, 'they do select some more important victims . . .'

'Oh, yes . . . One or two files come up out of the pile, occasionally, I admit, but they always seem to pick someone who's helped in his career by the shameful publicity instead of ruined by it, as they'd fondly hoped, and even that sort of prosecution's getting rarer every day . . .'

We chewed the cud on this.

'I tell you, Hop,' I said, 'if ever the law *was* changed, nine-tenths of your queer fraternity would immediately go out of business.'

He gazed at me with his lovely, languorous eyes. 'Oh, of *course*, child,' he said. 'With the law as it is, being a poof is a full-time occupation for so many of the dear old queens. They're positively dedicated creatures. They feel so naughty, in their dreary little clubs and service flatlets. Heavens, don't I know!' Despite the summer heat, the Hoplite shuddered.

The ex-Deb reached out eight encircling arms and gave the Fabulous a big kiss, which he accepted bravely. 'Don't weaken, beautiful,' she said.

'I *won't*,' said the Hoplite, rising.

I gave him a lift west on my Vespa, but untied his arms and dropped him off where he couldn't see my own destination, because this was a very private and, in fact, rather weird occasion, namely, my annual outing with

159

my Dad to see *H.M.S. Pinafore*, at the late afternoon performance.

In the far distant days before hi-fi and LPs, my Dad used to have, in our home-sour-home up in the Harrow Road, a contrivance that he'd made himself out of old bicycle parts and clocks and jam tins, on which he would play, to anyone who'd listen, which was of course us kids, a selection of records that he'd come by, most of them with hardly any grooves left, so that you needed sharp ears, and a lot of experience, to tell what voice or instruments were playing, let alone the tunes. And among this collection, which Dad kept, like a miser's hoard, in a locked steel trunk under a table in the cellar, were a stack of G. & S. things which we all adored, and could sing every word of that we could make out from the records. And so, before Vern and I grew up to hate each other, and to learn from the other kids that all this G. & S. stuff was square and soppy, he and I used to sing duets, and sometimes old Dad would even join us in a trio, or sing the chorus parts that bored us, or were too difficult to understand. All this, I may say, took place when Ma was out, or very busy.

This *Pinafore* one was always my and Dad's special favourite, I think chiefly because it has such a really miraculous opening – friendly and sweet and gay and completely crazy – and many's the time we've sung the Captain's number with his crew together, even since I've grown to man's estate, and even when out, he and I, in some public place. So every year, when Dad's anniversary comes round, we go off to the matinee to see it, Dad of course telling nobody, and sit eating chocolates and ices in a state of rapture, surrounded by the other G. & S. cats.

These cats, unless you've already seen them, you would really not believe are real. The chief thing about them is that though, presumably, they must live somewhere in the capital, you've never seen anything like them anywhere until this G. & S. celebration brings them all out of hiding. The thing is, although they're by no means all old-timers, there's not a single one of them that looks as if, in any way, he belonged to the present day. Their clothes aren't old-fashioned, exactly, but *home-made*. And though they're lively enough, to judge by their applause, they seem so completely neuter, I can only call it. They look very good, of course, but only because no one has ever told them that there's such a thing as bad.

In fact, come to think of it, they're rather like Dad: he fits in here, among this audience. When I glanced along the row, I saw his face shining and smiling just like theirs, and his hand beating time with his programme-souvenir, and his lips forming the words just underneath his breath – and sometimes above it, too, when it came to the ninth encore, or to the rousing choruses. And when the Captain sang that wonderful ditty with his crew, I knew my old Dad's greatest dream was to be up there beside him on that quarter-deck – yes, here and now my poor old battered parent was really having a tremendous ball.

Come the intermission, I asked my Dad for news of

Mum and Vern. 'Your mother,' he said, 'keeps saying she wants to see you.'

'She knows my address,' I said.

'I think she's expecting you to call around at home.'

'I bet she is. Well, you tell Ma the GPO run an excellent service, and a postcard will cost her 3d.'

'Don't be too hard on your Mum, son.'

'You say that!'

'Yes, son, me. I don't like your taking a liberty where your mother's concerned.'

'Liberties! She's been taking diabolical liberties with all of us for years!'

This little argument with Dad flared up quite suddenly and unexpectedly, as these often do, particularly among relatives, and I could see, of course, that poor old Dad could never admit to me Mum was a bitch without admitting all the mistakes that he himself had made, and sacrifice his dignity. It was also that Dad's very conventional, and comes the *father* sometimes, or tries hard to, and you can hardly let him down.

So there was a pause, and we looked round at the G. & S. cats, jabbering delightedly away.

'And Vern?' I said fairly soon.

'He's got himself a job.'

'No!'

'In a bakery: night work.'

'I give up eating bread from this day forward.'

Dad smiled, and the little film of ice was melted. 'And the tenants?' I asked him next.

'There have been changes,' Dad said carefully. 'The

Maltese are out. She's got some Cypriots instead.'

'Mum's certainly loyal to the Commonwealth.'

This just got by, and Dad, said, very decidedly, 'The Cypriots are gentlemen.' I asked him why, and he said, 'They don't despise you like the Maltese do. You can see, how they behave, they come from a people, not a tribe.'

I wanted to lead up to the question of Dad's health, but this was tricky, because no one is more secretive than my poppa, and also, how could I do it so that he wouldn't guess that I had anything to fear about him?'

'And how you been personally, Dad?' was all I could find to say.

'How I been?'

'Yes. I mean, how you been feeling in yourself?'

Dad stared at me. 'As usual,' he said, whatever that meant.

Actually, ever since Mum's disclosure, I was hatching a bit of a plot concerning Dad. It's like this. A year ago, when I was still quite a kid, I had food poisoning. That's what I had – but that's not what the doctors told me. What they *said* I had was almost everything *except* food poisoning. Believe me, I'm not making this up. When the local expert at the surgery threw in his hand, I went into hospital on the national health, where at least three of them probed me, gave me pills and injections, and discharged me as cured, exactly as before. For days I ran temperatures, and vomited almost hourly. I nearly went home again just then, back to my Mum and Dad, because I was beginning to get really scared.

Then I had an inspiration. Everybody knows that Harley Street and thereabouts is where the best doctors ply their trade, and so I thought – why shouldn't they ply it now on me? I went up there one day, and decided that I'd choose the same street number as the day of the month it happened to be, and ring on the bell, and see what happened. The trouble was there turned out to be six bells – so I rang them all. If you don't believe this fable, please recall that I was drunk with fever, and just didn't care what happened: all I wanted was to reach somebody who *knew*. Well, the six bells were all answered by the same person: i.e. a sort of nurse-secretary (I'd say nurse as far up as the bosom, and secretary above that), and I didn't have to choose which of the six medicos, because I collapsed in the marble hallway, and Dr A.R. Franklyn chose me.

This was the medical cat who cured me. When I came round, vomiting again, and got him into focus, I saw a tall, serious young-looking man who asked me to tell him all about it, which I did. He gave me an hour's examination, and then said, 'Well, I don't know what's the matter with you, but we must find out.' I can't tell you how much these words of Dr F.'s impressed me. Because all the other Emergency-Ward-10 numbers had assured me they knew *exactly* what the matter was (though they were very vague about the details of it), but Dr A.R. Franklyn of Harley Street said he didn't know – and got an ambulance and whipped me inside one of those eighty-guinea-a-week clinics where they pierce your ear-lobes, or change your sex for you, for three-figure fees

– all without any mention of who was eventually going to pay what.

To cut a long whatsit short, with two days of poking things into every gap I owned, he found there was an abscess, and pierced it, and down went the temperature, and that was that, except that I had to stay on another week inside the hospital, which I didn't really enjoy exactly, on account of the nurses. I know nurses are wonderful and everything, and the whole damn community would collapse without them, but they're bossy. They know every man remembers that, way back in time, when he was an infant, he was bossed about by women, and when they get you on that rubber mattress, between those sheets starched like cardboard, and never enough blankets, they work on those babyhood memories, and try to make you feel you're back again in that cosy little cot where females used to rock you, and push bottles at you, and take every kind of liberty. But I got by. And every day Dr A.R. Franklyn would call in to say, 'Hi!', and he always treated me, in front of those stacks of nurses, as if I was a cabinet minister or someone – I mean, he was so wonderfully *polite*. Considering who he was, and me, I really think he had the nicest manners I have ever seen in anyone, and I shan't forget it.

But the day they turned me loose, he didn't show up at all, and so I didn't have a chance to thank him, or to raise the tricky question of how all this medical luxury was going to be paid for. I wrote him, of course, but though he answered very nicely, he didn't refer at all to the financial aspect. So I did this. While I was in the place, I'd whiled away many a weary moment with my Rolleiflex, and some of the snaps I took of everyone were really rather intimate and funny, so I picked out the best, and made enlargements, and put them in an album, and dropped it in at Harley Street, and he wrote back and said, if ever I fell into his clutches again, which he sincerely hoped I wouldn't, he'd make sure my Rolleiflex was confiscated first.

You must see by now what was in my mind: it was somehow to get Dr F. to see my Dad without Dad exactly knowing why.

By this time, of course, we were back in the auditorium, but in the second half of *H.M.S. Pinafore* the marvellous magic of the first half gets lost somehow . . . I dare say old G. & S. were in a bit of a hurry, or felt the whole thing was becoming something of a drag – anyway, the plot of the musical doesn't thicken, but evaporates. We both knew, of course, that there'd be this bit of an anticlimax, but it was a disappointment all the same, and we came out into the night air together feeling a little bit lost and cheated.

'Well, there you go,' I said.

'Have a wet with me?' said Dad.

'Excuse me, no, Dad, I have to pound around a bit tonight . . .'

'Oh. See me to my bus, then?'

'Sure.'

I took his arm, and he said, 'How's your work? You've not been using your darkroom much of late, I've noticed . . .'

I expect even Dad was beginning to guess what must have been obvious to anyone, namely, that having a darkroom at Ma's Rowton House was only an excuse to keep in touch with him . . . well, yes, and I suppose in a way her, too . . . because up in my shack at Napoli, there were dozens of places I could develop in, and as for darkrooms, the electric fused or packed in at the meters with such monotonous regularity there'd be no lack of rooms dark enough to operate in for hours.

'That trip!' I said to Dad, to take his thoughts away. 'That ship trip up the river. Don't forget, you promised we'd do it this year for my birthday – all the way up to . . . where did you say it was?'

'Reading.'

'There you go! Well, that's a date, then? You'll book the tickets?'

Dad said yes, he would, of course, and I hoisted him on his number something bus, and waved him out of sight, and stepping back on to the pavement, was nearly crunched by a Lagonda.

'Careful, teenager,' cried the driver, and he pulled up sharply at a red.

I get so tired of characters in motor vehicles behaving like duchesses, when usually the car's not even their own, but part-paid on the never-never, or borrowed from the firm without the board of management's permission, and all they really are is human animals travelling much too fast with their arses suspended six inches above the asphalt – that I stepped round smartly to give this Stirling Moss a bawling out, and saw it was the advertising monarch, Vendice Partners.

'Oh, hullo, trade wind,' I said to him. 'Where did you blow in from?'

'Come and have a drink?' the Partners person asked me, opening his noiseless, squeakless door.

I held my hand on it. 'You haven't apologised,' I said, 'for trying to take my life.'

'Jump in. We're very sorry.'

'Come along, the lights are changing,' said the cat sitting by his side.

I thought quick, oh well, my Vespa will look after itself, and perhaps this V. Partners will be of use to me over my photographic exhibition, so I climbed in the rear seat, with a fine view of their stiff white collars and Turkish-bathed necks and un-hip Jermyn street hairdos, and Vendice half turned and said. 'This is Amberley Drove.'

'Don't *turn* like that, Vendice!' I cried. 'How do you do, Mr Drove.'

'You're nervous?' the Partners number said.

'Always, when I'm not driving.'

'Then you must be nervous very often,' said my fellow passenger, in a great big booming 'friendly' voice, and treating me to a doglike grin. 'The London track,' he continued, 'is becoming a real menace.'

'Some day, it'll just seize up,' I told him. 'It'll just get stuck, and everyone will have to walk home.'

'I can see you're an optimist,' he said.

'You bet,' I told him.

As you can see, I wasn't hitting it off with this

Amberley Drove creation. I could see he was marked down by fate as one of those English products such as you'd make a circuit of five miles to keep away from, not because he's dangerous at all, really, but because these hefty rugger-bugger types are so damn *boyish*, and beneath their thick heads and thin skins, such bullies, longing, I expect, for the happy days in the past when they could bash the heads of juniors at their academy, or the future ones when they hope to bash someone else's in some colony, provided they're too small and powerless to hit back.

'Amberley,' said Mr P., 'is much concerned with questions of the moment. He's a leader-writer.'

'Is that so,' I said. 'I've always wondered what they looked like. It doesn't trouble you,' I asked the Drove one, 'that no one ever reads that stuff of yours?'

'Ah, but they do.'

'Who do?'

'Members of parliament . . . foreign newspapers . . . City people.'

'But anybody *real?*'

Vendice laughed. 'You know, Amberley,' he said, 'I believe the young man's got something.'

The Drove let out a laugh that would chill your bones, and said, 'The leader columns are angled at the more intelligent portions of the population – few though they may be.'

'You mean I'm a dope,' I said.

'I mean you talk like one.'

We'd pulled up outside one of those buildings down

by Pall Mall that looked like abandoned Salvation Army hostels, and Amberley Drove got out, and carried on quite a long conversation through the car door with Vendice that was evidently way up above my head, then said to me, 'I tremble to think, young man, that our country's future's in hands like yours,' didn't wait for an answer (there wasn't going to be one, anyway), and leapt up the steps, three or more at a time, and disappeared into his clubman's emporium.

I climbed over the back seat beside Vendice. 'He's too young to act like that,' I said. 'He should wait till he's a bit more senile.'

Vendice smiled, did some fancy stuff among the traffic, and said to me, 'I thought you'd like him.'

I wanted to broach this photographic topic, but the fact was, I found V. Partners rather paralysing. He was so cool, and polite, and sarcastic, and gave you the impression, so much, that he just didn't believe in a damn thing – not anything – so all I could find to say to him, after a while, was, 'Tell me, Mr Partners, what is advertising *for*? I mean, what *use* is it?'

'That,' he replied immediately, 'is the one question we must never pause to answer.'

We'd now stopped outside a classified building in the Mayfair area, and he said to me, 'I've got some papers to pick up. Would you care to look inside?'

I can only describe the atmosphere of the joint by telling you it was like a very expensive tomb. Of course, all the staff had left, and the lights were dim where they ought not to be, which made it all a bit sepulchral, but it did look, as a tomb does, or a monument, like something made very big by people who want to prove something that they don't believe in, but desperately need to. Vendice's office was on the second floor, all done in white and gold and mauve. The papers were laid out on the table in coloured folders with perspex covers, and I asked him what their contents were all about.

'About Christmas,' he told me.

'I don't dig.'

He held up one of the folders. 'This about a product,' he said, 'that will be flooding the stores, we hope, at Yuletide.'

'But this is July.'

'We must plan ahead, must we not.'

I admit I shuddered. Not at the notion of his cashing in on Xmas, particularly, because everyone does that, but at the whole idea of the festive season, which comes up like an annual nightmare. The thing that's always struck me about Merry Xmas is that it's the one day of the year when you mustn't drop in on your friends, because everyone's locked tight inside his private fortress. You can smell it already when the leaves are getting golden, then those trashy cards begin arriving which everyone collects like trophies, to show how many pals they've got, and the horror of it mounts right up to that moment, round about 3 p.m. on the sacred afternoon, when the queen addresses the obedient nation. This is the day of peace on earth and goodwill among men, when no one in the kingdom thinks of anyone outside it, let alone the cats next door, and everyone is dreaming cosily of himself, and reaching for his Alka-Seltzer. For two or three days, it's true, the English race all use the streets, where they never dare to loiter for the rest of the long year, because then streets are things that we must hurry through, not *stand* in, students sing ghastly carols in railway stations and shake collecting boxes at the peasants to prove the whole thing's charitable and authorised, not bohemian, and when it's all over, people behave as if a disaster had just overtaken the entire nation – I mean, they're dazed, and blink as if they'd been entombed for days, and are awaking up to life again.

'You look thoughtful,' the Partners number said.

'I am! I mean, the idea of planning for all that in mid-July. I'm really sorry for you.'

'Thank you,' he told me.

Then I took a swift grip of myself, and, sitting down firmly on a sprung white leather sofa, so that he couldn't throw me out before I'd ended, I told him of my plan for the exhibition, and asked what he could do about it to help. He didn't laugh, which was certainly something, and said, 'I've not seen any of your photographs, I believe.'

'Dido's got some . . .'

'Oh – those. Yes. But have you anything more exhibitable?'

I whipped out a folder from my inside breast, which I'd been carrying these days for emergencies like this, and handed it over to him. He looked at them carefully against the light, and said, 'They're not commercial.'

'Of course not!' I cried. 'That's the whole point about them.'

'They'd need presentation,' he continued. 'But they're very good.'

He put them down, looked at me with his 'amused' smile (I could have smacked him), and said, 'I'm a very busy man. Why should I do anything for you?'

I got up. 'The only possible reason,' I said, looking him as coolly in the eye as I was able, 'would be because you want to.'

'It's a very good one,' he said. 'I'll do it.'

I shook his hand. 'You're a nice cat,' I said.

'There, I'm afraid,' he told me, 'you're really very much mistaken. Shall we have a drink?'

He went slowly to a mirrored chest. 'Tonic for me,' I said, 'and thank you.'

I turned down V. Partners' offer of a meal, because I've always found that, whenever someone's done you an unexpected favour (I mean, as unexpected to them as it has been to yourself), it's best to keep right out of their way for just a moment, so that their promise can bite into their consciences a bit, otherwise they're apt just to talk the thing away to death immediately. So I said goodbye to him for now, and headed it out of the deserted Mayfair area, because I wanted to look in at a jazz club, for purposes best known.

You'll have dug, of course, that the Dubious, which I referred to earlier, is not a jazz club. It's a drinking club where some of the jazz community foregather, but a jazz club is a much bigger place where fans go to dance and listen, and not drink at all, except for softs and coffees. The one I was calling at is the Dickie Hodfodder Club, which consists of an enormous basement, a flight of concrete steps leading down thereto, a commissionaire, who does nothing, a ticket vendor who sells tickets, the aforesaid soft and coffee bars, several hundred fans of either sex and, of course, the Dickie Hodfodder ork, led by Richard H. in person, playing away merrily a sort of not very tidal mainstream and, alternating with them, on certain evenings, a group called Cuthberto Watkyns and Haitian Obeah, of which the less said (and heard) the kinder. My object in going was therefore not artistic, but because I thought I might catch a character called Ron Todd.

This Ron Todd is a Marxist, and closely connected with the ballad-and-blues movement, which seeks to prove that all folk music is an art of protest, which, fair enough, and also – or, at any rate, Ron Todd seeks to – that this art is somehow latched on to the achievements of the USSR, i.e. Mississippi jail songs are in praise of sputniks. Ron has some powerful contacts on the building sites, and what I wanted to ask him was if we could somehow arrange to hoist the ex-Deb and the Hoplite and my own good self and camera, up on top of one of those mammoth cranes along the south bank, and take some snapshots of the scene. Why I thought I might find him in the Hodfodder place was that I knew he admired the male vocalist in the Cuthberto Watkyns ensemble, who had some songs in dialect French about the resistance movement to Napoleon, I think it was, of the last King of the Zombies, which Ron wanted to have him perform at a ballad-and-blues festival he was

Mc-ing in the ice-rink up there on Denmark Hill.

But, as a matter of fact, when I got down into the sub-soil, the first person who accosted me wasn't Ron, but the last one I expected, which was Big Jill. She was wearing her suedette jeans and a woollen cap with a long hanging bobble, and was sitting at a table with some empty Pepsis, looking miserable. But when she called me over, her voice sounded loud and clear above the Hodfodder combo.

'Alone, Jill?' I said. 'All the young starlets too busy to keep you company a while?'

'Sit down, stud,' she said, 'and feast your eyes upon a vision.'

'Where?' I asked, thinking she could hardly mean the personnel of the R. Hodfodder band, though she was staring intently in their direction. 'In just a moment now,' she said.

So I stared too, over the hundred heads of the kids whipping it up in the small central space for dancing, or standing around, all in their sharpest garments, the boys tapping a knowledgeable toe or rocking slightly, the chicks looking a bit restless, eyes wandering, because, say what you like, the birds don't go much to the clubs to *listen*. When after a bit of nonsense on the drums, R. Hodfodder gripped the mike, and told us his vocalist, Athene Duncannon, would now be with us.

Big Jill rose four inches off her seat and gripped a Pepsi bottle.

Miss A. Duncannon was quite okay, and the kids certainly enjoyed her, but I must say I do think it's a mistake for young white English girls to try to give an exact imitation of Lady Day, since the best possible imitation that's conceivable would come about two million miles from what Billie H., at her best, can do to you, which is turn you completely over, so that you can't bear to hear any other singers, at any rate for an hour or so after. However, from Big Jill's point of view, I could quite see the situation, because this Athene D. was a highly flexible creation, who wore her dress tighter than her skin beneath it, and glared at the assembly in that imitation-woman manner that's getting to be fashionable among white US female vocalists, if you can judge from the poses on the LP sleeves.

'Oh!' cried Big Jill.

'Where have you been hiding yourself?' said a voice.

This was Ron Todd, who'd come up and stood by the table, looking scruffy and disapproving, in the correct ballad-and-blues manner, and who also was one of those people who believe that, if they haven't seen you for a while, then you must certainly have been out of town, or died, because they see *everyone*.

'Yes, long time no see,' I said to him. 'Come over here, I want to talk to you.'

But when I got him in a fairly vacant corner, and started my spiel about the mammoth crane, I could see he wasn't listening, but glaring across above the innocent and cheery faces of the Hodfodder fans at a number who was coming down the steps, wearing some very fancy schmutter: mauve, button-two tuxedo, laced shirt, varnished pumps with bows, and, on his arm, a nameless dame.

'That's Seth Samaritan!' cried Ron.

This was more or less how K. Marx himself might speak of the head of the Shell Oil company (if there is one), because S. Samaritan is the number-one villain of Ron's picture-book – and not only of Ron's – the reason being, that he was the first to see, a few years back, that jazz music, which used to be for kids and kicks, had money in it, and opened clubs and signed up bands, and brought in talent from afar, and turned it all into minks and Jags and a modest little home at Teddington. I tried to get Ron back on top of that South Bank crane again, but it was heavy labour.

'I'd like to put him in!' cried Ron, waggling his briefcase because, like a lot of musical cats this summer, he had a thing of carrying one without a handle, but a zip complete with lock and key.

'Take it easy, Ronald. Put it all in a song.'

He stared at me. 'You've got an idea, there, you know,' he said. 'What rhymes with pieces of silver?'

I racked my brains, but had to admit I couldn't help him.

'This place is bad enough,' Ron said, waving his briefcase round the musical establishment, 'but just imagine it if Seth Samaritan moves in.'

'You're right,' I said.

Ron glared at me behind his Gilbert Harding lenses. 'You say so,' he cried, 'but do you mean it?'

'Well, yes, I do. I mean you're *right*.'

'I am?'

'Well, yes, you are. I mean there's *source* music, isn't

there, and period music, that feeds on it, and just comes and goes.'

'That's it!'

'In England, most of what you hear is period. Not much source.'

'There you go!'

'And that applies as much to you ballad-and-blues puritans as it does to the jazz cats.'

This didn't go down quite so well. 'Our art's authentic,' Ron Todd said.

'It was,' I told him. 'But you don't think up enough songs of your own. Songs about the scene, I mean, about us and now. Most of your stuff is ancient English, or modern American, or weirdie minority songs from pokey corners. But what about *our* little fable? You're not really trying – any more than Dickie Hodfodder is.'

'What a comparison!' cried Ron, in high disgust.

But I saw I was breaking one of my golden rules, which is not to argue with Marxist kiddies, because they *know*. And not only do they know, they're not *responsible* – which is the exact opposite of what they think they are. I mean, this is their thing, if I dig it correctly. You're *in* history, yes, because you're budding here and now, but you're *outside* it, also, because you're living in the Marxist future. And so, when you look around, and see a hundred horrors, and not only musical, you're not responsible for them, because you're beyond them already, in the kingdom of K. Marx. But for me, I must say, all the horrors I see around me, especially the English ones, I feel responsible for, the lot, just as much as for the few nice things I dig.

But, as I thought this, my eyes had strayed away from Ron, a foot or two to that commissionaire I spoke of, who, not being interested, I suppose, in the performance, was reading an evening paper, I don't blame him, and I caught a headline. I just said, 'Excuse me,' and took the paper from him, and looked at a photograph of Suze and Henley, and ran up the steps into the street. Quite honestly, I don't know quite what happened then, because my next quite clear recollection was batting along a highway on my Vespa, which went on for miles and miles, I don't know where, until the petrol ran out, it stopped, and I was nowhere.

So I got off the vehicle, which I cared about no longer, and sat down on the verge, and watched the car lights flash by occasionally. I thought of an accident – yes, I did – but not for long, because I wasn't going to be rubbed out by a gin-soaked motorist returning to his bed out in the suburbs, and I thought of leaving the country, or dragging some chick or other to the registry and getting wed myself – I thought, in fact, of anything but Suze, because that would be just too horribly painful at the moment, though it was really an agony not to do so – I mean not think of her – in fact practically impossible: because even when I *didn't* think of her, I felt the ache of that I wasn't – really a torture. And at that point, the verge I was sitting on turned out not to be a verge, but a pile of metals for the roadway, and the bloody thing collapsed and I slid down in a cascade on to the Vespa, overturning it.

A car pulled up, ten feet away, and a voice inside it said, 'Are you all right?'

'No!' I yelled back.

'You hurt?'

'Yes!' I cried out.

There was a bang and a thump and some feet came along, but I couldn't see the face above them in the glare, and the cat the feet belonged to asked me, 'You been drinking?'

'I never drink.'

'Oh.' The cat came nearer. 'Then what's the matter?'

At that, I let out a hysteric shout, and shrieked with laughter like a maniac. 'You *have* been drinking,' said the cat, disapprovingly.

'Well, so have you,' I said.

'As a matter of fact, you're right, I have.'

The cat lifted up my Vespa, shook it and said. 'You've run out of juice, that's what's your trouble. No juice left in this toy.'

'I've run out of juice all right.'

'Well then, it's simple. I'll siphon you some out.'

'You will?' I said, getting interested at last.

'I've said I will.'

He pushed my Vespa up by the car's arse, and rummaged in the boot, and fished out a tube and handed it to me. 'You'd better do it,' the cat said. 'I've swallowed enough strong liquor for this evening.'

So I sucked away, and spat out several mouthfuls, and the damn thing actually worked, exactly as advertised, and we listened to it gurgling into the Vespa.

'Something's just struck me,' said the cat.

'It has?'

'I've only got a gallon or so left myself. We don't want to have to siphon it all back again, do we.'

'No,' I said, making a swift bend in the tube.

'I guess you've got enough to take you back to civilisation.'

'Thanks. Where *is* civilisation?' I asked.

'You don't know where you are?'

'Not an idea.'

The cat made *tst-tst* noises. 'You really should lay off the stuff,' he said. 'Just turn about, follow the catseyes half a mile, and then you're on the main road into London. I suppose you want London?'

I handed back the tube. 'I want the whole damn city,' I said, 'and everything contained there.'

'You're very welcome to it,' said this benefactor. 'I'm from Aylesbury, myself.'

So we shook hands, and patted each other's backs, and I saw him off, then got on my Vespa and turned back. I reached a garage before long, and got a proper fill, and had a cuppa at a drivers' all-night caff, and resumed my journey into the capital, like R. Whittington. And as I sped along, I said to myself, 'Well – goodbye happy youth: from now on I'm going to be a tough, tough nut, and if she thinks she can hurt me, she's bloody well mistaken, and as for the exhibition, I'll go ahead with it just the same, and make some loot and catch her when she falls, as she will, you bet, and then we'll see.'

I soon hit familiar sections, and found myself heading

down to Pimlico, because – I have to admit it – I wanted some miracle to happen and that squalid old Mum of mine to grasp what had happened to her second-born, and maybe suggest something, or even do something, or, at any rate, *say* something about it all. I reached the area, and went down the street in low, and sure enough, the lights were gleaming in her basement, so I parked the Vespa, and stepped carefully down, and took a glimpse through the window where, as you might have expected, I could see her drinking something or other with a lodger. Dad may have been right about the Cypriots, but it looked to be the same old beefo Malt to me, and honestly, though I wanted to chat Ma – I mean, in a way, I even felt I owed it to *her* to give her this opportunity – I just couldn't face opening the whole theme up with the Malt there in attendance, even though, no doubt, she'd have got rid of him, so I went up the area steps again, and headed home to see if Big Jill was back now by any chance.

Big Jill was not – at least, there was no light on – but someone else was there: guess who! It was Edward the Ted, none other, carrying a parcel, and coming out of the front door (which, as I've said, is always open) just at the moment I came in. He backed away at first until he saw that it was me, then said, 'I gotta see yer,' so I invited the goon to come up into the attic and have a natter.

I turned on the subdued lighting, of which I'm rather proud (because a theatrical kid I know, who scene-shifts at the Lane, created it all for me for ten pounds, plus the costs), and I poured the brave, bad Ed a glass of lager-and-lime, that I keep there for such visitors, and turned on C. Parker low, and took a look at him. He was wearing his summer uniform – i.e. slept-in jeans, four-inch prowlers, tiger vest and blue zip jacket (collar, of course, turned *up* – he must use whalebone), with lawn-mower hairdo and a built-in scowl. But something about Ed-Ted put me on my guard: he wasn't as beat about as he used to be, the snarl was a bit more real, and the shoulders hunched with a bit more power in them.

'Fuss ov all,' said Ted, 'abaht vese platters.'

'What platters?'

'Vese there.'

He pointed at the parcel. The soil in his nails must have been inlaid.

'What are they?'

'I wanter flog thm.'

'Let's have a look.'

Much to my surprise, they were an exceedingly hip collection.

'I didn't know you had such taste,' I said to Edward. 'In fact, I didn't know you had any taste at all.'

'Eh?' he said.

'They're knocked off, I suppose.'

A crafty grin cracked over the monster's countenance. 'Nachly,' he said.

'And what are you asking?'

'You name a figger.'

'I said, "What are you asking?"'

'Ten.'

'S.P. too high. I'll give you four.'

183

'Errrr!'

'Keep them then, sonny.'

'Ten, I sed.'

I shook my head. 'Well, that was fuss ov all,' I reminded him. 'What was second?'

Now Ed looked very sure of himself indeed, and said, 'Flikker sent me.'

'Did he. Who's Flikker?'

'You dunno?'

'That's why I asked you.'

Edward looked very contemptuous. 'If yer liv up ear,' he said, 'and don no oo Flikker is, yer don no nuffin.'

'Yeah. Who is he?'

''E eads me mob.'

'I thought you'd done with mobs. And they'd done with you. How did you work your passage back?'

'I don work.'

'How'd you join the mob?'

'They arst me.'

'On bended knee, did they? I wonder why?'

Ed stretched, then took from his zip jacket a small chopper, such as the butcher trims the cutlets with, unwrapped a bit of rag from off its blade, rubbed it, and said, 'I did a job.'

'You'll do a stretch, as well.'

'Not me. Ver push give me cuvver.'

I got up, went over, held out my hand, and looked at Ed. He slapped the chopper down, blade sideways, quite hard, on my palm. When he saw I was taking it, he tried to snatch it back.

'I'll just put it there,' I said, laying it on the floor. 'I don't like to talk during meal times.'

Ed kept some eyes on the weapon, some on me. 'Well, vis is it,' he said. 'Flikker wonts ter see yer.'

'Tell him to call round.'

'Yer don *tell* Flikker.'

'*You* don't, I'm sure. Listen, Ed-Ted. If anyone wants to see me, I'm available. But I'm not being summoned by anyone except the magistrate.'

Edward arose, picked up his chopper, dangled it, returned it to his grease-gleaming jacket, and said to me, 'Orl rite. Okay. Ill tell im. An this stuff ear?'

'I'll give you four.'

'Ten's wot I sed.'

'And I sed four.'

As a matter of fact, I was getting anxious about this visit and also, I don't mind telling you, a bit scared. Because you can be as brave as a lion, which I don't pretend to be, but if fourteen of these hyenas set on you, at night, in an empty street (as they always do, and that's always about the number), believe me, there's absolutely nothing you can do, except book a bed in the general hospital. So best is, keep out of their way if you possibly can, which is fairly easy, provided you don't provoke them (or they pick on you), because if there *is* an incident, I can tell you from experience – I mean, I've seen it often enough – *no* one will help you, not even the law, unless they're quite a number too, which generally, in an area such as this, they aren't, except for traffic duty.

'I'll give you five,' I said, which was my big mistake.

'Ten.'

'Forget it, then.'

'I won't . . .' said Ed. 'Yer'll be earing from me agen, an ver lads, and Flikker . . . An so wul vat feller e wonts aht ov it . . .'

'Who wants who out?'

'Flikker wants Cool aht ov ear.'

'Why?'

'E don av ter say why. E jus wonts im aht ov ear, an aht ov ver ole sexter. An *you've* got ter tell im, tell Cool, an see e blows.'

I stared at this English product. 'Ed,' I said, 'you can go and piss up your leg.'

Strangely enough, he smiled, if you can call that thing a smile. 'Orl rite,' he said, 'I'll take five.'

And now I made my second big mistake, which was to go over to the cabin trunk where I keep a few odd valuables, and unlock the thing, and get out a bit of loot I had there, and next thing Ed's hands were there inside it, and when I grabbed at them he pulled back and hit me on the neck, twice, quick, with his hand held on the side.

Now, I hate fighting. I mean, I'm not a coward – honestly, I don't think so – but I just hate that silly mess which, apart from the risk of getting hurt yourself, may mean you damage someone else you don't care a fuck about, and land up in the nick for wounding. So I avoid it, if I can. But on the other hand, if I'm in it, I believe quite firmly in fighting dirty – no Gentleman Jim for me

– because the only object I can see in fighting, if you've got to, is to win as quickly as you can, then change the subject.

So though in great pain, my first act, while Ed was still jabbing at my neck, was to grab his jacket by both hands so that he couldn't get his paws back on the chopper, and my next was to struggle up, while he was still bashing at my face, and jump on his feet with all my nine-stone-something, and then kick him hard as I could on both his shins, just as I felt some teeth rattling and blood flowing in my eyes. He bent down, he had to, and I let go his jacket, and grabbed the lime bottle, and cracked it on Edward's skull as heavy as I knew how, and he wobbled and melted and fell over, where I kicked him in the stomach, just to make perfectly sure.

'You wasted mess of a treacherous bastard!' I exclaimed.

Ed lay there moaning. I got out his chopper, staggered over to the window, and flung it into the Napoli night, then turned up C. Parker, on account of the neighbours hearing what they shouldn't and wiped some of the blood off with a sheet, and the door opened, and there was Mr Cool.

'Hi,' Cool said. 'I heard some turmoil.'

I pointed at Ed-Ted. 'That's it,' I said.

Cool walked across and looked at him. 'Oh, that one,' he said. 'Excuse me not arriving earlier.'

'Better late than never,' I said. 'You can help me dispose of the body.'

Cool looked me over. 'You'd better go in the bathroom,'

he said. 'I'll see him off.' And he took hold of the neck of Edward's jacket with two long, lean, very solid hands, and started dragging him across the floor, and out the door, and I could hear them bumping down the stairway like the removal men shifting the grand piano for you.

In the bathroom, I put myself together, and found all was well, except that I felt terrible, and I went back to my room, and took the top record from Ed's packet out of its sleeve, and put it on, and it was the MJQ playing *Concorde*, very smooth and comforting.

Cool reappeared, nodded at the music, said, 'Nice,' and asked if he could wash, and I went with him in the bathroom. 'Where'd you stow Ed?' I asked.

'In the area. Next door. Behind the dustbins.'

'I do hope he's not dead, or dying.'

'I don't think so,' said Cool, drying his long hands. 'He'll *die* another day,' and he gave me a not very pleasant smile. As we went back in the room, I told him what Ed had been on about during his kindly visit.

'Wilf told me the same,' he said, '—my brother.'

'He's with that lot?'

'He'd like to be, but they won't have him, on account of me.'

'And this Flikker,' I asked Cool. 'You know him?'

'I know his appearance . . .'

'Tough number, is he?'

'Well, there's four hundred teenagers, they say, up here, who he can beckon.'

'*Four hundred*? Don't kid me, Cool.'

'Believe me. Four hundred or so.'

'And *teenagers?*'

'Well, Teds, semi-Teds . . . you know . . . local hooligans . . .'

I wish you could hear the spite Cool put into that last word! 'Well, what you think about all this?' I asked him.

Cool lit a fag. 'Something's happening,' he said.

'You mean now?'

'Something's cooking . . . Excuse me, but you wouldn't notice, son, not being coloured . . .'

'Well, tell me: what?' Because shit! I didn't want to believe this whole thing at all.

'For instance: they've taken to running us down with cars. And motorbikes.'

'Accidents. Drunks. You *sure?*'

'It's happened so often. It's deliberate. You have to skip fast when you see them coming.'

'What else, Cool?'

'Well, there's this one. They stop you and ask you for cigarettes. If you offer them, they take the whole pack, and grin. If you don't, they take a smack at you, and run.'

'"They." How many "they"?'

'Little groups . . .'

'This thing has happened to you?'

'Yes. Also this. Few days ago, down by the tube station, they stopped me and said, "Which side you want your hair parted?"'

'And you said what?'

'Nothing.'

189

'You were alone?'

'Two of us. Eight or nine of them.'

'What then?'

'They said, "We hate you".'

'You answered?'

'No. Then they said, "Get back to your own country".'

'But this *is* your country, Cool.'

'You think so?'

'By Christ, I do! I tell you, man, yes, I bloody well do, it *is*!'

'That's what I told them.'

'So you answered?'

'When they said that, I did, yes.'

'What happened then?'

'They said I was a mongrel. So my friend said, "When your mother wants a good f–k, she doesn't bother about your father – she comes to me."'

'How'd they like that?'

'I don't know. Because when he said that, my friend also pulled his flick on them, and told them to come on.'

'And they did?'

'No, they didn't. But that time, they were only eight or nine.'

A look had come into Cool's eyes, as he stared at me, just like the look he must have given those Teds. 'Don't glare at me like that man,' I cried. 'I'm on your side.'

'You are?'

'Yes.'

'That's nice of you,' said Cool, but I saw he didn't mean it, or believe me.

I turned off the MJQ. 'So what's going to happen next?' I asked him.

'I don't know, boy. I wish I could tell you, but I can't. All I *do* know, is this. Up till now, it's been white Teds against whites, all their baby gangs. If they start on coloured, there's only a few thousand of us in this area, but I don't think you'll see there's many cowards.'

I couldn't take all this nightmare. I cried out, 'Cool, this is London, not some hick city in the provinces! This is London, man, a capital, a great big city where every kind of race has lived ever since the Romans!'

Cool said, 'Oh, yeah. I believe you.'

'They'd never allow it!' I exclaimed.

'Who wouldn't?'

'The adults! The men! The women! All the authorities! Law and order is the one great English thing!'

Here Cool made no reply. I took his shoulder. 'And Cool,' I said. 'You – you're one of us. You're not a Spade, exactly . . .'

He took off my hand. 'If it comes to any trouble,' he said, 'I am. And the reason I am is that they've never questioned me, never refused me, always accepted me – you understand? Even though I am part white? But *your* people . . . No. The part of me that belongs to you, belongs to them.'

And after he said that, he went out.

So what with all this, I spent an evil night: sometimes waking with pains and itches, and the red-purple glow

191

hanging in the sky outside the window, sometimes dreaming those dreams you can't remember, except they're horrible, sometimes lying thinking, and not sure if it was me or someone else . . . But when I did wake, round about midday, I knew there were two things, anyway, that I must do: number one, call Dr A.R. Franklyn, on the pretext of tending my wounds, but actually to fix that rendezvous with Dad, and number two, to track down Wiz: because about all that Cool had told me, the only person who would really know – and who could match his danger, if he wanted to, with Flikker or anybody else – was Wizard. Also, I wanted to see the boy again.

When I went out, to rent a call box, the sun was busy at it, and the day was calm. But whether it was what I'd heard, or just that I was weary, there did seem a *silence* in the air; together with a sort of *movement:* I mean, as if the air was shifting not by the wind, but by itself, to and fro, then pausing. On the steps, after a while to take this in and wonder, I called down to Jill a moment to ask if she knew Wiz's number, then checked in the area next door to see if Ed was there (he wasn't), and set off up the street to where the phones are. The glass of one box, which lord knows, is tough as iron, had been splintered in most squares of it, and in the other, the mouth-and-ear thing had been ripped out at the roots. So I went back in the cracked one, and dialled Harley Street.

I got the secretary-nurse, who said she remembered me, and how was I, and that Dr F. was on his holidays, down there in Roma, at a congress, but back in a week, she thought, and would I call again? Meanwhile, was there anything? My head seemed just a chemist's job to me, so I said no, best regards to the doctor, and best to her, and thank you, I'd try another time. Then I got on the line to Wiz.

Now, as a matter of fact, I was a bit anxious about this call. In the first place, would Wiz like it? And in the second . . . well, I'd never exactly belled anyone in that kind of business before, and who would I get first on the line? The boy? The girl? The maid? One of the clients? So as *bzm-bzm* went the bell, I practised my possible openings. But I needn't have bothered, it was Wiz, he said Big Jill had told him I'd be calling, and when was I coming round? He gave me the address, and said to hit the bell marked 'Canine Perfectionist' up on top. So I buzzed off down there at once, and did that.

Another surprise was that, in addition to Wiz himself, there was Wiz's woman, who somehow I expected would be out of sight – I mean not receiving me so socially, like someone's auntie. She looked very young to me, and, as they say, 'respectable', in fact, if I'd seen her at the local whist drive (supposing I'd been there), I doubt if I'd have rumbled anything. The only point was, she had a way of *looking* at you as if you were a possibly valuable product – I mean a cake of soap, or leg of chicken, or something of that description. I suppose, too, I'd half expected to find all sorts of orgies going on – judges and bishops having a ball on voluptuous divans – but in fact the whole set-up was very ordinary – even a little prim and dainty or, as Ron Todd would say, boogewah.

While Wiz's woman was getting us a cuppa, and some

Viennese gattos, I told him of Ed and Cool and Flikker and the whole scene up in Napoli. 'There seems to be something *wrong* up there,' I said.

'An what you want *me* to do?' Wiz said, not very nicely.

'I don't know, Wiz. Maybe come up and have a look.'

'Why, kiddo? In this profession, you mustn't get mixed in anything except you must.'

'No, I suppose not.'

'What you worrying about, anyway, boy? You're not a colour problem . . .'

I saw I wasn't getting my thing across to Wiz at all. There he sat, curled like a cheetah, dressed up in casuals that cost far more than usuals, smiling and smirking and fucking pleased with himself, I dare say.

'It's just, Wiz,' I said, trying a final bash, 'that I thought what I told you would disgust you, too.'

'Well,' he said, 'as a matter of fact, it does. It does, boy, it does – all these *mugs'* activities disgust me: hitting without warning, for example! The *games* people play!'

I apologised for that, and wanted to say he'd played a few, and still was, if it came to that, but you have to remember, with the Wizard, that the kid, somewhere there inside, is so very *young*. Really, in many ways, he's just a short-pant product.

He'd got up, to play some music that he'd captured on his tape-recorder. 'I know this Flikker kid,' he said, pressing button A, or B.

'Oh? Come on then, Wizard. Tell.'

He did. The Wiz, it turned out, and Flikker, were both old boys of an ecclesiastical baby farm in Wandsworth, down by the common there – which was news to me about the Wizard, as well as about the Ted. According to Wiz, the infant Flikker had been noted for his meek and mild behaviour, and much scorned for such by the other young lost property toughies, until the day came when, at the age of eleven, he'd drowned a junior in the Wandle river, by launching the nipper in an oil drum and dropping rocks in it till it submerged. Henceforth, the other kittens at the lost cats' home kept Flikker somewhat at a distance, which, according to Wiz's memory, surprised and pained young Flikker, who, it seemed, had no notion whatever he's done something out of the ordinary at all. Wiz told the tale as I've just done, for giggles, but even he didn't seem to think it all that laughable, I could see.

'And then?' I asked. Then, said the Wiz, the child had been sent away to all the delinquent cages that they have for the various age-groups, working his way upward year by year, until now, at the age of seventeen or so, he was as highly trained in anti-social conduct as any kiddo in the kingdom, and the law were only waiting for his next major operation to put him away for a really adult stretch. Heaven help, said, Wiz, the screws wherever they sent him to, because unless they beat him up and turned him mad, which they probably would do, the kid would certainly do one of them, the trouble being, so it seemed, that the boy wasn't so much exactly bad, as having no grasp at all of what being bad really *meant*. Meantime, his chief exploit, since his last home leave from the ministry, had been to wreck the Classic cinema in the Ladbroke basin, and, with some of his four hundred, drop the law's coach-and-four into a bomb site, while others engaged the cowboys in pitched battle with milk bottles and dustbin lids. 'In fact,' Wiz concluded, 'the boy should be put to sleep.'

'No one should,' I said. 'Not even you.'

At that point the phone bell rang, and Wiz's woman reappeared, and took over the captain's bridge from Wiz just for the moment very obviously, because this was business coming up. If you'd happened to hear her conversation, over crossed lines – I mean, only her end of it – it would have sounded completely ordinary, because of the careful way she chose her words, but if you knew the whole picture as we did, you could see how her spiel all dovetailed with the arrangements she was making with the randy cat at the far end of the blower. And you couldn't help wondering, from her answers, who this character might be – and whether he had any notion of the actual scene at the receiving end, and the matter-of-fact way his glamorous date was being organised for him, poor silly fucker.

After that, Wiz's woman looked at us politely, and didn't say anything, but after a while Wiz got up, as if that was what he'd been planning to do now for some time, and said why didn't he and I take a little stroll? and went out with me without saying anything to his woman, who didn't say anything to him.

There in the air, after a bit of silence, we turned into a private square, that Wiz seemed to have the key to – as a

196

matter of fact, within sight of the department store where I mentioned earlier how we used to go together – and we sat down on two metal chairs, there in the late afternoon sun, and Wiz said, 'Boy, it's a drag: I tell you, it's a drag. As soon as I've made a bit of loot, I'm cutting out.'

'Will she let you?'

'*Let* me?'

'She seems to like you.'

'Oh, she *likes* me all right!' He laughed – quite horrible. 'But I'm turning her loose as soon as I've got just that much I need.'

'And what'll you do with that just that much?'

He looked at me. 'Kid, I dunno,' he said. 'Maybe travel. Or start some business. Something, anyway.'

He aimed a pebble at a pigeon.

'Unless you get knocked off first,' I couldn't help saying.

He gave me a shove. 'Not likely, boy, honest, it's not likely. Your bird on the streets – yes, it's dodgy. But call-girl business – it's really not so easy for them to prove.'

'There's a first time for everything, they say.'

'Oh, sure they do.'

He aimed another pebble, and scored a bull.

I said, 'You don't mind if I ask you a question, Wizard?'

'Shoot, man.'

'Your chick's had, let's say, x men. The day's work is over, and you come home to sleep. How do you feel about it?'

'About what?'

'The x men she's just had.'

Wiz looked at me: I swear I really wanted to *do* something for the boy that moment – give him a thousand pounds and see him off to some lovely South-Sea island, where he could have a glorious, carefree ball. 'I don't feel about it,' he said.

'No?'

'No. Because I don't *think* about it. I don't let myself – *see*.'

Some kids were running to and fro, and the flowers and everything were blooming, and the birds strutting – even the one he'd scored on – and I couldn't bear it. 'See you, Wiz,' I said. 'Come up and visit me.' He didn't answer, but when I turned back at the gate to look at him, he waved.

By now it was the evening, and I wondered whether to keep my date with Hoplite. Frankly, I was quite exhausted, and not only that, I wasn't sure I really wanted to see Hop display himself in front of the TV cameras to the nation. The fact was, you see, that Call-me-Cobber had decided the Lorn Lover thing wasn't quite the suitable vehicle for Hoplite, but the kid was such a telly natural that they'd have to place him somewhere, which they were going to do this evening in a magazine series called, *Junction!*, where they threw unexpected and unsuitable pairs and groups together in the studio, to see what happened.

But after a quick bite at a Nosh, and two strong black coffees, I felt up to the ordeal, and headed it out to the studios in a taxi. I got past the commissionaires and women at desks with cobra glasses by means I've always found effective: which is, walk firmly, boldly in as if anyone who *doesn't* know what your business is just doesn't know his own (this shames them), go smartly up the stairs, or take a lift and press some button, then knock at any door whatever, say you're lost, and you'll find a pretty secretary who'll put you on the right track, and even show it to you personally.

The one I fell on took me along to Call-me-Cobber's office, where the Aussie looked just a bit surprised to see me, but not much, because already he had a bunch of strange characters on his hands. There was Fabulous, of course, who ran up and hugged me, which was embarrassing, and four others who, I learnt from the secretary, were all going to be separately rehearsed from five quite different characters who were hidden somewhere else inside the building, and then be put together at the actual performance, so that we'd see Hoplite with a rear-Admiral, an Asian gooroo with a Scottish steak-house chef, an undischarged bankrupt and a cat from Carey Street, a lady milliner and a male milliner (that was a cute one, I considered), and finally, to wind the thing up before the commercials came on to bring relief, a milk delivery roundsman and an actual cow.

While our little lot were having gins-and-oranges, and triangular sandwiches with grass in them, of which I partook too, the Cobber one was busy with a stack of telephones, like the captain of a jet before his instrument panel, bringing the craft in for a tricky landing. I don't know what it is that comes over so many numbers when they use the blower: it must give them a power thing, like driving some tatty beat-up motor also seems to, because they take liberties on the blower they never would to anyone face to face. If they're calling *out*, they tell their secretary to catch all sorts of cats, and keep them waiting at the far end, like fish on hooks, until they're kindly ready themselves to say their little piece of nonsense. And if they're being called themselves, they'll never say, excuse me, won't you, to whoever's in the room, or tell the cat who's buzzing them they'll call back a little later, even if the number sitting in their office has something more important to tell them than the mug on the blower has. And when the damn thing rings, in any household, everyone flies to it, as if Winston Churchill's at the other end, or M. Monroe, or someone, instead of the grocer about the unpaid bill or, more likely, a wrong number. We're all too much set on gadgets, and let the damn things rule us, and that's why, back home at Napoli, I've always refused to have the blower in, but using Big Jill's or, if I don't want her to hear the message, then the public.

Well, all was rare confusion, with Call-me-Cobber using six green phones at once, and secretaries and junior male products explaining the forthcoming scene to the dazed performers, when in came a female telly queen in a dark blue suit with bits of clean, white, frilly linen sticking out at various neat and vital points, and a big, slightly wrinkled brow, and a too-powdered face and thin lips and lots of schoolteacher's calm, and a really dreadful smile, who evidently intended to straighten things out, and put us all at ease, and somebody said, just as you might say here was Lady Godiva, that this was Miss Cynthia Eve, C.B.E.

And while Cynthia Eve spread calm about, giving everyone nervous breakdowns, I had a natter with the Hoplite on an air sofa that let out a fart each time you sat on it, or even moved. 'You look glorious, Hop,' I said. 'You're going to kill them.'

'But an admiral! Baby, I shall *faint*!'

'You don't know your own strength, Hoplite. Just fire a few salvoes of broadsides at him.'

The Hoplite mopped his face, which was painted the colour of old orange peel.

'And the Nebraska kid,' I said. 'Will he be viewing? Or is he around here somewhere?'

The Hoplite gripped my arm. 'Oh, no!' he cried. Didn't I tell you, sweetie? It's all over between he and me!'

'Yes? It is? My heavens?'

'Over and done with!' cried the Fabulous with great emphasis. 'From the moment I saw him in a *hat*.'

'A hat, did you say?'

'Yes, a hat. Imagine it! Baby, he wore a *hat*. The whole thing faded instantly. I'm heartbroken.'

But now the sad lad, and his group of weirdie colleagues, were hustled out for their rehearsal, and I went along with the other stage-door gum-shoes to a viewing room, where we could observe the act when it finally came on. I thought about the dear old telly, and what an education it has been to one and all. I mean, until the TV thing got swinging, all we uncultured cats knew next to nothing about art, and fashion, and archaeology, and long-haired music, and all those sorts of thing, because steam radio never made them all seem real, and as for paper talk, well, no one in their senses ever believes that. But now, we'd seen all these things, and the experts and professors, and were digging their secrets and their complicated language, and having a sort of non-university education. The only catch – and, of course, there always is one – is that, when they *do* put on a programme about something I really know about – which I admit is little, but I mean jazz, or teenagers, or juvenile delinquency – the whole damn things seems utterly unreal. Cooked up in a hurry, and made to sound simpler than it is. Those programmes about kiddos, for example! Boy! I dare say they send the taxpayers, who think the veil's being lifted on the teenage orgies, but honestly, for anyone who knows the actual scene, they're crap. And maybe, in the things *we* don't know about, like all that art and culture, it's the same, but I can't judge.

Which makes me admit, it's all very well sneering at universities, and students with those awful scarves and flat-heeled shoes, but really and truly, it would be wonderful to have a bit of kosher education: I mean, to know what's up there in the sky: just up above you, like the blue over the umbrella, and find out whatever's phoney about our culture, and anything in it that may be glorious and real. But for that, you have to be caught young and study, and it's a hard task, believe me, to try to find the truth about it on your Pat Malone, because so many are anxious to mislead you, and you don't know exactly where to turn.

Well, excitement mounted, and now came the *Junction!* thing. First came some trains rushing at each other, then some racing cars doing likewise, and then some aircraft landing on the tarmac, and a voice bellowed 'Junction!' in an echo-chamber, and we found ourselves face to face with Call-me-Cobber. Believe me, the number was transformed! If you didn't know what an imbecile he was, you'd take him for a man of destiny, because he frowned and glared and spoke up so damn honest and convincing, just like W. Graham, and that nasal Aussie accent gave the exact tone of sincerity. He said life was a junction: the junction, he said, of composite opposites (he liked that group, and rifled it several times). From the shock of ideas, he told us, in this day and age, the light would shine! And the next thing we saw was the Hoplite with a cheery old geezer who'd obviously had four or five too many.

The Hop was terrific: boy! if they don't sign that cat up for a series, they're no talent-spotters. He hogged the camera – in fact, the damn thing had to keep chasing him about the studio – and spoke up like he was King Henry V in a Shakespearean performance. He told us that what he believed in was the flowering of the human personality, such as his own, and how could a personality flower in the boiler room of a destroyer?

At this point, Call-me-Cobber interrupted him – though he found it darn difficult, and for a while you couldn't tell who was saying what – and he brought in the old rear-Admiral. The ideas, as you'll have dug, was that this nautical cat should sail in with guns blazing, fling all his grappling-irons on the Hoplite, explode his powder magazine, and keel-haul him before making him walk the plank. But all the time that Fabulous had been speaking, the old boy had been jerking his bald head like a bobbin, and punching himself on both his knees, and when he spoke up, it seemed he couldn't have agreed more with all that Fabulous had said. He told us the navy wasn't what it used to be, by God, no! In his day, it seemed, you ate salt fish for breakfast, and shaved in Nelson's blood. What the fleet needed badly, he told the viewers, and the Board of Admiralty too, was a depth-charge let off under all their bottoms, and he was very glad to hear Hoplite's constructive criticisms, and would welcome him aboard any ship that *he* commanded. Hop said that was okay by him, except for the uniform which was too much like an old-style musical, and couldn't the admiral do something about streamlining it a bit, and getting pink pom-poms for bell-bottomed-Jack like those French matelots have got. They had a bit of an argument over that, with the admiral quoting Trafalgar and the Nile and something I didn't catch about Coburg harpoons, I think it was, and all this while Call-me-Cobber was trying to chip in, but when he did, they both rammed him immediately, the admiral bellowing 'Avast!', and the Hoplite saying, 'Keep out of this, *landlubber*,' till eventually they had to fade the couple out, and move on to the Asian gooroo and the Scotch steak-house products, though you could still hear Hoplite and the old admiral having a private ball somewhere off scene in the background.

Well, after all this, the whole circus (except for the cow) gathered in a reception room without any air or windows, and there was more booze on the house, and Cynthia Eve, C.B.E., clapped her hands together, and addressed us. The effort had been fine, she said. Magnificent, she told us. The viewers were buzzing in with complaints and congratulations, and she looked forward to seeing the viewing figures, and some of us must certainly come again (and she gave old Hop an eerie, dazzling smile). It wasn't often, she went on, she used the word 'magnificent': if things just ticked over, all she said was, 'Thanks so much for coming,' but this time – well, she'd say it again – the only word that fitted was 'magnificent'.

But the ghost at the wedding was old Call-me-Cobber. Maybe the cat was just tired out, which was understandable, but he seemed to be thoroughly wrought down, and I felt sorry for him, and wished the ex-Deb-of-Last-Year was there so he could weep upon her shoulder. Well, come to think of it, it must be sad to be a Call-me-Cobber: because without that little television box, you're nobody; and with it, you're a king in our society – a television personality.

Out on the road, though, Hoplite was a bit sad, too: the boy's a born artist, I'm convinced, and this taste of the telly magic had disturbed him. There was also his emotional upset, and he said, 'By the way, although it's all over with Nebraska, he's asked me to visit him at his base, and in spite of all my pangs, I just can't resist the opportunity. Will you come too? I'd love to see the occupation army.'

'It'll be air personnel,' I said. 'The army's left.'

'Well, tailored uniforms, and gorgeous work clothes, like their films of prisons. You're not tempted?'

I told him okay, but I had to leave him just for now, because if I didn't, I'd have to bed down there and then upon the pavement. Because the fact was, I was spent.

IN AUGUST

For our trip up the river, Dad and I decided that we'd settle for the bit in between Windsor castle and a place called Marlow. We chose the shorter run because we found that was about all we could manage what with travelling to and fro from London, and also because Dad's health was certainly far from brilliant – and also because I'd discovered (but this was a secret that I kept from Dad) that Suze and Henley had a house down by the Thames at a village by the name of Cookham, and though I'd no intention of dropping in for tea and buttered scones, I certainly wanted to have a look at the place, as our pleasure boat sailed by, if that was possible.

There we were, then, up in the front seat, and passing under Windsor bridge. I don't know if you've ever been in a Tunnel of Love – I mean in one of those boats that wind along it in at the amusement parks – but if you have, you'll know the whole point is to get in that front seat, right up in the prow, because if you do, you have the sensation as you glide along, that you're just hanging there over the water: no boat, just you and the surroundings. Well, this was the same (except, of course, that it was light, not dark – in fact, a glorious August day), the water sparkling so that I had on my Polaroids, the diesel chugging, and old Dad there, with his open-neck shirt and sandals, and his mackintosh in a roll (trust Dad!), and puffing away like an engine at his briar. Up there behind us, was the enormous castle, just as you see it on the cinema screen when they play 'the Queen' and everyone hustles out, and there out in front of us were fields and trees and cows and things and sunlight, and a huge big sky filled with acres of fresh air, and I thought, my heavens! If this is the country, why haven't I shaken hands with it before – it's glorious!

In fact, the only dark cloud on the horizon, was Dad himself. It's like this. By means of nagging and prodding and persuading, I'd managed to get him inside Dr A.R. Franklyn's consulting room in Harley Street. Honest, it was like getting a hip cat into a symphony concert, but I succeeded. While I waited outside, reading eighteen magazines from cover to cover, Dr F. gave my Dad a thorough go-over. But all he would tell us was that he *must* get Dad into hospital for a proper examination, which he couldn't do there in Harley Street even if he'd wanted to, but Dad turned this down point blank, and said he wouldn't go into hospital unless they'd tell him what was the matter – which, as I tried to explain to him (but it was like talking to a wall), was exactly what they wanted to find out, if only he'd only go inside there for a day or two. But Dad said once they get you in hospital, you're half dead already, and he wouldn't.

Well, there it was. I tried to forget it, on this sunny summer day, but there it was.

At this point, we went round a great U-bend, honking our horn like a truck in the Mile End Road, and round in the other direction came two hundred or so little boats – I swear I don't exaggerate – each with one kiddo in them, sitting the wrong way round, and rowing like lunatics: a club, it must have been, of athletic juniors, each in white vest and pants and brown legs and arms and a red neck – it was cyclists they made me think of, weaving their way at speed through the city traffic – and we, of course, had to slow down almost to zero as they shot by both sides of us in their dozens. And I got up and cheered, and even old Dad did. Wonderful kiddos on that hot-pot cracking day, racing downstream as if only the salt sea would stop them!

And as we went on, I was really astonished at all the different kinds of boats they had on this old river! Boy! There's a great life on this Thames you'd never imagine, if you only saw it down in the city among the cargo ships and barges. Moored beside the stream there were square things like caravans, with proper chimneys and cats emptying slops over the side, and out in the fairway there were powered craft – some of them, believe me, you could have sailed in to South America – and occasionally we met a real old-timer, with a funnel and steam engine, like the Mississippi things they show you on the LP sleeves. And a big surprise was that there were so many sailing boats: I mean, how did they do their criss-cross performance, like Saturday night drunks, in a river as narrow as old father Thames is up there? And canoes, of course, and eskimo boats with one oar made of two (I hope you dig), and even the craziest number of them all – a flat one like a big cardboard box the same size each end, where the chick sits on cushions in the front part, with a brolly, and her stud heaves the thing along with a hop pole, just like gondolas. And the biggest surprise of all, when we got a bit further up the river, was one really large sailing boat lying there in a sort of parking lot, which, according to Dad, must have been brought up there in bits and re-assembled – anyway, I can't tell you how peculiar it was to see this big ocean boat sitting there right in the middle of the English countryside.

Surprises? Believe me, there were plenty. Did you know those river cats drive their boats on the wrong side of the water? I mean, no keep left nonsense at all for them? And dig this one. Did you know, when you go *up* stream – I do hope I make this plain – you go up hill, and so you have to use a kind of staircase, which is called locks? This is the spiel. You form up in a queue, just like at the Odeon, then, when it's your turn, sail in at one end, into a sort of square concrete well, and they shut two big doors behind you, as if you were going away inside the nick, and there you are, like pussy at the bottom of the drain. Then the lock-keeper product – with a peaked cap, and an Albert watch-chain, and rubber boots – throws some switches or other, and the water gushes in, and you'd hardly credit it, but you start going up yourself! I mean rising like in a commercial lift. And when you've got up there, you find to your amazement that the river on the far side is way up there too: i.e. at the same level as you're at yourself now in the well thing. And the lock-keeper opens two more doors, by pushing against great wooden arms they have with his arse – and a lot of kidlets helping him to do so, or maybe hindering – and you get your release papers, and your civvy clothes back and your fare money, and see! you're out in the stream again away to freedom, except that now you're that much *higher* up! Boy! I certainly dig those locks! And most of them had little gardens, like in St. James's, and tea chalets, and river cats and onlookers all jigging around and shouting, and having a great, noisy, lazy, watery ball!

'What about a pint?' said Dad, who the sight of all this water must have been making thirsty.

'Why not? Come on, I'll buy.'

'You flush these days?' Dad asked, as we made our way past the excursionists, and the skipper at his tiller, and the technical kiddo who helped him by sitting on the rail.

'I've just had a sub,' I answered, as we cracked our heads on the low door leading down into the saloon.

'For doing what?' he asked me, when I'd got the wallop and the Coke.

It's weird, isn't it, how your elders are always so suspicious when they hear that you've made money!

They just can't credit that little junior has grown up a bit, and turned some honest coin.

'If you listen, Dad, I'll explain,' I said. But it was hard to concentrate, because through the portholes just beside our faces we were exactly at the water level, and you found yourself unable not to watch, just like the telly.

'I'm listening,' Dad said.

I told him how a character I knew called V. Partners, who's prominent in the advertising industry, had said he'd sponsor an exhibition of my photos if I'd agree he take the best of them to publicise a skin lotion he was marketing, called *Tingle-tangle*, which was targeted at the teenage market, and that he'd given me an advance on it of two times twenty-five.

'That's not much,' said Dad – very greatly to my surprise.

'You don't think so?'

'It's not all you could have . . .'

'You mean I should have asked more?'

'Not that exactly, no. Did you sign anything?'

'I had to.'

'You're a bloody fool, son. Also,' Dad added, 'he is, because you're a minor.'

Well!

'Listen, Dad,' I said, quite a bit vexed, 'I've not got your experience, but one thing I'm not, please, is a fool.'

'Apologies,' said Dad.

'Apologies accepted.'

But I wasn't pleased – no, not at all – the more so

as I thought Dad might probably be right. Vendice was very nice – and at any rate he'd listened to me, and not laughed – but of course he was in business for commercial purposes. I thought: I must get to know a lawyer.

'What time we get there?' Dad asked.

'Marlow? You thinking of that already? About six.'

'We might stay down there for tea.'

'If you want to, Dad, but I'd like to get back to the smoke, if you don't mind, because I want to take in a concert, second house.'

'That jazz?'

'Yeah. That jazz.'

'Oh, all right. Where we have midday grub?'

I thought quick. 'Well,' I said, 'we could have it here on the Queen Mary, or we could stop off at one of the little villages, and catch the next boat on.'

'Our tickets let us?'

'Oh, certainly. I've checked.'

'Well, we'll see,' he said.

'Okay.'

That brought back thoughts of Suze. And much as I love old Dad, taking him all in all, I couldn't but wish that, at that very moment, he wasn't there, but she. Glory! How fabulous it'd be to make this river trip with Crêpe Suzette! And why in creation didn't I think of it, back in the earlier days?

Wow! I really had a shock! Because a face – a human face – flashed by a porthole, just outside. But then I saw what it was, which was a bunch of bathers knocking themselves out in the surrounding drink, and Dad and

I went upstairs to get a closer dekko. There they were – scores of them – diving off the bank, thrashing about in the river, and making the skipper swear at them by coming too near to his transatlantic. Yelling and splashing or, if they had any sense, roasting their torsos up there on the green, or just standing in plastic poses, watching. 'Good luck to you!' I shouted at an Olympic number who'd flogged it across the water in front of the ship's bows. 'Help! but I'd like to join them,' I told Dad.

After this we passed a quieter bit, with big houses with their front lawns on the river, and sometimes quite lonely, with only an angler or two sitting like they were statues, and swans coming out to hiss at us, just like alligators when the paddle-steamer sails up the Amazon, or the Zambesi, or wherever it is, to gnash at the explorers. As we passed tall banks of rushes, they seemed to bow to us, because they sank several feet, then rose again when we'd gone by. And sometimes hills popped up unexpectedly – and what was even more peculiar, popped up again (I mean the same hills) in some quite different location, because we'd gone round several mile-long bends. There were little bridges we could only just get under, like in corny films about baronial Scotland, and beside each of the locks, were weirs with notices saying 'Danger', and roaring noises like Niagara, or almost. In fact, the whole darn scene was as good as Cinerama in continuous performance, and much fresher.

The most famous of these locks, so Dad informed me – and he must have been right, because the skipper left his wheel to a skilful kiddo I admit I envied, and came along among the passengers to say the same – was one called Boulter's Lock. It had a little bridge, like in Japanese murder pictures, and a big wooded island, and according to Dad, in the days of Queen Victoria and King Edward and all those historic monarchs, it was the top hip rendezvous for the dudes and toffs and mashers, and their birds. Personally (though naturally, I didn't say so), I found it a bit gloomy – a bit sad and deserted and un-contemporary, like so many glorious monuments your elders-and-betters point out to you proudly from the tops of buses. And when we sailed on afterwards into a section they called Cliveden Reach (only you don't pronounce it that way, because it's a square thing to do with educated words), which apparently is one of the scenic glories of the nation, I admit I was considerably wrought down. It was like the canal at Regent's Park, only, of course, bigger: I mean great woods of dangling trees like parsley salad, wringing themselves out into the river, all rotting away gradually, and *old*: which, of course, England is, I mean all those ancient cities, but it seems even the nature part of it can look like that as well.

But now I was growing a bit nervous: because I knew when we'd get out of this Cliveden lily-pond, the next stop would be the place called Cookham. Now, when I'd imagined the whole scene, lying back at home upon my spring divan, I'd thought – well, I know it's foolish, but I had – I'd thought of Suze's house being a little white thing set beside the river, and the boat going slowly by, and she coming out just at that moment (without Henley, need I say), and seeing me there on the deck like the Captain in *H.M.S. Pinafore*, and throwing a kiss or two at me and pleading to me to alight, and the boat pulling in beside her garden, and me getting off into her arms.

Well, naturally, as the day grew older, I knew *that* wasn't going to happen, but I'd put off deciding exactly what I should do: e.g. get off or not, and how to find Suze's dwelling, if I did. But just after Cookham lock (which comes a bit before the place itself), while I was still hesitating about it all, and feeling kind of paralysed, and wondering if perhaps I even wanted to see Suze at all, it was Dad who came, unexpectedly, to my assistance – though in a very awkward way. Because when we'd set sail again after the lock thing, and I was already cursing myself for doing nothing, and we were just going to go underneath the metal bridge there, Dad slumped on to my shoulder, and passed out.

So I propped him up and ran and told the skipper, who wasn't pleased and said we could hop off at the next lock we came to. But I said no, that was no damn good, that Dad was a sick man, under Dr A.R. Franklyn's care of Harley Street, and that I had to get him to the Cookham doctor quick, and if he didn't stop his boat immediately, I'd hold him personally responsible. And then I turned round to all the passengers, and said in a loud voice my Dad was dying and the skipper didn't care a darn about it – in fact, as you've guessed, I became a bit hysterical.

Well, I know mums and dads by now, and if there's one thing any official person hates, it's when they turn on him in a body – or, so far as that goes, if there's anything like a *fuss*. Some nosey, interfering passengers, thank goodness, took a look at Dad, and said I was quite right – *they* wanted to get rid of him too, I could soon see, because nobody likes sickness, especially on a holiday. So the skipper slowed the boat down, and pulled in near the bank there, and bellowed at an old geezer who was mending boats just beside the iron bridge (or that's what his sign said he was doing), and the geezer rowed out in a little boat, and we got Dad down into it, and pulled off, and the pleasure boat sailed on.

By the time we landed on the slipway, Dad had fortunately recovered; which I was bloody glad of, because I did feel a bit guilty about bundling him into the little boat – and in fact, about my whole hysterical performance. The old geezer helped him into the boathouse, into the shade, and yelled at his wife to get a cup of tea, and get on the blower to the local national health representative, who turned up before long, not very pleased to be interrupted from his test tubes and hypodermics, and Dad not very pleased to see him either, because he said this was a lot of fuss about nothing, and we should have stayed up there on the boat, and what the hell: so neither of them was very cooperative with the other. And this Cookham doctor said there was nothing much wrong with Dad that he could see (I'd heard *that* one before!), and what he needed was a rest, and then get on the bus and go straight back home to bed, and slumber.

So the boat-building geezer fixed Dad in a deck-chair with a hood on it and tassels, and his wife came up with further reviving cuppas, and I said a bus would be too slow, and cost what it would, I was going to get Dad back to London in a taxi. The geezer said he'd phone through to the local car-hire, but I said no, just to give me the address, and I'd go off and fix things personally, and that would give Dad time for a short nap to set him up again, and me a chance to have a swift dekko at this lovely beauty-spot. So off I went.

This Cookham is a real old village like you see on biscuit boxes: with a little square church, and cosy cottages, and roads made of mud, and agricultural numbers trudging about them doing whatever it is they do do. I asked one or two for the address I wanted of the car-hire, and they were very relaxed and friendly, and didn't talk a bit like country people do in variety spots and things, and when I followed their directions, I came round a stack of corners . . . and wham! I saw Suze's house there! Yes. I mean, it was the same house I'd imagined in my vision, near enough . . . at any rate, I didn't ask any more directions, but just walked in through the front garden, and round the side to the lawn beside the river, and there, sitting on the grass listening to the radio, I saw Suze. And only Suze.

'Hullo, Crêpe Suzette,' I said.

She looked up, but didn't *get* up, and stared at me a minute, and said, 'Hi.'

I came up a bit nearer. 'You all right?' I said.

'Yes,' said Suzette.

'Henley well?' I asked.

'Oh, yes,' she said.

218

'Can I say hullo?'

Suze had got up on her two knees, and her hands falling down between them. 'He's up there,' she said.

'In London?'

'Yeah.'

I got down on my knees too. 'So I'll miss him,' I said.

'Yes,' said Suzette.

And then – well, it was like we were shoved at each other from behind by two great enormous hands. And there we were, all mixed up in a bundle, me clinging on to Suze, she clinging on to me, and Suze sobbing like a child – I mean, great dreadful sobs more like groans, it was really awful.

Well, that went on for quite a while, and I'm not conventional, but I thought, hell! there's windows all over the damn place, even though this is the country, so I kept saying, 'Suze, Suze,' and bashing her on the back, and kissing her face when I could get at it, and 'Suze, take it easy, kid, do relax, girl, please take it easy.'

So after quite another while, she got herself straightened out, and sat back on the grass, and looked at me with her face red as a tomato, as if I was suddenly going to disappear (which you can bet I wasn't), and I said to her, because I just couldn't damn well resist it – you must remember what I'd been through myself, and that I loved this girl Suze with all my heart – I said, 'And so it didn't turn out all right, then.'

She just said, 'No,' and then kept on saying, 'No.'

Now, you must realise, all this time, I had Dad's

219

health, too, in my mind, and the anxiety to get him back quite safe, though God knows how I wanted to remain there, so I got a bit brisk and businesslike, which I admit must have seemed very unfeeling to her, and said, 'Well, hon, why don't you skip?'

'I can't, darl,' she said.

'He can't stop you, Suze!'

'It's not that, I just can't!'

They won't give you a reason, will they! They won't ever give you a plain reason! 'Suzie, why not?' I cried.

Here we had another session of those dreadful sobs, which, honestly, were ghastly. 'Do *stop* that, Suzette!' I cried, banging the girl quite hard. Because honest, I couldn't take very much more of them.

'Because it's spoilt!' she cried, all mixed up with hair and bits of clothes, so as I could hardly dig what she was saying. 'I've spoilt what we used to be – it's gone!'

'Bollocks!' I cried indignantly. She'd got me in a grip like an all-in wrestler. 'It was a mess,' she kept saying. It was just a mess.'

I saw this was the moment for swift action. So I yanked her away from me so as I could *see* her (which most of the time had been quite impossible, because all I could see of her was her spine), and I said I had Dad there, and a car, and we'd both run her up to London – but though I said it at least half a dozen times or more, it just didn't register with Suze. She only kept on saying, 'No, no, no, no, no.'

So I got up and stood. 'Look, Suze,' I cried. 'I'm your boy – see? Your one and only. And I live up in London, and you know exactly where. And I'm waiting for you there, this evening, tomorrow, and every day until the day I die!' I grabbed both her shoulders, and joggled her. 'Have you heard what I said?' I shouted.

She said, yes.

'And have you understood me?'

Yes, she said, she had.

'Then I'm waiting!' I cried, and bent over and gave her a really fierce, everlasting kiss, then said, 'See you very soon,' and waved, and rushed off out of that garden like Dr Roger Bannister.

There in the road, I had to stop, because suddenly *I* felt faint, just like Dad, and had to sit down on the ground, which was the only thing I could find to sit on. Then I got up, and grabbed the first cat I saw, and asked him to lead me to the car-hire number – which he did, very nicely – and the cat was fortunately in (I mean the car-hire cat), and he came round to the boat-building place, and we collected Dad, and said goodbye and thanks very much indeed to the old geezer and his wife, and made it off for London, which the driver said would cost us exactly eight-pounds-ten.

Well, on the way home, Dad perked up quite a bit: in fact, he even started singing some George Formby numbers, and older songs he'd heard from his own Dad, of Albert Chevalier and historic old veterans like that, and apparently the Cookham driver knew quite a few of them too, and they had several rousing choruses, and argued as to which old music-hall artiste first sang what. But me, need I say, I didn't feel a bit like that, and was car-sick as well, which I've always been prone to if somebody else is driving, and in fact I wanted to tell Dad about my troubles, but you can see how I couldn't – and anyway, even at the best of times you can't tell even your father and mother anything that really *matters* to you.

Soon we were in the outskirts, and though I'd enjoyed the country, I was so glad to be back there in the town again – it was like coming home. And before very long we were in Pimlico, and when we pulled up, Dad had to go in and get the money, as even between us we hadn't got enough, and that brought Mum and Vern out on the pavement, and out of his second-floor window, the beefo Malt.

Nobody seemed to dig how dangerous it had been to Dad: all we got was exclamations about why had I taken him away without telling anybody, and where the hell had we both been to, and why did a taxi cost us eight-pounds-ten – even Vern chipping in with helpful observations – till I was so embarrassed, in front of that Cookham driver, and the Pimlico population, that I went up to the bunch of them in a fury, and shouted, 'If you're going to kill my father, don't kill him in the streets, but let him get into his bed!'

This changed the atmosphere, we all tramped inside, and got Dad stowed away, and then Mum turned on me, and said now she wanted to know exactly what all this was about, and I said okay, I'd damn well tell her, and Vern tried to join in the party, but we turfed him out and went down into the parlour.

'Sit down,' said my mother.

I got hold of both her shoulders (just like I had with Suze) and shoved her in a chair – though she's a darn sight tougher – and said, 'Now, *you* sit down, Ma, and just you listen to me.'

Then I let her have it. I said she was the most selfish woman I knew of, that she'd made Dad's life a torture ever since I could remember, that as for a mess like Vern he was none of my responsibility, but as for me, her son by Dad, she's brought me up so that I just hated her, and was ashamed of her.

'Is that all?' she said, looking back at me as if she hated me too.

'That's about all,' I said.

'You want to go now, son?' she said to me next.

This took me aback a bit. I said nothing, but just waited there.

'Well,' said my mother. 'If you can take it, you can stay and listen to this. Your father's been no use to me at all ever since I married him.'

'He produced me,' I said, staring at her very, very hard.

'He just about managed that,' she said. 'That was about his lot.'

Now at that moment, I wanted to strike my mother: like she'd done me, a thousand times or more, when I couldn't hit back, and I wanted to hit her real hard – hard, and get it over; and I took a step in her direction. She saw very clearly what was coming, and she didn't move an inch. And I'm very glad to say that, when I saw this – though of course, all this happened in a moment

– I didn't hit at her, but said, 'Whatever Dad may have been, or may not have been, you married him.'

'Yes, I married him,' she said, sarcastically and very bitterly.

'And whatever you feel about Dad,' I went on, 'if you made up your mind to have me, you were supposed to love me. Mothers are supposed to love their sons.'

'And sons their mothers,' my mother said.

'If they get a chance. There's not one that doesn't want to, is there? But they must get a bit of it back, a little bit of encouragement.'

At this old Mum just sighed, and gave me a crooked smile, and looked very *wise*, I must say, in her way, though very nasty, too.

'Now, you listen to me,' she said, 'and I don't give a b——r what you think. In the first place, I made you, here (and she banged her belly), and if you think that's easy, try it yourself some time. Without me, and what I went through, you'd not be here insulting me like you are. And in the next place, although your father means nothing to me at all, in fact just the contrary, I've stuck by him, not thrown him out, as I could have done a hundred times if I'd wanted, and made things very much easier for me by doing so. And in the third place, as for you . . .'

I interrupted. 'Just a minute, Ma,' I said. 'Why did you ask me, just two months ago, to come back here again, if anything went wrong with Dad?'

She didn't answer, and I pressed it home.

'Because you *can't* do without a man here – I mean, a *legal* man – and you know it, don't you. And you couldn't

224

have got rid of Dad, like you say you could, because I know you, Ma, if you'd been able to, you would have, but you couldn't help yourself.'

She looked at me. 'You're getting sharp, aren't you, boy,' she said.

'I'm your son, Ma.'

'Yes. Yes, I suppose you are. But let me tell you this. Since that night you turned up in the tube shelter, eighteen years ago, which I don't suppose even you remember, I've seen you're fed and clothed and brought up, best I could, till you can take care of yourself, as you seem to think you can, and that was quite an effort, sometimes!' She put her old, fetching face on one side, and said, 'You're not very easy, you know. You've not always been very easy.'

'I dare say not, Ma,' I said.

'As for *loving* you,' my mother went on, 'well. Listen, son. You don't love or not love because you choose to – even your own son. You love if you do, and if you don't, you just don't, and there's no good at all pretending. You'll find out it's true what I say when you grow older. Or I dare say you're so clever that you've found it out already.'

I sat down too, three feet away from her.

'Okay, mother,' I said, after a while, 'let's leave it at that.'

'If you say so, son,' she said to me.

Then Ma did a thing she'd never done with me ever before, which is to get up and go to the glass cupboard with the orange lace cover on it, which I remember so well from all our other addresses in their turn, and which we were never allowed to go within a mile of, and she got out a bottle of port, and poured two glasses in green crystal goblets, and handed me one, and said, 'Cheerioh.'

'I don't drink, Ma,' I said.

'Don't be a cunt,' she said to me.

So we had a tipple.

Then Ma said, what about my father? Well, then – I hope it wasn't betraying Dad, but I did think she ought to know – I told her all about Dr A.R. Franklyn, and how he really ought to go into hospital, and she listened without interrupting (the first time she'd ever done *that* with me in her life, either), and just shook her head, and said, 'He'll never go in there voluntary. But give me this doctor's particulars, and if he's taken really bad again, we'll just have to put him in.'

So I did that.

Then, when I came to go, just by the doorway, there was a sort of pause, and what was in both our minds was, should we have a kiss or not? We looked at each other, then both laughed together suddenly, and she said, 'Oh well, son, let's skip it, you're a real nasty little bastard, aren't you,' and I gave her a big clump and said, 'Well, Ma, *you* should know about that,' and hopped it quickly.

I looked up at the clock at the Air Terminal, and saw if I made it quick, I'd catch the latter portion of the Czar Tusdie concert, with Maria Bethlehem singing with him as soloist. The venue was up in the north part, in a super-cinema with academy of dance attached, so on the rank there I grabbed a taxi (who'd been hoping for transatlantics at the terminal, and wasn't pleased so much with only me), and shot off up across the town. I certainly felt in need of a lift and soothing music, after all the excitements of the day.

And that's what jazz music gives you: a big lift up of the spirits, and a Turkish bath with massage for all your nerves. I know even nice cats (like my Dad, for example) think that jazz is just noise and rock and sound angled at your genitals, not your intelligence, but I want you to believe that isn't so at all, because it really makes you feel good in a very simple, but very basic, sort of way. I can best explain it by saying it just makes you feel *happy*. When I've been tired and miserable, which has been quite more than often, I've never known some good, pure jazz music fail to help me on.

Now, I've explained a club for jazz people, and also a jazz club, but a jazz concert is something different still. In this, several hundred cats, and even often these days thousands, gather in as large a hall as the impresario can hire, and listen to the best selection of soloists and combos, English and American, that the impresario can offer for the price – which is by no means low. Of course, in these concerts, even the greats often disappoint you, because a big hall or cinema is no more the real place for jazz than a railway station would be for a tea party. But if your luck is in, they often overcome this disadvantage, and you hear some really marvellous sounds. And then what's so nice is to hear them in company with so many hundreds of like-minded kiddos – sharp, and eager, and ready to give of their best, too, if the performance is up to standard – and although I know jazz addicts are supposed to be a lot of morons, you'd really be astonished how these fans will all sit and *listen*.

Well, Czar Tusdie's, of course, is one of the great bands of all time, and American, and coloured. And as for Maria Bethlehem, I'd say that, second to a great like Lady Day (who, to my mind's right up there on an Everest peak all of her very own), she's the world's best female jazz singer that there is. So you can imagine I was thoroughly impatient in that vehicle, and kept advising the driver of short cuts and to accelerate, which he took no notice of whatever.

He dropped me on the corner just before the picture-palace, and so I had to walk past the dance academy, and there, on the pavement, I paused a second, because I saw a notice on the wall which said, and I said out loud, 'Boy, that one's us! Although me, after my experiences, maybe I'm going to move up a category or two!'

> *CURRENT CLASSES*
> *MEDALLISTS CLASS*
> *BEGINNERS PROGRESSIVE CLASS*
> *BEGINNERS PRACTICE*
> *ABSOLUTE BEGINNERS*

Well, as I went in through the foyer, and gave my ticket up to the appropriate cat, I heard, from outside, that really marvellous sound, which is the strains of jazz music when it's real and true: truly a heavenly sound, it seems to me to be. And honestly, when I die – when that day comes that must come – I'd wish for no other ending of it all than to hear that Czar Tusdie band playing for me as it did just then: because their sound was so strong and gentle, just like it would carry you right up on its kind notes to paradise. And then there was a roar and whistles, and the fans all applauded like a football crowd, and I went in and got my seat just in time to catch the entrance of Maria.

Maria is big, and no longer a young woman, but she walked on the stage just like a girl: quick feet, easy gestures, and a face that's so darn friendly, though it can also be kidding you, and sometimes quite severe. She's like a girl, yes, but she's also, in a strange way, just like everybody's Mum: she welcomes you all, takes charge of you all, and from the very moment she comes on, you know that you're all there with her in safe hands. And straight away she swings into the song she's chosen, no tricks, no crafty pauses, no hesitation whatsoever, and what she does to the songs is unbelievable: I mean, she takes even quite familiar standards and turns them inside out, and throws them right back at you as though they've become nobody's but her own – Maria's. And she can be witty as hell, throwing everything away and shrugging, but then, the next moment, rising like a bird, and sweet or melancholy. But whatever she does – and this is the whole thing about Maria Bethlehem – her singing makes you feel it's absolutely wonderful to be alive and kicking, and that human beings are a damn fine wonderful invention after all.

They rose to her at the end – all those hundreds of English boys and girls, and their friends from Africa and the Caribbean – and they practically had to gouge us all out of that auditorium. Cats I didn't know from Adam said, hadn't it been great, and one cat in particular then said, had I heard about the happenings at St. Ann's Well, up in Nottingham, last evening? I asked him, what happenings? not taking it very much in (because I was still back there with Maria Bethlehem), when I realised he was saying there'd been rioting between whites and coloured, but what could you expect in a provincial dump out there among the sticks?

IN SEPTEMBER

I was up very early on that morning, as if with a private alarm clock in my brain, and it was one of the most beautiful young days I've ever seen. The dome of the heavens, when I looked out up at it over my geraniums, was pale pink glowing blue, with nothing in it but a few stray leaves of cloud, lit up gold and green by sun you couldn't see behind the houses. The air was fresh, blown right in from the sea, and there wasn't a sound except from hundreds of thousands of pairs of lungs, still slumbering there in Napoli. Peace, perfect peace, I thought, as I sucked in the warm air of my native city. And it was also, as it happened, my nineteenth birthday.

I put on some music and abluted, then made two Nescafés and carried one down for Hoplite. The cat was absent. Waste not want not, I decided, so carried them further down to Cool. Another cat out on the tiles last night. No use disturbing Big Jill that early, so I drank both cups on the front doorstep, and stood there taking in the scene.

And I saw this. Coming down the street, from the N. Hill Gate direction, were a group of yobbos, who most probably had been out at some all-night jungle-juice performance too, and who straggled across the street and pavement in that *messy* way they have, and whose bodies were all *wrong* somehow – I mean with lumps and bumps in the wrong places – and whose summer drag looked hastily pulled on. And coming up the street, from the Metropolitan Railway direction, were two coloured characters – not Spades, as it happened, but two Sikh warrior products, with a mauve and a lemon turban, and with stacks of hair. Well, when the two groups met, the Sikh characters stepped to one side, as you or I would do, but the yob lot halted, so as it was difficult to pass by, and there was a short pause: all this just outside my door.

Then one of the scruffos turned and looked at his choice companions, and grinned a sloppy grin, and suddenly approached the two Sikh characters and hit one of them right in the face: with his fist pointed so that the top knuckles got inside the skull. So long as I live, I swear, I shall never forget the look on that Asian number's face: it wasn't at all fear, it wasn't at all rage, it was just complete and utter unbelief and surprise.

Then the other Sikh one shouldered up beside his buddy, and the yobbos drew away a bit, then both the two groups separated, and the oafo lot went off laughing down the hill again, and the Sikhs started chattering and waving their arms about. They walked on a little bit, then turned and looked back, then went off chattering and waving again up hill out of sight and sound.

Now, you will be asking, what about me? Did I run out and take a poke at the chief yobbo, and bawl the bunch of little monsters out? The answer is – I did not. First of all, because I simply couldn't believe my eyes. And next, because the whole thing was just so *meaningless*, I suddenly felt weak and sick: I mean I've no objection, really, to men fighting if they want to, if they've got a *reason*. But this thing! Also – I don't like to say this much, but here it is – I myself was scared. It doesn't seem possible such sordids as this lot could frighten you, and certainly one wouldn't, or even two or three of them . . . But this little group: it seemed to have a horrid little mind, if you can call it that, all of its own, and a whole lot of unexpected force behind it.

I ran down in the area and called Big Jill. She took a while coming to the door, and shouted had I no discretion, there were chicks sleeping on the premises, but I shoved past her into her kitchen and told her what I'd just seen. She listened, asked me several questions, and said, 'The bastards!'

'But what should I have done, Big Jill?' I cried.

'Who – you? Oh, I dunno. I'll make you a cup of tea.'

As she started banging crockery about, and pulling her red slacks on over her huge hips without any by your leave, I found that I was shivering. When she handed me the cup, she said, 'You might like to take a look at this.'

It was a leading article in the Mrs Dale daily which the Amberley Drove character, who you may remember, wrote for, and it was about the happenings a week ago up there in Nottingham. It said the chief thing was that we must be realistic, and keep a proper sense of due proportion. It said that many influential journals – including, of course, this Mrs Dale production – had long been warning the government that unrestricted immigration, particularly of coloured persons, was most undesirable, even if such persons came here, as by far the bulk of them undoubtedly did, from countries under direct colonial rule, and countries benefitting by the Commonwealth connection. But Commonwealth solidarity was one thing, and unrestricted immigration was quite another.

Then it had a word to say about the coloured races. England, it said, was an old and highly civilised nation, but the countries of Africa and the Caribbean were very far from being so indeed. It was true that the West Indian islands had enjoyed the advantages of British government for many centuries, but even in these the cultural level was low, to say the least of it, and as for Africa, it should be remembered that, a mere hundred years ago, some parts of that vast continent had never even heard of Christianity. In their own setting, coloured folk were no doubt admirable citizens, according to the standards that prevailed there. But transported unexpectedly to a culture of a higher order, serious difficulties and frustrations must inevitably arise.

'Must I go on reading all this balls?' I shouted at Big Jill.

'It's up to you,' she said.

Then it went on to give you the facts about the coloured communities who'd come to settle here in the UK. Many were toilers, it did not deny, as could be seen by those courteous and efficient public transport servants, but many were layabouts who thrived on the three-pounds-ten they got from the National Assistance. This led to labour troubles, and we must remember that the nation had been passing through a slight, though of course temporary, recession. Pressure on housing was another problem. It was true that many coloured folk – for reasons that were more than understandable, and need not be detailed here – found difficulty in securing accommodation in the better sections of most towns. It was also true that many West Indians, in particular, had saved up enough from their wage-packets, over the years, to purchase houses, but unfortunately these were generally speaking little other than slum property, which further deteriorated when they moved into them, to the disadvantage of the rate-paying citizens as a whole. Moreover, it was not unknown for coloured landlords to evict white tenants – often old-age pensioners – by making their lives impossible.

Then there was the matter of different customs. By and large, said the article, English people were renowned for their decent and orderly behaviour. But not so the immigrants, it seemed, or very many of them. They liked haggling in the shops, prodding fruit before they

235

bought it, leaving the hi-fi on all night, dressing in flashy clothes, and, worse still, because this made them more conspicuous, driving about in even flashier vehicles, which they had somehow managed to acquire.

Then there was the question of the women. (Old Amberley certainly went to town on this woman question!) To begin with, he said, mixed marriages – as responsible coloured persons would be the very first to agree themselves – were most undesirable. They led to a mongrel race, inferior physically and mentally, and rejected by both of the unadulterated communities. But frequently, of course – and this made the matter even graver – these tainted offspring were, in addition, the consequence of unions that were blessed neither by church nor state. More, said the piece. The well-known propensity and predilection of coloured males for securing intimate relations with white women – unfortunately, by now, a generally observed phenomenon in countries where the opportunities existed – led to serious friction between the immigrants and the men of the stock so coveted, whose natural – and, he would add – sound and proper instinct, was to protect their women-folk from this contamination, even if this led to violence which, in normal circumstances, all would find most regrettable.

But this was not all: it was time for plain speaking, and this had to be said. The record of the courts had shown – let alone the personal observations of any anxious and attentive observer – that living off the immoral earnings of white prostitutes, had now become all too prevalent among the immigrant community. No one would suggest – least of all this journal – that in each and every such immoral union, the guilty male was a coloured person since, of course – as figures published recently in its columns had unfortunately made it all too clear – the total estimated figure of active prostitutes in this country did not itself fall far short of the total numbers of male coloured immigrants of the appropriate age. Nevertheless, the disproportionate number of coloured 'bullies' could not be denied.

'Christ!' I said, putting the damn thing down. 'I just can't go *on* with this!'

'Stick it out,' Big Jill said. 'I'll make you another cuppa.'

Several conclusions, this Drove one continued, flowed inevitably – and urgently – from these grave matters and, more particularly, from the recent disturbances at Nottingham, which everyone – and especially his Mrs Dale daily – so greatly and so vehemently deplored. The first was, that immigration by coloured persons, whether having an identical citizenship status as ourselves or not, should be halted instantly. Indeed, the whole process should be reversed, and compulsory repatriation should be given urgent and serious consideration by the government. Meanwhile, it went without saying, law and order should be enforced most rigorously and impartially, however great the provocation may have been – and there may well, it must be admitted, have been provocation on both sides. But it was only a minority – chiefly persons known by the name of 'Teddy boys' – who had actually been guilty of a physical breach of the Queen's peace, and these youths should undoubtedly be restrained: though many might feel that such young people – who were far from being characteristic of the youth of the country as a whole were psychopathic cases, in greater need of medical attention than of drastic punishment by the courts of law.

The occurrences at Nottingham, A. Drove wound up, could in no way be described as a 'race riot'. No comparison with large-scale disturbances in the southern states of America, or in the Union of South Africa, was therefore tenable. By the swift and determined action of the Nottingham authorities, we could rest assured that no more would be heard of such lamentable incidents – which were entirely alien to our way of life – provided, of course, immediate action along the lines suggested by the Mrs Dale daily was taken without fear or favour.

I put this thing down again. 'The man isn't even funny,' I said to Jill. 'And I don't believe he's even stupid – he's just wicked!'

'Take it easy, breezy,' said Big Jill.

'And there's quite a lot of things that he's left out!'

'I don't doubt you're right,' she said to me.

'And the whole point is – he's not denounced this thing! Not denounced this riot! All he's doing is looking round for alibis.'

Jill sat down and started on her nails. 'He's just ignorant,' she said, 'not wicked.'

I cried out: 'To be ignorant, and *tell* people, *is* wicked.'

She looked up from her nail polish. 'All it comes to,'

she said, 'is if you've got a black face in a white or off-white neighbourhood, *everything* you do's conspicuous. You just stick out like a sore thumb.'

'Everything you do!' I said, picking up the Dale daily and rolling it into a tight sausage. 'But what *do* they do, different from all the hustlers living in this slum?'

'You tell me,' said Jill.

'Look! There's more coloured unemployed than white. Everyone knows that. And not only layabouts: you see them queueing at the Labour every day for hours.'

'Yeah,' said Big Jill.

'And you know what it's like when they try to get a room: "no children, no coloureds".'

'I suppose,' said Jill, 'if you hate the one, you also hate the other.'

'As for white illegitimates, are there none around here, would you really say?'

'I don't know many myself who aren't,' Big Jill said.

'And what about white chicks?' I cried. 'Don't they *like* it? I mean, hasn't everybody seen them hanging around the Spades?'

'I've seen more than a few,' Jill said.

'And those ponces. Are none of the bastards Maltese, Cypriots, even home-grown products, just occasionally?'

'Plenty,' Big Jill said, looking up.

'Oh, sorry, Big Jill.'

'It's okay, baby.'

'What's the matter with our men?' I said to her. 'Can't they hold their own women? Do they have to get this

239

pronk' (and I bashed the Dale daily on to the chair back) 'to help them and protect them?'

'I should have thought,' said Jill, beginning on her right hand, 'there should be more than enough girls to go round for everybody.'

I stuffed the rolled paper among the tea-leaves. 'The whole thing, anyway,' I cried, 'is that what really matters is being missed. And here it is. If every Spade in England was a hustler, that's still no excuse for setting on them ten to one.'

Big Jill didn't answer me this time, and I got up.

'I don't understand my own country any more,' I said to her. 'In the history books, they tell us the English race has spread itself all over the damn world: gone and settled everywhere, and that's one of the great, splendid English things. No one invited us, and we didn't ask anyone's permission, I suppose. Yet when a few hundred thousand come and settle among our fifty millions, we just can't take it.'

'Yep,' Big Jill said.

'Upstairs,' I continued, 'I've got a brand new passport. It says I'm a citizen of the UK and the Colonies. Nobody asked me to be, but there I am. Well. Most of these boys have got exactly the same passport as I have – and it was *we* who thought up the laws that gave it to them. But when they turn up in the dear old mother country, and show us the damn thing, we throw it back again in their faces!'

Big Jill got up too. 'You're getting worked up,' she said.

'You bet I am!'

She looked at me. 'People in glass houses . . .' she said.

'What does that mean?'

'Listen, darling. Personally, I live off mysteries, and that doesn't give me the right to be particular. As for you, you peddle pornographic pictures round the villages, and very nice ones they are, I don't deny. But that makes it rather hard for you, it seems to me, to preach at anybody.'

'I don't dig that,' I said, 'at all. You can hustle, and still be a man, not a beast.'

'If you say so, honey,' Big Jill answered. 'And now I must turf you out, the chicks will be screaming for their breakfast.'

'Oh, fine then, Big Jill.' I went to the door, and said to her, 'You are on my side, though, aren't you?'

'Oh, sure,' she said. 'I'm all for equality . . . If a coloured girl comes in here she's every bit as welcome as the others . . .'

'I see,' I said to her.

She came over and put her hammer-thrower's arm across my shoulder. 'Don't worry, son,' she said, 'and don't take things too much to heart that aren't your business. The Spades can look after themselves . . . they're big strong boys. A lot of them are boxers . . .'

'Oh, yes,' I said. 'But remember what I saw just now. Put Flikker and twenty Teds inside the ring tooled up with dusters in their gloves, and there's a sort of handicap.'

'Flikker's been sent away,' she said.

'Oh yes? He has?'

'He's on remand in custody.'

'This is the first time I've liked a magistrate.'

Big Jill came out into the area. 'It's not the Teds you have to worry about,' she said, 'but if the men join in it, too. The men round here are rather a tough lot.'

'I've noticed that,' I said to her, going out to take the padlocks off my Vespa.

'Where are you off to, baby?'

'I'm going to take a look around my manor.'

As soon as you passed into the area, you could sense that there was something on. The sun was well up now, and the streets were normal, with the cats and traffic – until suddenly you realised that they *weren't*. Because there in Napoli, you could feel a *hole*: as if some kind of life was draining out of it, leaving a sort of vacuum in the streets and terraces. And what made it somehow worse was that, as you looked around, you could see the people hadn't yet noticed the alteration, even though it was so startling to you.

Standing about on corners, and outside their houses, there were Teds: groups of them, not *doing* anything, but standing in circles, with their heads just a bit bent down. There were motorbikes about, as well, and the kids had often got them out there at angles on the roadway, instead of parked against the kerb as usual, for a natter. Also, I noticed, as I cruised the streets, that quite a few of those battered little delivery vans that I've referred to – usually dark blue, and with the back doors tied on with wire, or one door off – had groups around them, also, who didn't seem to be mending them, or anything. There were occasional lots of chicks, giggling and letting out little yells, a bit too loud for that time of the morning. There were also more than the usual number of small kids about. As for the Spades, they seemed to creep a bit, and keep in bunches. And although they often did this anyway, a great number of them were hanging out of windows and speaking to each other loud across the streets. As I continued on, I came to patches once again where all was absolutely as before: quiet and ordinary. Then turn a corner, and you were back once more in a part where the whole of Napoli seemed like it was *muttering*.

Then I saw my first 'incident' (as A. Drove wrote it) – or, as you know, my second. Here it was. Coming along, pushing a pram and wearing those really horrible clothes that Spade women do (not men) – I mean all colours of the spectrum and the wrong ones put together, and with shoes like Minnie Mouse – was a coloured mum with that self-satisfied expression that all mums have. Beside her was her husband, I imagine it was – anyway, he was talking at her all the time, and she wasn't listening. Then, coming from the opposite direction (and there always seems to *be* an opposite direction), was a white mum, also with kiddie-car and hubby, and whose clothes were just as dreadful as the Spade mum's were – except that the Spade girl's looked worse, somehow, because you could see, at any rate, that she was *trying*, and hadn't given up all hope of glamour.

Well, these two met and, as there's no law of the

road on pavements, both angled their prams in the same direction, and collided. And that started it. Because neither would give way, and the two men both joined in, and before you knew where you were, about a hundred people, white and coloured, had appeared from absolutely nowhere. Quite honestly! I was watching the thing quite closely from near to, straddling my Vespa on the roadway, and one minute there were two (or three) people on each side, and next minute there were fifty.

Now, even then, if in normal times, the thing would have passed off, with the usual argument, and even then, if someone had stepped in and said, 'break it up,' or 'don't be so fucking idiotic,' all would have gone well – but no one said this, and as for coppers, well, of course there wasn't one. Then somebody threw a bottle, and that was it.

That milk that arrives mysteriously every morning, I suppose it brings us life, but if trouble comes, it's been put there – or the bottles it comes in have done – by the devil. And dustbins, that get emptied just as regularly, and take everything away – they and their lids, especially, have become much the same thing: I mean, the other natural city weapon of war. They were soon both flying, and I had to crouch behind my Vespa, then pull it over, when I got a chance, behind a vehicle.

Even then, it was still, in a way, if you'll believe me, rather *fun:* I mean, the bottles flying, and the odd window smashing, little boys and girls running round in circles shouting, and people weaving and dodging, like they were playing a sort of enjoyable, dirty game. Then there was a scream, and a white kid collapsed, and somebody shouted a Spade had pulled a knife. It's always those attacked who give the pretext – don't we know! Anyway, there was some blood for all to see.

Then, just as suddenly, the Spades all ran, as if someone had told them to on a walkie-talkie from headquarters somewhere – and they dived round corners and inside their houses, slamming doors. Honest! One minute there were white and coloured faces battling, and the next there were only white. There was a lot of shouting and discussion after that, and a few more bottles through the windows where a Spade or two was peeping out, and the white kid was carried on the pavement where I couldn't see him, and the law arrived in a radio-car and told everybody to disperse. And that was that. All over.

Then, a bit later, came incident number two – or three. Along another road I was prospecting, I saw driving along quite slow, because anyway it was pulling up, one of those 'flashy cars' A. Drove was on about, and four Spades in it – and the driver handling the thing in that way Spades often do, i.e. very expertly, but as if he didn't realise it was a *machine*, not a wonderful animal of some kind. Well, two of those delivery vans I spoke of sandwiched it like the law cars do in US crime films, and out from the back and front of them came about sixteen fellers – those from the back spilling out as if they were some peculiar kind of cargo the van had on board that day. And these were not Teds, but *men* – anyway, up in the twenties, somewhere, I should judge – and this

245

time there was no previous argument whatever, they just rushed at that vehicle, and wrenched the doors open, and dragged out the Spades, and crunched them. Of course, they fought back – though once again, there was that same brief hesitation as I'd noticed with the Sikhs, that same moment of complete *surprise*. Two were left lying, and got kicked (those boys certainly knew all about vulnerable parts), and two made away, one weeping; and about a hundred of my own people gathered round about to watch.

And about those who watched, I saw something new to me, and which you may find quite incredible – but I swear it's the truth I'm telling you – they didn't even seem to *enjoy* themselves particularly – I mean, seeing all this – they didn't shout, or bawl, or cheer; they just stood by, out of harm's way, these English people did, and *watched*. Just like at home at evening, with their Ovaltine and slippers, at the telly. Quite decent, respectable people they seemed, too: white-collar workers and their wives, I expect, who'd probably been out to do their shopping. Well, they saw the lads get in the Spades' car, and drive it against a concrete lamp-standard, and climb back in their handy little delivery vans, and drive away. And once again, that was that. Except that a few coloured women came out and tended the men lying there, who the bystanders I spoke of had come up a bit nearer to, to examine.

Then came another incident – and soon, as you'll understand, I began to lose count a little, and, as time went on, lose count a bit of what time was, as well. This one was down by the Latimer Road railway station, among those criss-cross of streets I mentioned earlier, like Lancaster, and Silchester, and Walmer, and Blechynden. In this part, by now, there was quite a muster: I mean, by now people realised what was happening – that there were kicks to be had if you came out in the thoroughfare, and besides, the pubs were emptying for the afternoon. And they all moved about like up in Middlesex street at the market there on Sunday, groups shifting and re-forming, searching. People were telling about what had happened here, or there, or in some other place, and they all seemed disappointed nothing was happening for them then and there.

Well, they weren't disappointed long. Because out of the Metropolitan Railway station – the dear old London Transport, we all think so safe and so reliable – came a bunch of passengers, and among them was a Spade. Just one. A boy of my own age, I'd say, carrying a holdall and a brown paper parcel – a serious-looking kiddy with a pair of glasses, and one of those rather sad, drab suits that some Spades wear, particularly students, in order to show the English people that we mustn't think they're savages in grass skirts and bones stuck in their hair, but twentieth-century numbers just like we are. I think he was an African: anyway, there's no doubt that's where his ancestors all came from – millions of them, for centuries way back in time.

Now, this kiddy must have been rather dumb. Because he evidently didn't rumble anything was at all unusual – perhaps he'd come down from Manchester or somewhere, to visit pals. Anyway, down the road he walked, stepping aside politely if people were in his way, and they all watching. All those eyes watching him, and the noise dropping. Then someone cried out, 'Get him!' and the Spade dug it quick enough then – and he started running down the Bramley Road like lightning, though still clutching his holdall and his parcel, and at least a hundred young men chasing after him, and hundreds of girls and kids and adults running after *them*, and even motorbikes and cars. Some heathen god from home must have shouted sense into his ear just then, because he dived into a greengrocer's and slammed the door. And the old girl inside locked it from within, and she glared out at the crowd, and the crowd gathered round there, and they shouted – and I'm quoting their words exactly – 'Let's get him!' and 'Bring him out!' and 'Lynch him!'

They cried that.

But they didn't get him. What they got, was the old greengrocer women instead, who came out of another door, and went for them. Picture this! This one old girl, with her grey hair all in a mess, and her old face flushed with fury, she stood there surrounded by this crowd of hundreds, and she bawled them out. She said they were a stack of cowards and gutter bastards, the whole lot of them, but they started shouting back at her, and I couldn't hear. But she didn't budge, the old girl, and her husband had got the shutters up inside, and by and by the law made its appearance with some vans as well this time, and they got through the crowd, and started milling round, and collected the young African,

248

and moved among the mob in groups of six and told it to disperse – with truncheons out this time, just for a change.

I went off after this to be a bit alone. I rode out of the area to the big open space on Wormwood Scrubs, and I sat down on the grass to have a think. Because what I'd just seen in there made me feel weak and hopeless: most of all because, except for that old vegetable woman (who I bet will go straight up to heaven like a supersonic rocket when she dies – nothing can stop that one), no one, absolutely no one, had reacted against this thing. You looked round to find the members of the other team – even just a few of them – and there weren't any. I mean, any of us. The Spades were fighting back all right, of course, because they had to. But there were none of us.

When this thing happens to you, please believe me, it's just like as if the stones rise up from the pavement there and hit you, and the houses tumble, and the sky falls in. I mean, everything that you relied on, and all the natural things, do what you don't expect them to. Your sense of security, and of there being some plan, some idea behind it all somewhere, just disappears.

I dusted my arse, and rode down Wood Lane to the White City, where the old BBC's building that, splendid modernistic palace, so as to send their telly messages to the nation. And I looked at it and thought, 'My God, if I could get in there and tell them – all the millions! Just take them across the railway tracks, not a quarter of a mile away, and show them what's happening in the capital city of our country!' And I'd say to them, 'If you

249

don't want that, for Christ's sake come down and stop it – every one of you! But if that's what you do want, then I don't want you, and for me, it's goodbye England!' Then I turned back again inside the area, inside those railway tracks that hem it in – out of White City into Brown Town and as I was travelling past the station there, I saw another small encouraging sight, and stopped and looked.

This was a small old geezer, with a cloth cap and a choker, who'd got hold of a young Spade so tight I thought at first he was arresting him, or going to damage him in some way. But no! Apparently this boy must have told the geezer he lived up in Napoli, and was a bit dubious about going home, and this old codger, feeling his youth again, must have grabbed him by the arm, and said, 'You're okay, son, come with me,' and set off holding the coloured boy with a look on his face as if to say, 'If you touch him, then you touch *me*, too!' And I wondered why it was the only two I'd seen who'd fought back had been old-timers?

But that gave me an idea. I rode back to the White City station, parked my Vespa, and went inside to have a look around. And sure enough, there was a young Spade standing there, and I went up to him, and gave a great big smile I didn't feel, and said, how's tricks? and would he care for a lift home on my Vespa? He seemed a bit doubtful, but I asked him where he lived and went on chatting him, because I've found if you keep on *talking* at anyone who suspects you, the mere sound of your voice usually wins them over, and he said Blenheim Crescent, and I said hop on then, and I'll see you there. As we went out, a ticket number said, was I carrying my iron bar, just in case? Real witty.

So I batted along, and I tried to make conversation with the kiddo, but he just clung on and said, 'Yeh, man!' to everything I said, and as we reached the groups of bystanders we got one or two yells and whistles, and the odd brick, and a few kids ran out on the road in front of us, but I weaved or accelerated, and we got through to Blenheim Crescent without trouble. I was keyed up, expecting motorbike chases, and big mobs, but nothing happened. And that was the extraordinary thing that day in Napoli! It all popped up here, and subsided, then popped up there, then somewhere else, so that you never knew what streets were frantic, and what streets peaceful.

Well, I saw the kid to his door, where lots of dark faces were peering through the curtains, and he asked me in a moment. Well, frankly, *I* was a bit dubious now. It wasn't that I was afraid of my own people seeing, so very much, but I was a bit scared of the Spades themselves! After all, one white face is so much like another – especially on a day like this. However, I thought I really *must* stop being scared, or I just wouldn't get anywhere, and so I said sure, why not, I'd be glad to, but could I bring my Vespa in there and park it in the hall.

Well, he took me down to the basement, and there I found a sort of war cabinet of West Indians in progress. The boy made it clear, right away, that I wasn't a POW or something, and they patted me on the back, though several still looked damn suspicious, and wouldn't talk to me. They gave me a glass of rum, and one said to me, what did I think about all this? And I said I was disgusted and ashamed. Well, one of them said, at any rate, I was the first white man they'd seen that day who looked them in the eye when he spoke to them.

And then the phone rang, and a tall Spade with a bald head picked it up – and would you believe it, he was through on the blower to Kingston, Jamaica! And he had quite a natter with the folks back home, and I didn't much like a lot of what he said, and I wondered how my own people, out there in Kingston, surrounded by thousands of black faces, would be feeling when the news of it got around? And I also wondered whether, all over Napoli, there weren't other Spades calling Trinidad, and Ghana, and Nigeria, and Christ knows where, and telling *them* the story? And how all the whites in all *those* places would be treated, too? Because one big mistake a lot of locals make is to think that all Spades work on the London Transport or on building sites – whereas stacks of them are business and professional men, who know all the answers: for example, this bald-headed character turned out to run a chain of hairdressing establishments.

Then one of the Spades who was still suspicious of me said, did I think it was the English way of life to attack 6,000-odd in an area where there were 60,000 whites or more, and if us white boys wanted to show how brave we were, why didn't we choose an area like Harlem, where the whites were a minority? I could think of a lot of answers to that, but the others shut him up immediately

– in fact, what amazed me the most, in the middle of all this, was how damn polite they all were to me. And then they started chatting about plans, and one said the law was no use whatever, they must set up vigilantes; and another said anyway, they'd got to organise as a community, and keep it that way in future; and another said up in Nottingham, they'd moved Spades out of certain areas 'for their own safety', but if anyone tried to move *him*, he was damn well staying where he was, because this was his house, and his wife and kids were born here, and he'd had a bash in the RAF, and he was one of the Queen's objects the same as any other. And I began to get embarrassed, as you can imagine, because of course I partly agreed with them, but also I wanted to stick up a bit for my own people somehow, if I could. And the hairdresser cat realised this, and he and the kid I'd brought there saw me to the door, and opened it cautiously, and said all was clear, and I trundled my Vespa down into the road. And the kid came out to the pavement, and said thanks for everything, and shook my hand and gave me one of those smiles that Spades can turn on when they feel like it.

Well now, I thought, I'd better look in back home, to see if anything was happening *there*, and also to find out if Cool was quite okay. So I started off, and made the corner, where eight or so crashed the bike, and slung me off, and next thing I was standing against a wall with faces six inches from me. And what I liked least of all was that the oafo nearest me was carrying something wrapped in a science-fiction magazine.

Now luckily, the happenings of the day had made me so indignant, I wasn't frightened any longer. And also, although I'm a nervy sort of number, when a crisis comes, I usually surprise myself by keeping calm – however much my ticker's pounding there inside. So I stayed still as a rock, and eyed the yobbos, waiting, with one hand in one pocket round my bunch of keys, and the third finger through the ring of it.

'We sore yer,' said an oafo.

'Darkie-luvver,' said another.

When I glimpsed the SF number unwrapping his chopper, I whipped my keys across his face, and kicked another you-know-where. Then it was on! I was tensing for the death blow as I thrashed about, when suddenly I realised I was not alone in this – in fact, for just a moment, I had nobody to fight with, because two other kids were fighting them, so without waiting to raise my hat and ask who the hell they were, I ran over to my fallen Vespa, grabbed the metal pump, and cracked it on some skulls, and see! The Teds were in flight, except for one lying whimpering on the pavement, and I was shaking hands with Dean Swift and the Misery Kid.

'Dr Livingstone, I presume,' said Swift.

'You bet your bloody life it is!' I cried.

'That feller *hurt* me,' said Misery, rubbing his hands and looking very pale and angry.

'My Gawd!' I cried, messing their hairdos for them and almost kissing them. 'It had to take *this* to bring you two together!'

254

The Ted on the deck was trying to get up, and the Dean pushed him down and held his neck with his Italian shoe. 'We heard there'd been happenings,' he said, 'and thought we'd come up and take a dekko.'

'It's all in the evening papers,' said the Kid.

Well, was I un-displeased! And was I glad it was two kids of my own age, and two jazz addicts, even if of different tendencies, and even if one was a layabout and the other a junkie, because this seemed to me to show their admiration for coloured greats like Tusdie and Maria really *meant* something to them.

The Dean had picked up my Vespa, and he checked the motor, and then said, 'Well, how we to now? What we go where we do?'

'What about this one?' I said pointing to the Ted, who the Misery Kid was holding by his hair.

The Dean approached him. 'You're full of shit, aren't you,' he said, whizzing his fist round within a half-inch of the zombie's face.

'Wot I dun?' asked the yobbo.

And that's it! He'd scare you stiff inside his little group, but now he looked such a drip you couldn't even get vexed enough to crunch him. 'Wot you dun?' said Dean Swift. 'What you've done's get born – that was your big mistake.'

The yoblet, seeing he wasn't going to get fixed, had plucked up courage from somewhere. 'Ar,' he said, 'so a few of ver blacks git chived. Why oil ver fuss?'

The Dean swung him round, gave him a Stanley Matthews kick on his striped pink jeans, and told him to beat it fast. At the corner, the thing cried out, 'Cum back termorrer fer ver nest lot!' and cut out.

Well then, as we were discussing this, and examining the yobbos' chopper, who should come round the corner but a cowboy: one of that youthful, pasty sort, with shoulder blades, and a helmet not too secure, and boots too big for his athletic feet – usually the least pleasant, those young ones, that is, if any are. And he looked at the Vespa, and we three, and the metal pump, and the chopper, and he said, 'What's this?'

'You're prompt on the scene, son,' said the Dean.

'I said, "What's this?"' the law repeated, pointing at the chopper.

'This,' said the Dean, 'is what the local lads you can't control tried to do my pal with.'

'What pal?'

'Me,' I said.

'And why you holding that pump?'

'Because I used it to defend myself,' I told him.

'So you were in it too,' the cowboy said.

'That's right.'

'But you say you got attacked.'

'You're beginning to dig, mate,' said Dean Swift. 'You're speedy.'

The copper stared at the Dean. But the Dean had carried that look often enough before, and stared right back. 'You call me "officer",' the cowboy said.

'I didn't know you were one, captain. I thought you were a junior constable.'

The cowboy looked round, as if wishing for

reinforcements, and said, 'You're all coming to the station.'

'Why?' asked Dean Swift.

'Because I say so. That's why.'

The Dean gave a crazy yell of laughter. And though I sympathised with his attitude, I wasn't pleased, because all I wanted was to get to hell out of here immediately.

'Look, captain,' said Dean Swift. 'Aren't you supposed to arrest the law-breakers? Well, that's the way they went – all the whole click of them.'

'If you don't shut your trap,' said the cowboy, 'I'll knock you off as well.'

'Why?' said the Dean. 'You afraid of Teds, then?'

'Take it easy, Dean,' I said.

'Boy, of course he is!' cried Swift, turning to Misery and me, as if he was explaining something perfectly well known to all. 'He's young, he's alone, he's not used to trouble of this kind – he's used to pinching parkers on the broad highway.'

This cop turned rather red, and, thanks to Swift's efforts, broke the number-one rule of the copper mystery, which is never to *argue*. Because as soon as the public hears a copper argue, and see he's a human being like any other (well, let's be generous), they know he's only a worried man in fancy dress.

'We're not afraid of trouble,' the young cowboy said.

'Oh, no!' cried the Dean, really getting in the groove now. 'If there's sufficient of you, certainly you're not. We all remember how you cleared the streets so thoroughly when old B. and K. came here, or Colonel Tito. But if you're a few, and the trouble rises round you, and metal like this lot's flying, you can't take it, and can't stop it! Not here in this dump you can't, anyway. If it was Chelsea or Belgravia, you'd stop it soon enough, maybe . . .'

Now, all the while he was needling the cowboy, Swift, we both saw, was edging a bit away from him, and throwing a glance or two at Misery and me, who were doing likewise, and suddenly the Dean shouted to me, 'Your place!' and pushed the chopper at the copper (handle first, though), and when he backed away a second, we all scattered, and while the Dean lured the law, I managed to make it off with Misery on my Vespa.

I yelled at him as we bowled along: 'Our city's dangerous! They don't know it, but our city's getting dangerous!'

'You too!' the Kid cried, as we shot a junction.

'They've got to know it!' I shouted. 'We've got to tell them somehow!'

'Yeah,' Misery answered, as we turned into my alley.

There were no signs of anything back home, and I made it up to the first floor and broke in on Mr Cool. There he was, sure enough, but with one white eye and strips of plaster, and his half-brother Wilf, who you may remember. 'Hi!' we all said, and I asked Cool for the fable.

They'd got him, he said, down by Oxford Gardens, where he's been visiting his Ma, when they threw burning rags in through the window, and Cool had gone out to make objections. And when the argument developed, his brother Wilf (much to my surprise, I must say) had shown that blood was thicker than prejudice, and sailed out and mixed in on Cool's behalf. A passing cat, who'd turned out, of all things, to be a county councillor, had given them a lift home in his jalopy, and there they both were for all to see.

'Well, what *you* think of all this, Wilf?' I couldn't resist asking the number.

'We ain't seen the end of it,' he said rather sourly, 'that's all I got ter say.'

'The law's losing its grip, if it ever had any,' said Mr Cool. 'The two lots are just going where it isn't, and having it out there.'

'Surprising!' the Misery Kid said.

'The law never settled much round these parts, any time,' said Wilf.

Well, now I had to do a thing I'd already decided, which was make a few telephone calls. So I collected all the fourpennies I could, and went down to Big Jill's, where I found nobody in, but got the key from its hidey-hole in the toilet cistern, and fetched out my pocket diary, and started business on that blower. Because I was determined to call every cat that I could think of, and *tell* them about what was going on.

At the best of times, when you call twenty numbers in a row, as you can do to fix a party, you don't get more than half of them, as is well known. And I only got a quarter – as well as those where I couldn't hack my way beyond the secretary, or even the switchboard starlet. I got V. Partners, who listened patiently, and made some intelligent comments, and said it was disgraceful, and I must get some snaps of it, if I could, for the exhibition. Mannie was out, but Miriam dug at once what I was on about, and said she'd get Mannie over as soon as she'd made contact. I got through to Dido at the Mirabelle, and she said I was a naughty boy to break in on her evening meal, but certainly, she'd tell her editor all I said, and a lot of her best friends were coloured. At the Dubious and Chez Nobody they seemed more interested, and said they'd spread the tale around.

By this time I was running out of pennies, and had to have a summit conference with the operator as to whether I could have all the calls I was entitled to if I put in silver pieces. I drew blank with Call-me-Cobber, which perhaps was lucky, and Zesty-Boy's secretary said she'd see he got the message – yes she'd written it all down. I even called Dr A.R. Franklyn, who listened carefully, and asked how was my Dad, and said would I please be careful of myself. Then I knocked off Big Jill's meter money from the rubber ashtray shaped like a bra she keeps it in, and called the Mrs Dale daily, and asked for Mr Drove. I got through, much to everyone's astonishment, and told him he might not remember me, but he was a lump of shit, and I'd do him if I ever saw his face again – whether carrying his furled umbrella, or not doing so. I felt better after this, and crash-landed, after the third try, at a session the ex-Deb was having out at Chiswick, and although she sounded raving to me over the blower, she said she'd be right along. I even, as well, thought of trying Suze and Henley at the Cookham place and in the London showrooms, but I skipped it. Of course I tried Wiz, but only got the dialling tone – not even Wiz's woman.

But even with the cats who dug it best, the great difficulty I had was in getting over what was *happening*: I mean, the scale of it, how serious, and that this was supposed to be the British Isles. Because even though most of them had heard something of it by now, there seemed to me to be a sort of conspiracy in the air to pretend what was happening in Napoli, wasn't happening: or, if it was, it somehow didn't signify at all.

I shot off after this up to my penthouse, to wash off the mud and blood, and have a lay down for a moment, and a bite. And while I was doing so, there was a little knock, and on me walked The Fabulous Hoplite. He was looking a bit diminuendo, and smiled rather nervously, and was wearing a beach-gown and his Sardinian slippers.

'My!' he said. 'What times we live in!'

'Sit down, beautiful. You can say that again.'

'You've been *bruised*, child,' he said, trying to grope my tribal scars.

'Hands off the model, Hop,' I told him. 'How have things been with you?'

The Hoplite got up, spun round so that the beach-gown did a Royal Ballet thing, and sat down again and said, 'Oh, no complaints . . . But I don't like all this.'

'Who does?'

'*Some*body must,' he said, 'or it wouldn't happen.'

'Clever boy. You been out at all?'

He let the gown fall open to reveal his pectorals. 'Once was enough,' he said. 'A glimpse, and I was in again.'

'Wise child.'

'I suppose *you've* been out fighting battles!' His eyes gleamed.

'The battles fought me.'

He folded the gown. 'I've heard some terrible tales . . .'

'Yeah?'

'Oh, yes. *Ecoutez-moi*. The whore at the sweet shop – the skinny bitch – said to me, "And when my husband got up, he was holding his back, and I saw there was a knife in it".'

'Whose knife?'

'A dark stranger's. Really, darling, I know you love them, but they're so *rough*. And somebody else I know has had thirty-seven stitches in his throat.'

'Just like a necklace.'

'Oh! Don't be so callous!'

The Hoplite once more arose. 'The innocent suffer for the guilty,' he said, with a little sigh. 'I expect all that most of the serfs who live in this sewer really long for, is just to be left alone – I mean, persons of both tints and textures.'

'Yep,' I said.

'Me, for example,' said the Hoplite. 'A pervert like me, with the fattest file, for my age, in the vice department's system, simply wants to avoid mud being stirred up needlessly.'

I got up too, and said, 'I love you, Hoplite, who

doesn't, but I really must tell you some day that you're a tit.'

'You think so?' he said, quite pleased.

'Or, in plain speech, a fool.'

'Oh, I don't like *that* . . . Not at all. You see, I set very great store by your opinions: even though they're sometimes so severe . . .'

'Well, if you do, Fabulous, may I say, I think the world's divided into those who, when they see a car crash, try to *do* something about it, and those who stand by and gape.'

'You looked like John the Baptist when you said that.'

'You never met him.'

The Hoplite smiled. 'But you, dear!' he said. 'We all heard you shrieking on the telephone, and isn't what you're doing exactly that? Bringing in a lot of gapers?'

'No,' I said.

'No?'

'No. I want witnesses. Friends who will witness this thing, and friends who'll show the Spades this two square miles isn't being written off as a ghetto.'

'And you think, sweet, that would improve matters?'

'Yes.'

'Really?'

'Yes. If they saw a few normal, healthy faces around here, it would lower the temperature they're all trying to build up. If the Spades saw a few hundred different kinds of kids who admired them, and the Teds saw a few hundred of the coloured nurses who'll have to stitch them up in hospital, it certainly would make a difference.'

'But they're not very *important* people.'

'Well, Hoplite, let's bring them in too! This is their big opportunity – the one they've been waiting for to prove their words about the kind of country this is! Let's have some of those public figures who haunt the telly studios, to advise us what to do! Let's have the thinkers of the left and right to tell us how they'd handle this one! Not from their home base, but from here! Let's have the bishops and ministers, to hold an inter-racial service in the open air! Isn't this their big chance? And let's have the queen in all her glory, riding through the streets of Napoli, and saying: "You're *all* my subjects! Each and every one of you's my own!"'

The Hoplite shook his head in pity, gave me a little wave, and blew.

I got my bend-torch out of a drawer, because it's always best to have a weapon, if you can, whose explanation's innocent, and I got my blood donor's card in its perspex folder (which I'd got when I started giving the pints after Dr F. had cured me), because this always seems to impress the law – not much, but just a bit – if they grab you and turn out your pockets, and I stuffed my new passport in my arse pocket as well, I dunno why, just for luck, I suppose. I took up my Rolleiflex, but put it down again, because it didn't seem useful any longer. Then I put on my buckle belt, and a zip jacket that's like a sabre if you swing it by one arm, and went down the stairs where, coming down as well, I ran into Cool.

'You taking the night air too?' I said.

'Yeah. I'll have a look around . . .'

'Be cool, Cool.'

'Oh, sure, white boy.'

I stopped the cat before the door, and took both his arms and looked at him, and said, 'I hope this isn't going to turn you sour, man.'

He smiled (quite rare with Cool). 'Oh, no . . .' he said. 'We don't turn sour – we must object. And you,' he added. 'I suppose it's not nice for you to feel your tribe is in the wrong.'

'Thanks, Cool,' I said. 'I bet you're the only Spade in Napoli who's thought of *us*.'

I slapped his arm, and we both went out into the dark, and this time I'd decided not to take my Vespa. On the pavement, without speaking about this, we shook hands and both went different ways.

There's no doubt night favours wickedness: I mean, I don't think the night's wicked, and I love it, but it opens the trap for all the monsters to come out. I went down by Westbourne Park station, and took a ride along the scenic railway to the Bush. The train was packed with sightseers from the West, who hopped out at different stations for the free display. From the height between the stops, you could see the odd fire and firemen and, at sudden glimpses as the train rocked by a street at right angles, the crowds, and law cars prowling, or standing parked with cowboys packed in them, waiting for action, like bullets in a clip. And when the train halted, at Ladbroke and by Latimer, you could hear loudspeakers blaring something harsh and meaningless, like at Battersea pleasure gardens, in the funfair there. And all along the ride there were patches of blue-black darkness, then sudden glares and flares of dazzling light.

But at the Bush, I was amazed. Because when I crossed over, beyond the Green, to that middle-class section outside our area – all was peace and quiet and calm and as-you-were-before. Believe me! Inside the two square miles of Napoli, there was blood and thunder, but just outside it – only across one single road, like some national frontier – you were back in the world of Mrs Dale, and *What's My Line?* and England's green and pleasant land. Napoli was like a prison, or a concentration camp: inside, blue murder, outside, buses and evening papers and hurrying home to sausages and mash and tea.

I bought a late night edition by the telly theatre there. They were playing it up – big headlines, no paper can resist that – but also trying to play it down. Reactions from Africa and the Caribbean, it said, had been unfavourable, but much exaggerated. There was a bit of gloating in South Africa and the US South, which, in this difficult situation, was greatly to be deplored. The cardinal fact to remember was that neither at Nottingham – nor even at Notting Hill, so far – had there been any loss of actual life. Meanwhile a cat at Scotland Yard had issued a message to discourage sightseers. I threw the thing away. The law never wants you to see what it can't handle. Then I went back inside the area again.

I walked down an empty street that was lit, as a lot of them are round there, by lamps put up in Queen

Boadicea's day, when I saw, coming along, three coloured cats, keeping together. I looked around to see if they were being chased or anything, but they weren't, so I went up and said, 'Hi, boys, what's cooking?' – when I saw that one of them had a spanner, it looked to be (anyway, something metal), and they made a rush. Boy, did I gallop! With those three sons of Africa racing after me and hissing! I made for a pool of light, and dodged round some vehicles, and batted across a road straight into Mr Wiz. 'Hold it!' he cried, and the coloured cats saw I had an ally, and melted like a falling gleam. 'Boy!' I cried, slapping the old Wiz like a carpet-beater. 'Am I glad to see your wicked face! Where the hell have you been, man, I've been seeking for you!' The Wizard took my arm, and said, 'Cool it, kiddo,' and just round two corners we found ourselves in the middle of a large assembly.

This lot were being addressed by a thing from the White Protection League, whose numbers were also distributing leaflets round the throng. The speaker on the portable platform was a man of quite ordinary appearance – i.e. the kind you'd find difficult to describe if someone asked you after – except that now he was lit up and jet-propelled by a sort of crazy, electric frenzy. He wasn't talking to *anybody* – to any human cat you could imagine, even the very worst – but out into space, out into the night to some spirit there, some witch-doctor he was screaming to for help and blessing. And looking up at him, in the yellow-coloured glare, were the white faces he was protecting, all turned, by the municipal lamps above, into a kind of unwashed violet grey.

I nudged Wiz. 'He's round the bend,' I said.

Wiz didn't answer.

'I said he's flipped, boy!' I shouted, above the noise of the loudspeaker.

Then I looked at Wizard. And on my friend's face, as he stared up at this orator, I saw an expression that made me shiver. Because the little Wiz, so tight and sharp and trim and dangerous, had on a little smile, that showed his teeth a bit, and his wiry little body was all clenched, and something was staring through his eyes that came from God knows where, and he raised on his toes, and shot up his arms all rigid, and he cried out, shrill like a final cry, 'Keep England white!'

I stood there a moment, while the mob roared too. Then I grabbed Wizard's neck clothes with all the strength I have in my body, and I yanked him round about off balance, and I hit him with all my life behind it, and he stumbled. Then I looked round quick, and saw how it was, and ran.

Luckily, I knew Napoli: and I got away easier than I'd hoped and feared. Round by Cornwall Crescent, I ran into an area, and stood there, panting. Then I crossed Ladbroke Grove, and made it up the rise, keeping along the railings.

Under a light ahead, I saw a peculiar figure: it was an African trader well known round the area, a long, lean old number who runs a little shop let specialising in imported products that the Spades like for their cuisine.

He usually wears an antique suit and a battered Anthony Eden, but tonight he was in his full regalia – I mean, he had on his African robes, and was standing outside his house there, all alone, and waiting.

I went up and said 'Hi!' and asked him what the score was. He said this was his home, and his wife and children were inside it, and he didn't want to hurt anyone, but if anyone wanted to damage them, they'd have to have a word with him first. He'd been standing out there all day, and meant to continue standing there, he said, as long as these hooligans were around. I loved the way that old boy said that word, 'hooligan'! It came right out of his stomach, and he threw it up through his big lips like it was a nasty mess he was vomiting up. I said to him, 'stick to it, daddy,' and I liked his robes, and as soon as I got a chance I was going to Africa to see all the cats wearing theirs like on the travelogues, and from out of somewhere there he fished a panatela for me, and I lit it, and made it up the road again.

Soon I could see lights. So I hurried on, and came on the outskirts of another crowd, and found they were gathered round the Santa Lucia club, which is a BWI clip-joint about as glamorous as an all-night urinal. There were several hundred milling there: and what added joy to the whole scene, was the presence of newsreel and TV cameras, with arc lamps and the odd flare and flashlight, as if the crowd were extras on a movie lot. And directing the whole lot, standing on a car roof with a microphone, was – yes, you've guessed it – Call-me-Cobber. That certainly was the evening of his career – the big scoop, our dauntless reporter right there in the firing line! And as for the Teds and hooligans, well, they can smell a camera, even a press one, from a mile away, and there's nothing they like better than seeing their moronic faces next morning in the tabloids, so this was their big opportunity as well.

'Child!' shouted someone, and I looked across, and there, standing up in the back of a cream vintage Bentley, was the ex-Deb-of-Last-Year. I struggled across, and found she was with a bunch of Hooray Henries, who seemed, I will say this for them, a bit doubtful if all this was really so damn amusing. And as for the ex-Deb, she leant out of her vehicle, and said, 'That crowd's nothing but a lot of bloody scum.'

'You're telling me,' I said.

'And what *is* that place?' she asked, waving a hand at the Santa Lucia club.

'A local nitery. You like to take a spin around in there?' I asked a bit sarcastically, I must admit, because if the yelling crowd outside didn't do you, the Spades down in there, if there were any, most certainly would, if you attempted to *get* in.

'Certainly!' she cried, and she spoke up a bit loud even for my liking. 'I'd love to have a dance with someone African! They're the best dancers in the world!'

So she told me to get in, which I did thinking, 'Oh, well!' and the Henry at the wheel got the car up near the entrance, with everyone, when they saw the ex-Deb and the Henries, imagining, I suppose, that this was some item in the television programme. The ex-Deb and I got out, with a Hooray or two in tow, and shouldered down some steps into the basement area, and the ex-Deb banged with both hands on the locked door.

I admit I was petrified, but also so damn hysterical by now the whole thing struck me as quite funny, so I had an inspiration, and went in the outside can there, and got up on the pedestal, and, taking a chance, I shouted through the ventilator, 'Cool, if you're there, let us in, we're customers!' Then we waited a bit more outside the door, and the eye-shutter opened, and there was a noise of bolts and ironmongery, and the door opened eight inches, and we squeezed inside – but not the Hooray numbers, who got barred.

Well, down in the Santa Lucia club, they were certainly putting up an old troupers' show-must-go-on performance. Because they weren't cowering in corners, or putting up barricades, but hopping around to the strains of the jukebox, and sitting at tables drinking double rums: West Indians, a few GIs, and a small herd of brave hens from the local chickery. And all this while, from beyond the walls, that *other* noise that scared them, I hope, less than it did me. A GI nine feet high cut me out with the ex-Deb, and I sat down to have a breather. And then – out of the chicks' toilet, there walked Crêpe Suzette.

For just a minute, I was shaken rigid. Then I leapt up, shot over, and grabbed the girl. She was shook rigid too, but only a second, and we hugged like two Russian bears, then fell on two contemporary chairs.

'Crazy girl!' I shouted. 'Spill it quick! What the hell—'

271

She kissed me still, and said, 'I came up a week ago.'

'And you not told me? Bitch!'

'And when I heard this, I came right over.'

I looked at her. 'To be among the boys?'

'Yes.'

I kissed her at arm's length. 'Now, crazy, Suze!' I cried. Brave girl! Nice chicken! But it's mine you are now, not theirs.'

She shook her head. 'Not while all this goes on,' she said.

'Well, it won't forever, hon,' I told her.

'But while it does, darl, I'm staying here.'

'So long as it's clear I've got the option.'

We laughed like two hyenas, and I went and fetched two drinks, and the side window crashed, and a petrol bomb came in and rolled among the dancers and exploded, and the electrics all cut out, and there were shouts and screaming.

Then, there was a noise like thunder on the stairs outside, and a crashing and hammering on the door, and by the light of the bomb flare you could see the law rush in, and the fire service, not as if they were coming in to rescue anybody, but to capture an enemy position. Cats were being grabbed, and others weaving in all directions, and I'd lost Suze and the ex-Deb, so I followed a Spade in through the ladies' toilet, and we climbed out the window, and into a dark garden, and over a back wall.

There, this Spade and I, we both stood panting. And I said to him, 'Okay, *white trash*?' And he said to me, 'Okay, *darkie*,' and it was Cool. We both laughed –

Ha! Ha! Ha! – then crept up to somebody's back door, opened it and tiptoed through the corridor to the front, and out down the steps where a kid was lying groaning, and I shone my torch on him, and I saw blood, and the blood belonged to Ed the Ted.

'Well!' said Mr Cool.

'Yeah,' I said too, and we just left him there, and went round in the street.

And there, there was a pitched battle. The Teds had got the law hemmed up against the railings – anyway, I suppose they must have been hemmed – and the rest of them were struggling with the Spades and one another, with razors and stakes and bike-chains and iron bars and even, at times, with knuckles. And soon I got scooped into the thing, and I heard a cry, 'Nigger's whore!', and through arms and bodies I saw Suze, and they'd got hold of her, some chicks as well as animals, and were rubbing dirt all over her face, and screaming if that's the colour she wanted to be, she'd got it. And I screamed out too, with all my lungs, and I fought like a maniac and couldn't get at her, and next thing I was slugged and staggered, and was vomiting.

Then someone heaved me up, and it was a Hooray Henry, and he said, 'Are you all right, old man?' And I said, 'No, old chap, and will you for Christ's sake try and get my girl.' Well, they had. Some more Hoorays and the ex-Deb had dragged her into the vintage vehicle, and I piled in too, and the Henry at the wheel said, 'Where to now?' and I said, 'Home!'

It was all I could do to keep them off the premises

once we got there, because they were high and the ex-Deb, in particular, wanted to help Suze, but I said, thank you all very much, but would you please all fuck off, and leave us, which they did, and we staggered up, arm in arm, falling all over each other, and there, when we got up to my place, sitting holding his dreadful hat, was my half-brother Vern. 'Where you been?' he cried.

I didn't answer, and we both flopped. Vern came over, looked at us, and said, 'Your Dad's nearly gone. Ma said you got to come down there right away.'

'In a minute, Vern,' I said.

Then I kissed Suzette, vomit, and black face, and all.

'You got to come!' Vern kept saying, tugging me.

'In a *minute*, Jules,' I said. 'Do beat it now, boy, I'll come right down as soon as ever. Do get *out* of here just now,' and I pushed him through the door.

Then I came back to Suze and said, 'We'd better wash you.' She got up, looked at herself in the glass, and said, 'No, I like it this way. It suits me.'

'Hell, no,' I said, and went and got the bowl and things, and washed her all over, and I kissed her between, and there in my place at Napoli we made it at last, but honest, you couldn't say that it was sexy – it was just love.

Then I whipped up some eats, and we sat on the bed scoffing like some old married couple, and I stopped, and stared at her, and said, 'You're a mad girl, you know.'

She gave me a look.

'Yeah,' I said. 'And now it's going to be wedding bells.'

'Not for three years,' she said. 'There's got to be a divorce.'

'Oh, to hell with three years!' I cried, and grabbed her left hand, and pulled off Henley's Bond Street ring, and went over to the window and threw it out there in Napoli. 'No reward for the finder!' I cried to the early dawn.

Then I turned round. 'What about Wiz?' I said. 'What is it makes you betray?'

'Some like it,' she said. 'It's a big kick to some,' then she went on eating.

'Well,' I said, 'old Wiz must sort it out with Satan when he meets him.'

'You believe in all that?' she said, getting up too.

'I certainly believe in Satan after tonight,' I told her, then came over again and said to her, 'The new Napoli Flikker. I hope the Spades sort him out.'

'Or you,' she said.

'No, not me, Suze. I'm cutting out of Napoli, and so are you.'

She looked at me again.

'We're off on our honeymoon,' I said, 'tomorrow. No, I mean it's today.'

She didn't let go, but shook her head. 'I'm not leaving here,' she said, with her pig-headed look returning, 'until it's over.'

I grabbed her hair and wiggled her head about. 'We'll talk about that,' I told her, 'a bit later. Now I must get down to Dad.'

'Now?'

'Yes. Bed down, chicken, I'll be back to bring you in the milk.'

I can't tell you what I felt, seeing Suze lying there on my bed, where I'd so often thought of her, and I ran back and kissed her till she struggled, then beat it out into the area and early morning.

But in the area, no Vespa! 'Good luck to them!' I cried, and started off on foot along the road. I guessed I'd have to make it up to the Gate to get a taxi, and I certainly wasn't going back into the bullring to ask any sort of motorist whatever for a lift. So I hoofed it along, and the streets were very quiet, like the silence after the crash of broken glass, and the green trees had the light on them again, and looked fresh and everlasting. Then some cat tried to run me down.

I whipped round, ready to murder this one, weak though I was, but who should it be but Mickey Pondoroso, at the wheel of his snazzy CD Pontiac. 'Mickey!' I cried. '*Buenas* dias! What the hell you doing in this asylum? You been studying some more conditions?'

Well, believe it or not, the diplomatic number had been doing exactly that: touring the area, poking his damn nose in everywhere, and he'd ended spending two hours at the section house, because there'd been some little arguments over his car – and, would you believe it, too, on whether his dark face was Negroid or not, and this had infuriated the Latin American cat, because apparently his grandma *was* a Spade, and he was very proud of her and of her race, and he had stacks of cousins in the national football team which, I must know, had won the cup this year in 1958, and, by God! was going to win it next year too, and those hereafter.

I cut the cat short. 'Mickey P.,' I said, 'you're hired! You're driving me down to Pimlico, please, and it's very urgent.'

On the way, I asked Mickey which of the countries that he's been in had the least colour thing of any, and he said at once, Brazil. And I said, okay by me, the moment I've got the loot, I'm heading it out to Brazilia forever with my bird.

Because, in this moment, I must tell you, I'd fallen right out of love with England. And even with London, which I'd loved like my mother, in a way. As far as I was concerned, the whole damn group of islands could sink under the sea, and all I wanted was shake my feet off of them, and take off somewhere and get naturalised, and settle.

Mickey didn't seem to approve of this, although I'd thought the cat might be flattered. He said once a Roman, always a Roman, and in *every* country there were horrors as well as felicities – that was the word he used.

I said, that what had happened up in Napoli, could happen once again. That once you'd done some people, or group, or race a wicked injury, especially if they were weak, you'd come back and do it again, because that was how it was, and with people, too.

And he said, but didn't I realise these things could happen anywhere?

I answered to this, I didn't mind so much its *happening*. But what I did mind is, that ever since Nottingham, more than a week ago, nobody had reacted strongly: so far as the government and top cats who control things were concerned, these riots might just not have happened at all, or have been in some other country.

Well, he delivered me at the door, and I said farewell, and thanks for the Vespa once again, I don't know what I'd have done without it, and he cut off like Fangio wherever he was going to.

The door opened up at once, and it was Ma, and I could see immediately that Dad was dead. 'Where is he?' I said, and she took me up the stairs. Ma didn't say anything, except just as we went inside the door, 'He kept asking for you, and I had to tell him you weren't there.'

I don't know if you've ever seen a corpse. As a matter of fact, it was my first time, and it really wasn't impressive very much, except for the whole thing about death and dying. I hope that's not disrespectful: but as I knew for sure, before I got there, Dad would be dead, I hadn't very much feeling left for what I saw there lying on the bed. All I felt, as a matter of fact, was so very much *older*. I felt that I'd moved one up nearer to something, now he was gone.

Old Ma was crying now. I had a good look at her, but it seemed perfectly genuine to me. After all, they'd been quite a while together, and I dare say time by itself makes something, even when there's no love at all. I gave the old girl a kiss, and rubbed her a bit, and got her downstairs, and said what about funeral arrangements. And she said she knew all that had to be done.

Then I said to her I was sorry, but I wasn't coming to the funeral. She didn't like this at all, and asked me why. I said, so far as I was concerned, Dad was what I remembered of him ever since I was a child, and I wasn't interested in corpses at all, and if she wanted flowers and hearses, that was up to her. She just stared at me and said she'd never understood me, and then she said a thing that shook me a bit in my determination, which was, had I considered what Dad himself would have wanted? So I said I'd think it over, and let her know, and meanwhile, goodbye, I was pulling out. She just looked at me again, said nothing, and went into her parlour and shut the door.

But as I was moving off, old Vern delayed me, and said he had to talk to me alone. I said I was very tired, but he pulled me out the back where I used to have my darkroom, and shut the door, and locked it, and said, 'You got to hear your father's secret.'

I asked him what.

He didn't say, but out of a corner he got the old metal box – the one you may remember where Dad used to keep the G. & S. gramophone records – and from it he took a large paper parcel, and he said, 'This is your Dad's book, he told me to give it to you personal if anything should happen.'

I opened it up, and there it was – hundreds of sheets all grubby and altered and corrected, except for the first one, where he'd written on a single page, 'History of Pimlico. For my one and only son.'

Well, then I broke down. I sobbed like a boy, and Vern left me alone a bit, but I could see he hadn't ended, and he dragged the tin chest out and said, 'Look inside,' and there, on the bottom of it, were four big envelopes, and I opened them, and they contained stacks of pound notes.

'What's this?' I said.

'Your father's fortune. He saved it year by year.'

I looked at Vern. 'What did he say to do with it?'

Vernon swallowed a bit, didn't look his best, and finally said, 'Give it to you.'

'All of it?' I said.

'Yes.'

'And it hasn't been touched?' I said.

Old Vern looked really narked at this. 'You little bastard!' he said. 'You don't trust your own brother!'

I didn't answer that, but just looked at all this loot, and imagined Dad hoarding it and hiding it. 'And he managed to keep all that from Ma?' I said. 'Well, one up to old Dad!'

Vernon said, 'You know all this should go into the estate?'

'It should?' I said.

'That's the law,' Vern told me.

I picked up two of the envelopes, and handed them to Vern. He hesitated, then took them. 'Aren't you going to count it?' he said.

'You want to?'

'Oh, no.' He frowned. 'This is quite all right with you?' he said, very dubiously.

'I've given it to you.'

'And you won't tell Ma?'

I grabbed my two envelopes, and the *History of Pimlico*, and I held out my hand and said, 'Not if you don't, brother,' and he shook it, and managed to raise a smile, and then I beat it out of that house forever.

Up by Victoria, I bought a holdall at a lost luggage, and put in the book and money, and made it to the Air Terminal. Because what with this all, my present feeling was I'd leave Dad's body to Ma, and Suze to get over loving Spades, and me, I was going away for a while, and perhaps not coming back.

At the Air Terminal, all was bustle. I went into the gents, and sorted out the loot which, so far as I could see, sitting counting it on the pedestal, was about two hundred, plus or minus. Then I had a wash, and grabbed my holdall, and went up to the wicket and asked for a single ticket to Brazil.

Where in Brazil? the cat asked me.

I said, anywhere.

He said, could he see my passport – and I whipped it out, and he said I hadn't got a visa.

I asked him what the hell a visa was, and he said it was a thing you couldn't fly to Brazil without, and I said, okay, where *could* I fly to without a bloody visa? And the cat answered, quite politely, not to South America, but to parts of Continental Europe, I could, so I say okay, give me a ticket to one of those.

The wicket number told me this was the wrong terminal for Europe, I'd have to go up to Gloucester Road, and I said, okay, and went out and got a cab, and drove there, and on the way, I'd decided I'd go to Norway, because I'd often heard from seamen Spades that they were nice to them up there.

Well, at Gloucester Road, everything easy. They gave me a ticket to Oslo, and by now I was getting crafty, and said how much loot could I export there? and they said up to £250, but I'd better get a bit of local currency, so I did that at another wicket, and found I had an hour to wait, so I had a cuppa and a meat pie, and read the morning newspapers.

The Napoli thing was big stuff all right that morning. They had it all over the place, and most of last night's occurrences, and a lot of columns in the leader sections. They were still on about unrestricted immigration, and how unwise it was, just as if it wasn't they who'd allowed it in the first place, and patted themselves on the back for the old mother country's generous hospitality, so long as everything went swimmingly. They said Welfare was an urgent consideration, and what was needed was a lot more experienced welfare officers to iron out awkward misunderstandings. A bishop had said on the radio, Home Service, that 'various tensions and taboos divide us almost as strongly as those of race and creed in other countries.' There'd been some charges made at last, and the magistrate had advised people to stay indoors at night: meantime, the coloureds, it said, were having to get white friends to do their shopping for them. Ministers were going to fly in from the Caribbean, and from Africa, to scan the scene, and the High Commissioner of somewhere had protested. Best news of all – really heartening – was that the cabinet minister in charge of home security had received reports of all these happenings at his country house, and was studying them closely, and said the utmost strictness will be observed in the impartial enforcement of the law. Always 'enforcement': never condemning! As for me, I always thought laws had some idea behind them, some sort of principle, and it was this you should shout out above, not police courts.

Well, then the loudspeaker said it was all aboard for Oslo, and the strangest bundle of cats you can imagine got in a sort of bubble-coach which was half double-decker, and I sat up in the arse part and surveyed the streets of London as we sped. Goodbye, old town, I said, good luck! We passed quite near Shepherd's Bush, where everything seemed free from tensions and taboos, and we made it out to the airfield which, I must say, was a splendid spectacle.

But I hadn't all that time for spectacles, because they fed us into a sort of sausage-machine of escalators and officials, and I had to think fairly quickly, because my idea was, to try and find where the Brazil flight began and, if I could, dodge the Oslo flight, and get on the Brazil one instead. Because experience has taught me that the more highly planned a sausage system is, the easier to feed yourself through the wrong part of it, if you keep your nerves about you.

So we went through the customs, where they seemed surprised I had only a holdall with a handwritten book in it, but I said I had an auntie out in Norway to look after me. And at the currency check, they said wasn't that a lot of money for so young a feller, and I said, wasn't it just! and got by that one. And at passports, they said was this my first passport, and I said my very first, and how did they like the photo, I'd taken it myself, and didn't I look a zombie? And after that, we all went into a great hall thing, overlooking the airfield through huge glass panels, and the loudspeaker announcing departures, and me keeping my ears skinned.

I got a Coke, and went and gazed, and it certainly was a sight! All those aircraft landing from outer space, and taking off to all the nations of the world! And I thought to myself, standing there looking out on all this fable – what an age it is I've grown up in, with everything possible to mankind at last, and every horror too, you could imagine! And what a time it's been in England, what a period of fun and hope and foolishness and sad stupidity!

Then they announced the flight to Rio. I joined the wrong queue, just like I was a regular traveller to there, and we had no check at the exit, nor when we walked across the tarmac to the aircraft, until we met a chick who stood with a board beside the staircase, asking people their names as they got on. I put myself in between a family, hoping they'd think I was cousin Frank or someone, and the chick asked my name, and I pointed at her list to a name she hadn't ticked, and she said, could she have my embarkation card, and I said what embarkation card? and she smiled politely and said one like all these, and so I gave her up mine, and she said, tut, tut, wasn't I a silly boy, that one was for the Oslo flight, and I'd better hurry back or I might miss it.

But I stayed down there, and watched the great plane taking off for Rio. And just as it became airborne – crash! down came the rain in torrents out the heavens, and I held up my arms in it, and opened my mouth and cried, 'More! More! More! That'll stop it up at Napoli! That'll do what the ruling olders can't do! That's the only thing to keep the whites and blacks and yellows and blues of Napoli indoors!'

Well then, just as I was going to get back into the sausage-machine to reconnect with Oslo, in taxied a plane, quite close to where I was standing, and up went the staircase in the downpour, and out came a score or so of Spades from Africa, holding hand luggage over their heads against the rain. Some had on robes, and some had on tropical suits, and most of them were young like me, maybe kiddos coming here to study, and they came down grinning and chattering, and they all looked so damn pleased to be in England, at the end of their long journey, that I was heartbroken at all the disappointments that were there in store for them. And I ran up to them through the water, and shouted out above the engines, 'Welcome to London! Greetings from England! Meet your first teenager! We're all going up to Napoli to have a ball!' And I flung my arms round the first of them, who was a stout old number with a beard and a briefcase and a little bonnet, and they all paused and stared at me in amazement, until the old boy looked me in the face and said to me, 'Greetings!' and he took me by the shoulder, and suddenly they all burst out laughing in the storm.